D0330824

The Valley of Light

ALSO BY TERRY KAY

Taking Lottie Home

Special K: The Wisdom of Terry Kay

The Kidnapping of Aaron Greene

The Runaway

Shadow Song

To Whom the Angel Spoke: A Story of the Christmas

To Dance with the White Dog

Dark Thirty

After Eli

The Year the Lights Came On

TERRY KAY

The Valley of Light

A NOVEL

ATRIA BOOKS
NEW YORK LONDON TORONTO SYDNEY SINGAPORE

ATRIA BOOKS
1230 Avenue of the Americas
New York, NY 10020

This book is a work of fiction. Names, characters, places and incidents are products of the author's imagination or are used fictitiously. Any resemblance to actual events or locales or persons, living or dead, is entirely coincidental.

ISBN: 0-7434-7594-1

First Atria Books hardcover edition October 2003

10 9 8 7 6 5 4 3 2 1

ATRIA BOOKS is a trademark of Simon & Schuster, Inc.

Manufactured in the United States of America

For information regarding special discounts for bulk purchases, please contact Simon & Schuster Special Sales at 1-800-456-6798 or business@simonandschuster.com.

This book is dedicated with affection to
Marjorie Ammons

A gifted teacher, a gentle and caring lady,
and the first great influence in my life other than my own family.

AUTHOR'S NOTE

I seldom go fishing, though I have memories (and a photograph) of fishing in the small branch that ran through our farm in northeast Georgia. Catching a finger-long minnow was an accomplishment of great pride.

Truth is, I have no talent for fishing. Sometimes a little luck, but no talent. I have never caught anything on an artificial lure, for example.

But I have a son—Scott—who has a remarkable gift for catching fish. Once, when he was very young and we were on vacation at a lake house, I saw him go to the lake and kneel down and place the palm of his hand on the water's surface, like a ritual in an innocent religious ceremony. He began fishing—and catching. I stood beside him. Used the same kind of equipment, the same bait. Fished within inches of where he was casting. I don't remember getting a nibble.

That gesture of touching the surface of the water has stayed with me for years, and it is the leaping-off point of this story.

Yet, this is not a story about my son or about fishing, but about the mysticism of being gifted. It is a trait that has always inspired me—seeing that person who, by nature, had a way of doing something that was, in the long run, inexplicable, yet thrilling. The artist. The musician. The gardener. The mechanic. The engineer. The chef. The anything.

It has always been my practice to fictionalize the setting of a story, yet I have chosen an actual area for this offering—that region around Hiawassee, Georgia, and Hayesville, North Carolina. However, the valley created for this purpose—the Valley of Light—is purely fictional, and the characters are residents only in my imagination.

In that area, there is a peculiarity in the spelling of the Hiawassee River. In Georgia, it is *Hiawassee;* in North Carolina, it is *Hiwassee.* In order to keep readers from being confused, and to keep editors from scribbling question marks in the margins of my manuscript, I have chosen to use *Hiawassee.* Call it prejudice on behalf of my home state.

In this story, there is a great bass and a lot of catfish. Regard the obsession with catfish another prejudice. As a young boy, when I fished Beaverdam Creek and the Broad River, it was for catfish. To me, the catfish is a noble creature and, when properly prepared, a memorable feast, even if my digestive system now tends to quarrel with me when I leave one of those wonderful, all-you-can-eat fish cafés that help define the culture of the South.

The Valley of Light

ONE

He made his way to the lake watchfully, crossing the bulldozer-built dam that was covered in weed-grass across its ridge and in trash trees growing on the waterside. It was late afternoon. The sun was behind him, his shadow making a long ghost that wobbled over the weed-grass. Grasshoppers sailed away from his footsteps.

At a clearing among the trash trees on the east end of the dam, he stopped and surveyed the ground. The lake had not been fished in a long time, he believed. Weed-grass grew high, with no look of being trampled. Left-behind bait cans were old and rusty. A coil of nylon line dangled like a spider's silk from a limb of one of the nearby trash trees, causing him to smile a smile that did not show on his face, knowing the spit of frustration the miscast had caused in some fisherman. A child's cast most likely. Not easy for a child to make a cast with nylon. Would be better to teach him with braided line.

He thought about the fishermen who had abandoned the lake. Once, they had come to it from the logging road, he reasoned, bringing their families in wagons or trucks, chairs to sit on, fishing early to late with long bamboo poles and cork floats, eating their sausages and sardines and baked sweet potatoes, and at day's end taking home their stringers of bream and bass and catfish, muscle-weary, smelling of fish slime and worms.

The water of the lake was the color of dark tea in the late-day shadows. Acid from trees. He closed his eyes, listened. The water lapped softly against the bank, rolled in, seeped back. The lapping sound was like a slow and lazy pulse beat. A dozing lake. Not much different from an old man sleeping in sunshine. Just enough breathing to keep alive.

A good place. A good place.

He wondered if it was the lake he had heard of. His sense told him it was.

A hundred yards or so up the east side of the lake, he had seen a small frame building that seemed empty from his distant view, though it was hard to tell since it had a screened-in porch, the screen hiding whatever was behind it. Probably a shack used by hunters, he had reasoned, remembering such shacks from his childhood. If somebody lived in it full-time, they did a good job of making it appear deserted.

Whoever it was that owned the lake and the shack had a good place.

He squatted at the lake's edge, placing the fishing rod he carried on the ground, and then he leaned forward and lightly touched the palm of his hand on the surface of the water.

Tell me, he said silently, said inside his mind.

The water was cool. Against his palm it had a ticklish feel of silk.

Yes, a good place.

He pushed his fingers into the water and wiggled them, paused, let his eyes scan the lake.

Forty feet away, against the bank, the water roiled, quivered like a muscle.

He smiled again, held his fingers in the water, watched the roiling ripple toward him in perfect circles. Soon, the first ring touched him. He pulled his hand from the water and lifted it to his face and inhaled slowly, taking in the scents of the lake. Algae. The decay of trees pushed over by wind storms and dropped into the water. Hickory, oak, beechnut, sweet gum. Silt of leaves and wash-off of wood dirt. Frog and snake and turtle. And fish. The sharp, almost metallic scent of fish.

He rubbed his hand across the front of his shirt.

A very good place.

He stood and slipped the army knapsack he wore off his shoulder, then picked up the rod and pulled loose the line on the bait-casting reel, letting the lure dangle before him. It was an old lure, turned like a small minnow with silver flecks on its sides. He had caught many fish with it before snipping off the hook with a pair of wire cutters. It was now a lure for holding his line on the rod and for teasing.

One cast, he thought.

One cast to let Mr. Fish know he was there.

Enough to anger Mr. Fish, to make him restless.

Make him coil and leap at anything moving near him.

He tilted his rod to the water, dipped the lure, wetting it. Then he made his cast near the bank where the fish—a bass, a large-mouth, he believed—had rolled. He watched the lure slap the water, dive and disappear, and then he began his slow reeling-in of the line. He could feel the lure drag through algae and he flicked his wrist twice, giving the line a jerking motion.

A cloud skimmed the July sun, dimmed it. He felt a puff of air against his face and stood motionless to let the air pause on his skin. A sense of peace settled over him as though he had marked the place he stood on a map and, after a long journey, had arrived at his destination. He wondered what day of the week it was and the date marking the day. Thought: What does it matter?

For more than two years, he had walked into days and weeks and months without knowing them by calendar, only by season. The season he read in trees—lime-green buds in spring, full-leaf in summer, colors of hot embers in autumn, the dark limbs of winter. He had walked and fished, leaving behind war and the burial ground of his parents and the sadness of his brother and the open and the secret experiences of his boyhood. Walked far enough to stop looking over his shoulder to see if his history tagged after him like a scolded yard dog. Now it was only memory, and memory had a way of rubbing down most of the rough edges.

Still, he had always believed there would be a place to stop the walking, to stay, to become his own forest, show his own seasons.

And there, with the air on his skin, he wondered if he had found that place.

Three weeks earlier—in Kentucky, he believed—he had come upon an old, white-haired man with bowed shoulders fishing from a bridge over a wide, slow-moving river. They had made nods to one another and he had gone below the bridge to the riverbank and made his touch of the water, and then had joined the old man on the bridge and unreeled his own line over the bridge's railing and they had fished together for a long while, paying more attention to the talking that went on between them than to the fish that swam in the water below them.

The man, who offered his name as Hoke Moore, had put him on the path to the valley. Had said it was a good place to find fish and rest if a person could avoid certain elements of the population. "It's called the Valley of Light by some, Bowerstown by others. Where I was born," he had added in a voice that had the sound of longing. "They's some good people there, and some you'd just as soon not get caught with. Mostly good, though. Mostly good. You need a hand, they'll give it."

And then Hoke Moore had begun telling of a great lake called the Chatuge, built some years earlier as part of a government project called the Tennessee Valley Authority. Said word of the lake gave it good enough marks for fishing, though there were still too few fish for all the water pooled up behind the dam. "Takes time for fish to find out where they want to be when they's so many places to go," he had speculated.

He had never fished the Chatuge himself, Hoke Moore had

admitted. Liked smaller places, something he could walk around and not lose sight of where he'd started the trip. "They's another little lake over there—twenty or twenty-five acres, I'd guess—that's got the biggest fish I ever seen in it. A bass, it was. Must have been fifteen pounds. Maybe more. Used to try and catch him, but all he'd do was spit water on me. He'd jump up out of the water, like he was trying to swim through the air, mad as a wet hen. Never seen a bass do that. Not one that big. Not coming out of the water high as he did. It was like he was telling me I weren't good enough to catch him."

Hoke Moore had paused and turned to look in the direction of the far-off mountains in the southeast—the direction he had given as the location of the valley—and he had added, "Must be big as a whale now, if it's still alive. You just wandering around, you ought to go down there and try to catch him. You might can do it. Might can. You a fisherman, sure enough. I can tell that in any man just by studying him a little bit. If you go down there and you catch him, you look him in the eye when you drag him up and you tell him Hoke Moore's been thinking about him for a long time."

He had smiled, had said, "Yes sir. I get down that way, I'll do that."

"You got to take your time with him," Hoke Moore had said. "Got to aggravate him some. Got to make him want you, much as you want him."

"Yes sir, I've seen fish like that," he had replied. And it was true. Even as a child, he had known fish liked to fight, some more than others.

And then Hoke Moore had chuckled and made another soft cast with his line, watching the hook disappear under the pull of the sinker. After a moment, he had said, "I wonder if they doing the fish-off in the Chatuge these days."

He had asked, "What's that?"

"What I call it—a fish-off," Hoke Moore had answered. "Used to be on the river. Been going on over there for twenty years or more. Got started by the school as a way of making some money to pay teachers. First year they done it, they was catching fish fast as they could drop a line. Not much need to bait the hook, they was catching fish so easy. Had the biggest fry at the school I ever saw. You'd of thought Jesus had blessed them fish, they was so many of them. Everybody pays a dollar or two to get in on it and the man that catches the most fish by weight gets a cash prize. Used to be ten dollars. Guess it's more now. When they get through with the fishing, they have them a fish fry and everybody in the valley shows up. That's where they make the money."

Hoke Moore had paused, wagged his fishing rod over the water; then he had added, "Won it myself two or three times." Had laughed softly over the thought.

"When's it held?" he had asked.

"Right along now," Hoke Moore had answered. "July, August. Date changes about—or it used to. Tell the truth, I don't even know if they do it no more. War changed a lot of things." He had paused, clucked with his tongue, shook his head slowly, had added, "Had me some ups and downs there, but I miss the place." He had gazed again at the distant mountains. "You just going place to place, you ought to head down that way. Get in on that fishing if they still doing it. Catch that fish of mine while you there."

"Maybe I will," he had said after a moment of thinking about it.

"What you ought to do," Hoke Moore had urged. Had said again, "You a fisherman. Yes sir, you are. One thing I know about is fishing. Some people just born to it. Others can't do nothing but drown worms. You born to it, boy. You born to it. Just like I was."

"You going back over there someday?" he had asked, wanting to be friendly.

And Hoke Moore had turned slightly to look at him in an old man's studying way before answering, "About all I ever think about, you want to know the truth of it, but it's a long way off for old legs. If I go back, somebody'll have to throw me over his shoulders and carry me. You take a mind to go on down there, I'll consider I'm along for the ride." And he had smiled and turned back to his fishing and to his low-voice way of talking.

He had listened with interest to Hoke Moore, had found something pleasing in the description of the valley and had made his turn in the direction of Hoke Moore's pointed finger, walking toward the far-off mountains, so distant and pale gray on the horizon, they had the look of a lace hem on the blue skirt of the sky. Had made his journey at a languid pace, catching an occasional ride in a farmer's truck, stopping often to fish. One river in Tennessee—the Ocoee—had held him for three days with its hypnotic run of water over rocks and with the satisfying look of the mountains around it. Good fishing, too. If Hoke Moore had not told such a happy story about the valley near the Chatuge, he would have liked staying longer on the Ocoee.

But maybe Hoke Moore had been right. The valley had a natural feel to it. Coming into it, he had got an idea of the people living in it by studying the washings hanging on clotheslines. Reading a clothesline had always been an easy thing for him to do—a trick taught to him by his mother. If you read it with some careful attention, you could tell if the house belonged to a couple just starting out, or if it had children, or old people, or whether they were fat or skinny people. Could come close to guessing how much money the people might have by the new or faded look of their clothing and bedsheets and towels.

The clotheslines of the valley left him believing it was a place fairly well off, with people more or less settled in, happy enough to be where they were and who they were.

It was little wonder that Hoke Moore had a yearning look when he pointed out the direction of the valley.

He saw the water behind the line heave and bubble, and he raised the tip of the rod. He knew what was about to happen.

"Take it," he whispered.

The fish erupted from the water, flinging itself high, like a god becoming flesh, a spray of water spinning from its silver head, its tail fins dancing over the shattered surface. For a moment—a flash—the huge mouth flared open in outrage at the tasteless lure and he could see the orange of the gills shining in the sun.

He had never seen a lake fish so large.

The fish fell hard against the water, making a belly-flopping slapping sound, a sound like a sudden thunderclap, and then it disappeared. Water rippled again in circles and the late sun filled the circles like ringlets of liquid gold.

Hoke Moore's fish, he believed.

Hoke Moore's fish announcing itself, coming out of the water like that. Not the habit of bass to leap up, though it depended on the spirit of the fish, he guessed. He had seen such leaps. Not so high, though. Not from such a large fish.

Soon, he thought. Maybe tomorrow. Soon, I will catch you and see if you are the giant Hoke Moore says you are.

The fish would bring good money, being so big. Feed a good-size family, though it might not be easy finding somebody wanting a bass as big as a small pig. Most country people he knew—white and colored—liked the taste of catfish more than bass. So did he. Catfish—small ones, the length of his hand, wrist to fingertip—were as tasty as any fish he had ever eaten if they were cooked right in seasoned meal and melted lard. Some of the colored men he had fished with in his boyhood would come close to fighting over a string of catfish. One he knew—Runt Carter was his name—had a habit of collecting the heads of catfish and stringing them across his barn with binder twine, saying the fish kept away owls. Runt Carter had so many catfish heads dangling on binder twine, his barn had the look of wearing a necklace.

He wondered if there were many colored families in the valley. Doubted it, being in the mountains. Most colored people he knew were workers in cotton fields, and there was little cotton grown in the mountains. He had seen only one colored family in the last two days. They lived in a small house—if it could be called house, for it was more barnlike than houselike. Remembered watching three or four small, knobby-shouldered black children at play as he came upon the house, and then seeing them become suddenly quiet, suddenly motionless, like small deer going on guard, their eyes following him as he walked past them.

It was a family that would like catfish, and maybe he would catch some and take a stringer to them. It would be easy enough to do, though the walk to where they lived was a good distance. Still, he knew there were catfish in the lake. Knew by the scent of the water. Bass and catfish and bream. He would catch stringers of each, enough for a good sale, or for trades.

Soon, he thought. Soon.

First, he must find his place for sleeping.

Around him, birds made cheerful throat music. Redbirds, he guessed. Coming off the hill to the dam, he had seen some. And wild canaries, yellow as the bloom of a jonquil. Blackbirds with scarlet-tipped wings. Sparrows. Brown thrashers. A hawk, balanced on invisible cushions of air like a war glider, crying its war cry. He stood, holding the rod, the line still in the water, and listened. A breeze stirred in the trash trees, making its whisper. A squirrel chattered from a laurel bush. A frog made a jump from the bank of the lake, landing with a dull belly splash in the slush of water and mud. And then he heard the faint braying of a mule and he believed there was a farmhouse not far away, one he had not seen from the hillside above the lake, one probably resting on the hump of a knoll, hidden by trees.

He reeled in his line and locked it down, the lure snug against the eye at the tip of the rod, and then he lifted his knapsack and slipped it over his shoulders.

It was likely the owners of the farmhouse were also the owners of the lake. If he could find the house and the owners before dark, maybe he could make a trade of fresh fish for sleeping in the lake shack. Could even be a cot in the shack. Such a place would bring good sleep, better than the ground and a mattress of raked-up pine needles. He would have to be careful, though, approaching a farmhouse so late in the day, and he would have to be forthright about his offer. Mountain people were all right if you were straight with them. Try to fool them and they could turn rough.

On the edge of the lake a black snake slithered against a washed-up limb, curled, buried its head beneath a wad of decaying oak leaves. It was a good sign, a black snake.

He paused in the fringe of the woods, his soldier's training still with him, and surveyed the farmhouse. It was as he imagined it would be—off the road on a knoll, tucked under oaks, a tree line of pine and hemlock along the road gully, hiding the house from travelers. At one side of the house was a barn with a barbed wire fence, and near the barn, a smokehouse and a corn crib that had sheets of tin fashioned around its stone pillars and nailed to the underneath to keep rats from gnawing through the flooring.

Being summer, and the oaks in full leaf, the house was as camouflaged as a deer, and could easily have been missed by some stranger walking past, not paying attention to what occupied the right and left of his or her vision. The house surprised him. It was larger than he thought it would be—add-ons, he guessed—and had been recently painted a light gray that reminded him of troop ships. He had thought that it, and the barn with it, would be small, the same as the house and barn of his childhood—clapboard and tin, the clapboard unpainted, aged with weather, the tin roof coated in rust, its nail spots making rust freckles. Just room enough for what was needed. His mother—in despair, as he remembered it—had once said of their home, "No reason to go to dreaming, son; there's no room here to fit one in." And it had been true. He had not missed the home of his childhood, not after the death of his father and mother, not after the jailing of his brother. Once his childhood home had seemed as permanent as mountains. Now it seemed as distant as stars.

He stood patiently, himself camouflaged, and watched for the outside appearance of someone belonging to the house, seeing only the shadows of movement behind windows that he guessed to be at the kitchen. The light, fading in the sun's fall behind the mountains, was tricky. He could not tell if the movement was from man or woman. Woman, he believed, from the size and shape of the shadows. Near the front of the house, there was a car, a Ford of recent model, he thought.

He looked for dogs, but did not see any, and thought it strange. Most homes had dogs for hunting or for keeping guard with their barking.

In the pasture leading to the barn, he saw two tan cows and a white mule standing near the fence, each claiming a familiar space, each casting a gaze toward the house. The mule was old, as was one cow. The other cow was younger, had birthed one calf, he judged, but the calf was not in sight. There was still a sleek coloring to its coat and an alert lift to its head, as though it understood the time for being milked was soon. The older cow seemed sleepy, the mule weary from years of harnessed labor, having a used-up look about its drooping head, its bowed back, its ribbed sides. He saw the bobbing heads of chickens prancing in the yard near the barn, making the pecking that filled their gizzards with grains of sand.

The cows and the mule and the chickens could have been from the farm of his childhood. The cows, the mule, the chickens, the house, the barn—all that he saw was as familiar to him as the reflection of his own image in a mirror. It was the look of the South in the years after the war. The only changes seemed to be the number of tractors in fields and the lights from electricity that bloomed like the buds of flowers through the windows of the houses.

He saw the door to the house open, and a woman carrying a milk pail stepped outside. She crossed the yard to the barn, her stride showing purpose. He moved to step from the woods—to call out—then moved back. Was pushed back. Not by his own action, but by a force he could not explain, yet was familiar to him.

It had been with him through the war, invisible, though present. Something he had learned to trust. Once, he had talked of it to an army chaplain and also to his sergeant. The chaplain had reasoned it to be an angel, saying he had seen such angels drifting like holy medics among the dying, their wispy bodies floating over battlefields in the stagnant air of gunsmoke, the gunsmoke taking shapes that carried wings. His sergeant had called it gut instinct, the thing that bullets could not strike and bayonets could not penetrate. He believed both were right. Sometimes, he was certain he could see the angels.

He turned and left, made his way back to the lake and went to the shack and examined it, finding the door to the screened-in porch unlatched and the door to the house unlocked. On the porch was a rocking chair and a narrow cot, but without a mattress. He pushed open the door of the shack and stepped cautiously inside, noticing a sag in the floor near the doorsill. Let his weight test it and found it strong enough to hold him, though he did not think it would take much to make the underpinning give way. The inside was a single room with a small woodstove in one corner, one that could be used for heating as well as cooking. Beside it was a wood box with a few sticks of split wood peeking up over the sides. Oak, he guessed. Maybe hickory. Not far from the stove was a pie safe containing a few dishes and glasses and eating utensils and an iron skillet and a coffeepot and a pot for boiling water. A handmade eating table was in the center of the room with two chairs. A kerosene lamp was on the table, having a chipped dish under it. Another cot with a mattress and pillow and blanket was pushed against another wall. He saw a broom leaned in the corner, near the cot. A framed picture of Franklin Delano Roosevelt was hanging from one wall.

The room had a slight musty smell to it, like a place that needed airing out, or a place that had gone too long without somebody staying in it, leaving the scent of having been there—of cooked food and coffee and tobacco and soap and perfumed skin lotions. A lived-in place gave off its own odors, the same as the earth did.

It would be a good place to stay, he thought, but he would not—not without permission. To do so would be like house-breaking, and he knew the law on housebreaking. He had a brother in jail because of it.

He found a large beechnut tree in front of the shack, between the shack and the lake. A carving head-high on its trunk read:

And now this tree
Belongs to me
A W

The carving seemed several years old, the way it had crusted over, and it made him think of the beechnuts where he had carved his own initials as a boy. He wondered if the trees still stood, still held his initials, or if they had scabbed over and disappeared.

He made a bedding of pine straw under the tree and covered it with his sleeping bag. Put together a circle of stones and started a stick fire to boil water for his coffee. He ate from a can of sausages, sandwiched between soda crackers, and as he ate and took his coffee, he pondered over the force that had pushed him back into the woods as he watched the woman. Was it something his senses had seen, or not seen? Where was the man? Still in the house? Would the man have come from the house and chased after him with a gun?

A half-moon, bright in the clear air of the mountains, nudged itself over the trees, made a dull light around him. He wedged himself into his sleeping bag and pulled the mosquito netting over the pyramid of sticks he had jammed into the earth and tied with a string. The netting filtered the moonlight, gave it an eerie glow. From his position, he could barely see the carving on the tree. Wondered who A W was, or had been. He closed his eyes and let sleep follow.

• • •

He dreamed of Hoke Moore and the fish as he slept.

Hoke Moore stood at the lakeside, making a long cast with his rod, calling out to the fish, "I come for you." The fish rose up from the lake, split the water in a graceful leap, dove, split the water, dove. Then, in the sudden, unknowing way of dreams, the bass was hanging from the limb of the beechnut, a fishing line laced through its mouth and gills. Below the tree, Hoke Moore looked up, watched the fish quiver against the line, watched its soul spin out of its body like a dancing white flame and then reshape itself into a see-through ghost-fish with the faint coloring of pale yellow. A soft wail, moan upon moan, came from Hoke Moore, the same sound he had heard in Dachau from the chests of men so thin it did not seem possible that the chests could hold any sound at all. Then he saw a cloud of fish ascending from the lake. Thousands of fish suspended eerily in air, water dripping from them in moonlight, and the yellow-colored see-through bass, its torso twisting grotesquely, flew over them, and the fish followed, soaring above the trees, making the moon dark, so many of them. And then they were gone, and the water of the lake became calm, and the wail of Hoke Moore became a great cry.

The cry woke him.

He sat up, his head nudging against the mosquito netting he had fashioned over his bedding. He was perspiring, a condition that had marked his dreams since the war. From the lake, he heard the monotonous bellowing of frogs, and from nearby, the singing of cicadas and an owl's solitary announcement of itself. There was a scent of water in the air and he wondered if it was from a warning of rain or from the fog cap of the lake. The lake, he hoped. He had not pitched his pup tent, believing in the cloudless sky. Yet, if it rained, he could take shelter on the porch of the shack, trusting that if anyone found him there, they would not call it a break-in.

He glanced up, through the netting, through the limbs of the beechnut, saw the limb of his dream and believed he saw the fishing line that had held the fish. He blinked and the line became a twig. The sky through the tree was still cloudless.

He let his body drop again on the mattress of needles, turned to his side. He could smell the dead fire in the circle of rocks and the left-over coffee from his coffeepot. Tomorrow, he would need to find a store and buy more coffee, he thought. Coffee was his great luxury. In the war, he had never had his fill of coffee.

The owl sailed from the dark bark of a pine thirty yards away—less maybe; twenty maybe—and feathered a landing on the ground. The owl's wings had an astonishing reach, wings that could have been robbed from a sleeping eagle, and he propped up on one elbow, wondering what the owl had trapped on the ground. Field mouse doing its night feeding, most likely.

He eased again against the rolled coat he used for a pillow and imagined the fish of his dream hanging above him, turning lazily in the breeze. In the war, he had seen a hanged man at the death camp called Dachau. More boy than man, though. Dressed in the uniform of the SS. His eyes bulging, his arms hanging limp. An old Jew wearing the rags of prison stripes had stood near the dangling body, moaning like the moans of Hoke Moore in his dream.

Thirty yards away—twenty, maybe—the owl made its slaughter with a beating of wings that could have belonged to an eagle.

TWO

He saw the store from the road that ran parallel to the railroad track. A sign on the store gave it, and the place, a name: Bowerstown Community Store. He remembered that Hoke Moore had said the valley was called the Valley of Light or Bowerstown, and he knew he had been right about his guess of being where he wanted to be.

A few cars and trucks, dust-covered, were parked under the shade of two water oaks that fronted the store. It was a setting he knew well, and the gathering of men and boys on the porch of the store—some standing, some sitting in cane-bottom chairs and others on the porch steps—meant to him the possibility of pleasant company, though he had never been comfortable in a crowd of people. From the voices he heard at a distance—voices eased by laughter—he believed he would find high spirits. He knew the men to be farmers having good crops standing in the field. Corn, mostly, he judged, remembering the many fields of corn he had passed. A little tobacco, too. Milk cows grazing from thick grass in clearings that once had been timberland. The corn had a dark green look of health to it, as though it had been fed nitrate of soda at the right time, hand-pitched to the bottom of each stalk, just before a steady rain. The promise of good crops made upbeat feelings, and there would be boasting and laughter among the men, and the purchase of not-needed items solely for the celebration of the moment.

The talking, the laughter, stopped when he approached, as he knew it would. In the South, a stranger had to be studied, measured. In the South, silence hid many judgments behind faces that could have been carved from hardwood. A stranger could not walk his way past the gaze of such men. He slowed his step to make his own study, take his own measure, searching for the one man who would be spokesman among them. His eyes stopped on a man sitting in a chair, center of the gathering. The man was dressed in the farmer's wear of work pants and field shirt buttoned to his throat, felt hat on his head. His face was furrowed, having the look of age made by work and weather, yet a smile rested comfortably among the creases. His eyes were the eyes of a man who had a feisty nature among other men.

"Welcome, friend," the man said. His voice had energy, was cheerful.

He nodded, said, "Good morning."

"You wouldn't be lost, would you?" the man asked, leaning forward in his chair.

"Never been here before, so I guess I am," he answered. "A little bit, at least."

The man laughed. He turned to the others. "Looks like we got us a wandering sheep here," he said in a loud voice. Then he turned back. "You in the good state of North Carolina, friend, no more'n a long throw of a flat rock from the Georgia line. County name of Clay, county seat called Hayesville, six miles to the north of where you standing. Old courthouse, some stores on the four sides around it, some filling stations, schools, and a few churches. Where you standing right now is the Bowerstown community. Some call the Valley of Light, the way it's all spread out and taking to the sun like it does. The river that runs through it goes by the name of the Hiawassee, coming out of Chatuge Lake. Runs north, and that'll puzzle your senses to you get used to it. Used to be Cherokee Indian land, before Andrew Jackson had them moved off. But old Andy's boys didn't get them all. A bunch just hid out in the hills and they still around, like Marshall Hawk, over there." He motioned to a stocky man with bronze skin and high cheekbones and chocolate-colored eyes. All Indian features. The man smiled, said, "How," and the other men laughed.

"There's them that swears there's gold by the sackful buried in the hillsides, but I been looking for it for about a thousand years and I ain't found it yet," the man continued. "Some specks in a pan, but that's about all."

The man paused, let his smile work over his face. He pulled himself from his chair. "Name's Whitlow Mayfield," he added, extending his hand. The smile in his eroded face deepened. "When I'm not out looking for gold or walking behind a plow, I run for sheriff of this county. Been running so long I don't even have to put my name in the hat, but this sorry bunch of boys keep voting for the other fellow." His smile became a short laugh. "They all scared of what I know about them."

The men laughed easily. Chuckle laughs. Marshall Hawk said, "Other way around, if you want the truth of it."

Whitlow Mayfield's grip was surprisingly strong. A shine flashed in his small, blue eyes. "They just jealous. I got my own bloodhounds and them dogs know the hiding place of every still in twenty miles. These boys know that once they put a badge on my shirt, I'm coming after every one of them with my dogs, and they'll have to go to growing corn for nothing but cornmeal and mule feed." He paused, let his smile bloom. Then: "And what name do you go by, young fellow?"

"Noah," he answered, releasing the grip. "Noah Locke."

"And where you from, Noah Locke?" Whitlow Mayfield asked.

"Georgia. Down near Elberton," Noah answered.

Whitlow nodded, and the nod seemed to swim through his body. "I been there," he said. "Had a cousin that lived down there, named Wally Mayfield. You know of him?"

Noah said he had heard the name, but did not know the man.

"You didn't miss much," Whitlow said dryly. "Sure couldn't call him one of your leading citizens." Then: "You in the war?"

"I was," Noah answered simply.

"Japs or Hitler?"

"Hitler," Noah said.

A shadow seemed to fall across Whitlow's face. His forehead furrowed. "What group was you with?" he asked in a quieter voice.

Noah hesitated before replying. He again glanced at the men who were listening. There was something expectant about them, something he could not read in the dark coating of their eyes. "The Forty-second Infantry," he said.

Whitlow dipped his face, nodded slowly, rolled his lips together; then he looked up and pushed a smile across his face in a motion that carried pain. "You looking for some work, Noah Locke?"

"Not especially," Noah told him.

"You got a farmer's look about you," Whitlow said.

"I done my share of it," Noah replied.

"Sharecropping?"

"Yes sir."

"You quit it?"

Noah thought of the question, wondered if people quit farming, or if farming quit people. "Just never went back to it after the war," he said.

"It's nineteen forty-eight. That's been three years," Whitlow said. "What you do for a living?"

Noah again hesitated, considered how his answer would sound; then he said, "I pick up a job here and there, but mostly I do some fishing."

A look of surprise flashed in Whitlow's eyes. "Fishing?"

"Yes sir," Noah said.

"How you make a living, doing that?"

"Sell the catch, make some trades."

"People buy fish, when they can go out and catch them on their own?" There was astonishment in the question. The men listening offered smiles.

"Some do," Noah said.

"Well, now, that's a new one on me," Whitlow said. "I've heard of just about every kind of job a man can do, but never met a man who was a walking-about fish seller. Hard to see how a man can make a go of it as a living."

"I get by, that's about all," Noah replied.

"You must be pretty good at it, then," Whitlow said playfully.

"Good enough, I guess," Noah told him.

The smile that Whitlow wore wiggled across his face. "Friend, if you good at it, you come to the right place at the right time."

Noah did not reply, sensing he would hear the same story told to him by Hoke Moore. No reason to mention Hoke Moore, though, he thought. A man telling a story wanted to think it was his own. There was no harm in letting Whitlow Mayfield have the stump to himself.

"We got a little fishing contest that goes on here every year," Whitlow explained. "Cost two dollars to get in on it. We meet over at the river and spend the day fishing and acting fools, and then we have us a fish fry that goes on into the night long enough for some of the boys to get rowdy when the good people go home. Draws a crowd and we wind up with a little money to help out at the school. It's coming off in a week from today. You good enough, you could walk away with twenty dollars, since the man that catches the most by the steelyard gets the prize."

Whitlow paused, sucked in a breath, then said, "We never had a man at the fishing that makes his living at it. Hope you'll stay around for it. It'll stir up some interest."

"I'll try to do that," Noah said.

"Guess we better let Littleberry know he's got some competition," an older man wearing an eye patch said with a drawl, making the syllables in competition sound like separate words. The man was squat and fat-heavy, and when he laughed at his saying his face turned red from the effort. A young boy—maybe fourteen, Noah judged—sat beside him. The boy had a narrow, pale face, wore thick eyeglasses, leaned forward to make himself part of the group. A lopsided grin rested on his face.

"That'd be Littleberry Davis," Whitlow said to Noah. "He's the best we got around here, if you go by how many times he's won our little contest. Last five or six years by my count."

"Six," said the eye-patch man. "And if I know Littleberry, he's spent this year's money before he's wet his hook."

Another laugh—easy, natural—spilled from Whitlow. He removed his hat and began to fan with it. His hair was thinning and sweat-stamped to his head. "You out looking for customers this morning?" he asked.

"Guess I always am," Noah answered, "but right now, I'm mostly looking to pick up a couple of things in the store."

"Well, around here this is the getting place," Whitlow advised. He gestured to the door of the store with his head. "You'll find a cousin of mine in there by the name of Taylor Bowers, more'n likely counting all that money he's got hid around in shoe boxes and tobacco cans, and if he's not got what you want, he'll try to sell you something else to take its place. Some folks are born-again Christians. Taylor's a born-again talker. Even worse than I am and these boys will tell you that's going some." He smiled broadly. "But, don't you go buying no sardines in a can. That'd put some holes in your story about fishing." He laughed again and the men around him also laughed.

Noah grinned, said, "I guess it would at that."

The eye-patch man leaned back in his chair and laced his fingers across his bulging stomach. "You go fishing around here, stick to the river, or go over to the Chatuge. They's a little lake up the road a piece, but you won't find no fish in it."

The men nodded nods of agreement.

"Used to be full of fish a long time ago, but they all gone now," the eye-patch man added. "Just up and disappeared."

Noah thought of his dream of the fish rising from the lake, following the ghost of the see-through bass.

"I'll make you a deal," the eye-patch man said. "You go over there to the river and catch me a mess of river cats and bring them back here before sundown, and I'll give you a dime a fish, if they big enough to fit in the fry pan. All this talking has made me catfish hungry. You can throw back the trout and bream and crappie. Just catfish, and a lot of them. I got a tableful of people to feed, like my grandboy here." He nudged the boy sitting beside him, and the boy nodded vigorously, his lopsided grin quivering.

"Sounds fair," Noah said. Not being good with figures, he had always accepted whatever offer was given. A dime for a fish even seemed high to him.

"Don't let him bait you, friend," Whitlow said cheerfully. "Fishing's been off around here for a few years. Hunting, too. All them fellows working on building the dam just about cleaned us out. You not knowing the river, I'd say you'd be wasting your time. You make a dime on that deal, you'll be lucky."

"He said it was fair," the eye-patch man said in an easy voice.

"It is," Noah told him.

"Well, there you go, friend," Whitlow said cheerfully. "You been here five minutes and already got you some business."

Noah made arrangements to deliver the fish to the eye-patch man, then went into the store with Whitlow to buy his coffee.

Taylor Bowers was a tall, middle-aged man of handsome features—a strong face carrying a small scar over his left eyebrow, dark blue eyes, a shock of rusty hair having the tint of dried corn silk, and like the man named Whitlow Mayfield, he had a permanent smile cut deep into his jowls, giving the two men a blood-link look. He was the kind of man who seemed familiar to anyone who met him, and Noah wondered if he had seen him in another place on his travels. He was behind the counter, leaned over, making sums in a ledger. "Adding up the day's take, I see," Whitlow said in a joyful bellow that was meant as humor.

"Trying to see how much you stole from me last month," Taylor replied. His voice was strong, friendly, matching the look he carried on his face and having a sound much like Whitlow Mayfield, but deeper in tone.

"A man running for sheriff don't have to steal," Whitlow said.

"I forgot," Taylor said. "When a man running for sheriff takes it, it's called a political contribution."

Whitlow laughed. He made introductions, calling Noah a handyman and a traveling fish seller who might stay around long enough to be in the fishing contest, giving Littleberry Davis a reason to worry, and then he launched a story about the only year there had ever been any trouble at the fishing. He had had to break up a fight between two men quarreling like boys over lines being crossed in the river. He named the names, gave the count of blows exchanged, the degree of blood coming from cuts. It was funny in memory, Whitlow said. Not so funny when one of the men left and returned later with his shotgun. "Had to bust him up a little bit before the fellow who was trying to be sheriff that year got there," Whitlow said. "But I wound up taking him a catfish supper to the jail. Me and him, we're good friends to this day."

Noah said nothing during the telling of the story. He listened patiently, nodded appreciatively, as men did in such situations. He could also hear the laughter of the men on the porch, knew they were telling other tales—repeated ones, likely—that held some pleasure.

Hoke Moore had been right, he thought. It was a good place.

And then the laughter ceased suddenly, so suddenly it caused Taylor Bowers to look toward the door. A woman wearing a simple blue cotton dress with a faded pattern of small roses entered the store, paused, took in a breath, then crossed to the men.

"Eleanor," Taylor said.

She nodded, said, "Taylor." Then she glanced at Whitlow, said "Whitlow."

Whitlow blinked once, slowly. He said, "Morning, Eleanor."

She did not look at Noah; still Noah recognized her as the woman he had seen the day before at the farmhouse.

"Anything I can get for you?" Taylor asked politely.

"I think I know where everything is," the woman said. She glanced at Noah, walked past him.

"Well, it's time I got on home," Whitlow said. He smiled at Noah, then turned to Taylor. "Don't go raising prices on our friend, here. Don't want him to go away thinking bad about us. He was a soldier against Hitler." A sad smile appeared again among the age ridges of his face and he added, "Like my boy was." He narrowed his gaze on Noah, said, "Bears a resemblance to him, don't you think?"

"He does at that," Taylor agreed.

"Like I said, don't go cheating him," Whitlow said.

"You the only one I cheat, Cousin," Taylor replied. "You know that."

The sad smile stayed on Whitlow. His eyes blinked rapidly. He mumbled, "Uh-huh, what I thought." Then, to Noah: "Sure hope you stick around long enough for the fishing. And don't go picking a fuss with Taylor. He used to be a boxer. There's many a good man from around here who's missing a tooth or two from when he was younger. When they make me the sheriff, I'm gonna make him my chief deputy."

"I'll remember that," Noah said.

Whitlow bobbed his head, glanced again toward the woman named Eleanor, then left the store.

"You really make a living fishing?" Taylor asked in a voice that held as much amusement as curiosity.

"Depends on what you'd call a living, I guess," Noah answered. "I eat a lot of fish."

Taylor laughed. "What can I get for you?" he asked.

"Coffee," Noah told him. "And a soap bar, I guess."

"That it?"

"I guess so."

"That's easy enough," Taylor said. He moved again behind the counter, took a bag of coffee from a shelf and a bar of soap from the counter. The soap, he explained, was homemade by an elderly woman who lived alone in the hills. All she made was herb-scented, but he only had rosemary. "It's better than any factory-made you'll find." He sniffed the soap and handed it to Noah, who also sniffed it.

"Smells good," Noah said.

"It'll cut down on the fish smell," Taylor said behind a grin. "Only thing I never liked about fishing—the smell it left if you caught any." He cocked his head, added, "I used to fish a lot when I was a boy, but I can't get away from here long enough to do nothing these days."

"I guess not. You got a crowd outside," Noah offered.

"It's Saturday," Taylor said. "They always come around on Saturday. Used to be a lot more would show up, but most people go over to Hiawassee or up to Hayesville, unless they just need a couple of things."

"I forgot what day it was," Noah admitted.

"I suspect that's the way it is with a traveling man," Taylor said. "You walk far enough, you walk out of where one day ends and another one takes up, I'd guess."

"There's some truth to that," Noah replied.

"Whitlow said you did some handyman work, too. You want to pick up a few days' work while you're around, you let me know," Taylor said. "I got to get the store painted, and nobody around here seems interested—not even enough to help pay off their accounts. I suspect they don't want everybody else seeing them swap a plow handle for a paintbrush. I'd do it myself, but it'd take me all summer, having to stop every few minutes. "

"I appreciate that. I'll keep it in mind," Noah said. He thought he would enjoy being around Taylor Bowers and felt an urge to say more about the offer, but did not. The woman named Eleanor approached the counter carrying a roll of gauze bandaging and two bottles, one of a woman's cologne and the other of iodine.

"You find everything all right, Eleanor?" Taylor asked.

"I did," Eleanor said.

"Want some candy this time?"

Eleanor paused before answering, made a glance to Noah, then said, "Yes."

"Hershey?"

"That'll be fine."

Taylor turned to the shelf behind him, took the candy from its box, turned back. "All right, one Hershey. Want me to put everything on the books?"

"Yes," she said, "but I can wait my turn." She spoke in a calm, even voice, soft-edged, but having force in the core of it.

Taylor smiled. "We just talking fishing," he said. He tilted his head toward Noah. "This man fishes for a living. Goes place to place. He's just passing through, like tinkers used to do."

Eleanor looked at Noah without expression. Her face, like her body, was slender. Her eyes were green, the green of a colored stone or of a jewel in a brooch. Her hair, a reddish brown, was in a bun that rested on the back of her neck. She was in her mid-thirties, Noah thought. Younger, maybe. Older, maybe. There was something unsettling about her gaze. Without reason, Noah thought of his mother, and it surprised him. The eyes, he guessed. Something about the eyes. Not the color, but something.

"His name's Noah Locke," Taylor continued. He looked at Noah. "I got it right, didn't I?"

"You did," Noah said uncomfortably.

"Well, Noah, this is Eleanor Cunningham," Taylor said. "She's got a place up the road a piece, sort of in the horseshoe of the river."

"Ma'am," Noah said, offering a nod. He remembered the smooth stride of the woman, going from her house to the barn.

Eleanor Cunningham moved her face in an answering nod.

"If you got a taste for some fish, he's taking orders," Taylor added merrily.

For a moment no one spoke, and the silence was like a chill. Then Eleanor said, "Thank you, but I don't eat much fish." She turned to face Taylor. "You see everything I got?"

Taylor glanced at the goods she held, handed her the candy. "I do," he answered. He wanted to ask about the iodine and the bandaging, but put the question aside. The reason it was needed was private, and he had long understood that it was bad business to be too nosy. "You take care of yourself," he added.

"I will," Eleanor Cunningham said. She looked at Noah, then stepped back, turned and walked across the store and out of the door.

"That's a fine woman," Taylor said softly. "Usually a lot more talkative, and she's got a smile you'll keep seeing a long time after she's gone when she's in a good mood, but she's had her share of trouble." Then he added in a manner that had apology to it—realizing he was talking to a stranger who did not know the facts: "Her husband's dead."

Noah felt his head dip in the ritual of acknowledgment, heard his voice speak from the ritual of response, "Sorry to hear that."

"Boyd—that was his name—was in the war all over Europe," Taylor continued. "Didn't get so much as a scratch that I ever heard tell of, then comes home and shoots himself about a year ago."

Noah took the news with surprise, a turn of his head toward Taylor. "Why'd he do that?"

"Nobody knows for sure," Taylor told him. "He got back from the war wearing the bars of a second lieutenant and carrying a lot more money than the government pays a soldier." He paused, shook his head, let his smile grow. "But Boyd always was the kind of man that'd make you want to check how many fingers you had left after you shook hands with him. Used to pay off everything with twenty-dollar bills so new you could cut butter with them. That's what I remember," he added. Then: "Anyhow, there's them who think that had something to do with it, thinking maybe he ran out of them new twenty-dollar bills." He paused again. "War does a lot of things to people, I guess."

"It does," Noah said.

"When Boyd killed himself, it left Eleanor in a bind," Taylor said. "She's had her place up for sale, but nobody's made any kind of offer that I know of."

Noah gave a small shake of his head as if to say he understood how it was to be holding something you didn't want. Then he glanced toward the door of the store.

"Well, I'm glad to meet you, Noah Locke," Taylor said, reading the look.

"Same here," Noah said. "How much I owe you?"

Taylor gave him the sum of the debt, took the money offered, and made change, saying, "My offer stands. You want some work while you're here, I got the paint stacked up in the back of the store. Pay you eight dollars a day, plus one feeding."

"I'll give it some thought," Noah told him.

It was a good day for fishing. Cloudless, warm. On the river the sun seemed embedded in the water like a pigment of color. Below the shoals where he fished, Noah could see the sun-colored water vaulting over a bedding of rock that stretched across the river before spilling into deep pools of eddies. Fish would feed in the pools, he had reasoned, and he had been right. Using worms he had dug with his folding army spade from damp soil near a seeping spring, he had caught fish steadily for an hour, mostly river cats, though some bream. The bream he released, the catfish he kept, threading them through their gills on long cords of binder twine. The cords were tied to trash trees, with the fish dropped back into the water. It was maybe two miles to the store, where the fish were to be delivered. They would die on the walk, but they would not spoil.

By three o'clock, he had seven fish worth keeping—five on one cord, two on another. He would take three more, making ten for the order. Ten fish would earn him a dollar, if he had counted right. And maybe he was wrong, he thought. It was not easy, making a sum. Other people could do it, but he could not. He could hear a thing, a saying, and often remember it clearly and exactly, as though the saying had taken root inside his ear and was growing there like a flower, yet he could not keep numbers straight. It had always amazed him to hear people talk numbers like a tobacco auctioneer, adding and subtracting and dividing in their minds, without pencil or sheet of paper. Travis, his brother, was smart that way. Could make sums easily and quickly, could say his multiplication tables like a person singing a song from memory. He knew he was slow at such things, and it embarrassed him, but it was how God had made him and there was nothing he could do about it. His father had thought him simpleminded, pitied him for it. His mother had sided with God. "When God shortchanges you in one place, he overpays you somewhere else," his mother had declared firmly.

It was his mother who decided that God had given him the gift of fishing. Had said it one night to his father when she did not know he listened, had said, "I swear that boy could catch fish with a safety pin. They just somehow go to him when he's out there with a pole in his hand." His father had called it luck. "God don't mind being called a person's luck," his mother had countered. "You ever watch that boy when he's fishing?" she had added. "Always puts the palm of his hand on the water before he starts. That's God's doing. Tells the fish he's there, that's what it does. Travis could wade neck-deep, naked as the day he was born, and wouldn't get a nibble." Until he heard his mother say it, he had never realized the habit. Afterward, he had never failed to do it. For his mother, maybe. For the fish to know he was there. Maybe for God. He did not understand why fish came willingly to his line.

He sat on a rock that jutted out over the river, above one of the pools made from water pouring off the shoals, and he watched the bobber on his line ride the gentle lapping made from the spill. In the gazing, in the hypnotic sound of the falling water, his mind wandered to the lake, to the great bass, to his promise of returning for the fight the bass would give him. It was a put-off promise, but one he would keep at the right time. His order had been for river cats, and that was his duty. An order was an order. The army had taught him that. Somebody gives you an order, you do it. The army had said there was honor in being such a soldier, and he had found it to be so. Even with so much killing around him, he had believed in the honor of doing as he had been told. There were times, remembering it, when he believed that following orders had saved his life. Even a slow-thinking man could do what he was told to do.

The float jiggled, then disappeared. He yanked quickly at the line, felt the weight of the fish, saw it bend the tip of his rod, watched the line flash to his left, then toward him. It was a fish of size and power, angrily trying to spit the hook or break the line. He laughed a chuckle laugh, began to turn the handle on the reel.

The fish weighed three or four pounds, he guessed. Maybe five. Its head was massive, its eyes fierce, its long whiskers like thin, limp horns, its back and side fins as sharp and deadly as ice picks, its skin as slippery as oil.

Too big, he decided. A catfish was best for frying when it was smaller, one that could be held comfortably by the eater, like an ear of boiled corn. Nothing was better than the fried tail fins of a small catfish, nibbled off.

He released the fish, rebaited, cast again into the center of the pool.

The sun was on his face and back, the smell of the water deep in his lungs. He closed his eyes, let the sun coat him. His muscles ached pleasantly. He was twenty-eight years old, his body still trim from years of farming and the rigors of war, yet there were moments—such moments as he now felt—when he imagined that he was many years older. As old as some of the men who had gathered at the Bowerstown store. He inhaled slowly, holding the sweetness of the sun-colored water in his lungs.

It was a good place, he thought again. A good place.

THREE

The book she was reading was John Steinbeck's *The Grapes of Wrath*. Rereading it. Steinbeck was her favorite American writer and *The Grapes of Wrath* her favorite Steinbeck book. It caused her to ache for the Joad family, and for all the families made to migrate from the near-nothing of their existence to the flimsy hope of some future holding promise, though none knew for certain what that promise would be.

She knew people who thought of the book as depressing, but she was not one of them. It was sad, jarring in some of the passages, yet she had always found something revealing burrowed in its pages. She accepted the Joads and all of the other families as survivors, some better than others, and the way Steinbeck gave them such delicate shadings of change, they were as real to her as her own life had been.

She, too, had been a migrant of sorts, going after dreams because they seemed to hold promise.

It had lasted almost a dozen years, her migration, and what she had to show for it was a farm littered with rocks and a husband in a coffin.

No child. Only the memory of an almost-child, one lost in miscarriage, one so briefly carried she had never mentioned it to her husband. There was no reason. The pregnancy had occurred in the last days of his furlough before he shipped off to war, and when the miscarriage came—before she had even written to him of the pregnancy—he had been in battle, with enough to worry about.

The doctor had called the miscarriage a blessing. Had said something must have been wrong with the pregnancy, or her body would not have rejected the fetus.

"A lot of women have miscarriages," the doctor had explained in a voice so bland he might have been describing a chest cold. "Some of them probably don't even know what's happened. They just think it's their time of the month, after they've missed it once or twice."

The way he made it sound, it was nothing compared to the suffering of the Joads.

And that was probably true.

The Joads had no choice in doing what they did. She could have become pregnant after the war, if Boyd had agreed to it. He had not. Was not ready for children, he had said. Maybe later. Maybe.

If she had a child it would be late in life, she thought, and most likely with a man she had not yet met.

She marked the book and closed it, knowing what would be waiting for her when she opened it again.

Chapter 15.

The chapter beginning with the description of hamburger stands along Route 66—writing so rich and rhythmic it needed the snappy sound of a wire-brush drumstick over a snare drum if someone wanted to say the words aloud. You could read the words and close your eyes and see everything the eyes of Steinbeck's fingers had seen as he typed out the lines.

It was the reading of such lines that made her want to become a writer, and it was also the reason she had never made a serious effort to do it; she believed she would never be good enough to match the worst sentence John Steinbeck would ever write.

She put the book on the side table next to her reading chair and sat thinking how it would be to get in a car loaded with everything you could carry and then drive away, following the wiggling, pencil-thin mark of a road on a map, not knowing where you might be in a day or a week, or who you might meet along the way.

One thing was for certain: staying where she was left no question about where she would be in a day or a week, or who she was likely to meet.

In the Valley of Light, she was known as one of the Three Widows—all wives of men who had been in the war. Two of the men—the husbands of Gladys Mabry and Martha Briggs—had been killed in battle, her own husband by his own doing.

Three widows waiting for new men.

There were men willing to approach her, and she knew it, but she knew also that they would keep their distance until she gave some signal that her time of mourning was over for her late husband.

She knew Taylor Bowers was one of those men, and the thought of him caused a smile that was as much amusement as pleasure. Taylor Bowers was friendly and handsome in his gangly way, and he had a manner of preening that reminded her of some of the characters she read about in her books. Always rushing to assist her in his store. Always asking if she needed anything done on the farm that required a man's muscle.

When she gave the signal that her grief had ended, Taylor would be first in line at her door, and she did not know how she would handle him. It was comfortable enough being around him, but he did not cause the kind of unrest in her she had sensed the first time she looked into the eyes of Boyd Cunningham. With all his faults—and there were many—Boyd had had heat in his eyes.

The heat had been deceiving, had burned out shortly after his return from the war, but the memory of what had been was still buried somewhere, and it was tender, and, she guessed, was the reason she had not given the signal of being finished with her mourning. She had merely stayed busy, caring for the old woman and helping at the school with students having trouble with reading and mathematics.

She liked the teaching. If she had finished college, she would have become a teacher. One year at Young Harris College had given her some credibility as a substitute, as a helper, but not enough to hold a job.

She taught by a method of her own enterprise, calling it the Eureka Method.

When a child accomplished something—made out a word in a reading book and said it correctly by breaking down the syllables and then pushing out the word like a pearl formed on his or her tongue, or when one of them added or subtracted or divided numbers and got the right answer—she would have them exclaim, "Eureka!"

It was a sound of joy to Eleanor.

"Eureka!"

"Eureka!"

She had found the word in the Young Harris College library in a story about the Greek mathematician Archimedes. The story said *eureka* meant "I have found it." What Archimedes had found was a way of determining the mix of gold and alloy in the crown of the king of Syracuse. She did not tell the students about Archimedes or the crown of the king of Syracuse. She wanted them to think of it as a word of magic, as a dot of light on a night as black as pitch.

The children of the mountains needed to believe in magic.

So do I, she thought.

She got up from her chair and walked to the kitchen to return the cup she had used for her nightly coffee, and she stood looking out of the window, at the haze of light from the moon and stars. She thought she could smell honeysuckle, and the sense of it—real or imagined—was as sweet in her mouth as the nectar hummingbirds fed on from the colorful throats of flowers.

She looked at the clock on the kitchen counter. Nearly eleven. After her bedtime. She would be up early, the next day being Sunday. She would be up early because the old woman would be awake early, somehow knowing—by some body clock, by some rhythm of habit that had never become muddled—that it was church day. And though they would not go to church—not with the old woman's confusion of being among many people—they would play the radio and listen to church music, and if the old woman was thinking clearly, they would hear a sermon by some preacher making the kind of cry that ticket hawkers at carnivals made, and the way he would paint God would be no more than that—God as a sideshow freak, caged in a tent, pacing like a tiger behind steel bars. *Yowsir, yowsir, yowsir* . . . Put your dime or your quarter or your dollar in the collection plate and take a peek at God. Won't believe your eyes, you won't. One of the great wonders of the world, God was.

And the old woman would listen intently, her head bobbing, her lips making words of praise that had no sound to them.

Maybe she was wrong about all the men who were waiting to call on her, she thought. Knowing about the old woman living with her—knowing the old woman's reputation for being blunt and mean and knowing how much time the old woman demanded—not many of them would bother to waste their time.

Not many at all.

Taylor Bowers, maybe, but few others.

She left the kitchen and went through the living room to the hallway leading to the bedrooms at the back of the house, paused at the closed door of the old woman's bedroom, then opened it quietly and peeked inside. The old woman was asleep, her breathing so shallow the movement of her chest was barely visible. Eleanor could see the bandaged hand, a hand cut by a kitchen knife when the old woman imagined she had a potato to peel. The old woman had watched the blood with a curious expression, as though it belonged to someone else. Sometimes she felt as though the old woman were a ninety-pound weight draped over her shoulders, and, later, she would always be depressed over such thoughts.

She closed the door and went to her own bedroom and dressed for bed, wearing only the tops of her pajamas. She stood before the mirror on the dresser, gazing at herself. The woman who gazed back at her no longer had the smile of joy worn by the girl who had been mesmerized by the heat of a man's eyes. The woman who gazed back at her was tired, had the beginning of crow's feet at her eyes. Her face appeared pale, carried a sign of surrender. Her hair seemed lifeless. She was in her early thirties. The woman gazing back at her had the hollow look of being ancient.

She touched her face with her fingertips. Her skin felt flushed.

She turned and left the room, moved through the house to the front door, opened it, stepped outside, lifted her face to the moonlight and inhaled slowly, taking the cool of the night into her lungs and with it, the scent of honeysuckle and pine and corn grown in the garden behind her home.

A deer moved under the low-hanging limbs of a hemlock in the tree line separating the house from the road, and she stepped back instinctively, knowing she was barely dressed. She had learned that lesson. Or thought she had. A few months after Boyd's death, she had seen a man peering into the window of her home as she undressed. The man had run away, but had been caught by the sheriff. A hiker from Atlanta, giving the excuse of being lost, saying he had only stopped by the house for directions, making it out to be nothing but a big mistake. He had paid a fine and had been warned to stay in Atlanta. Supposedly, the sheriff had said to him, "You show up around here again, looking in windows, and we're going to kill you. That's about as straight as I can put it."

Afterward, she had sensed eyes watching her from dark places.

Deer eyes were all right, though.

A breeze tickled her bare legs, slipped under the hem of her pajama top, spread across her skin.

An urge to laugh shimmered across her chest, an urge to find playmates, to listen to the bird-chattering voices of the friends of her childhood when promise was everywhere, before promise became confined to her husband.

The smile that had worked its way into her face from the energy of the urges faded. She did not have friends. Not really. She knew people, but she did not have friends. Not the kinds of friends who left little pieces of themselves with her after a visit, little pieces of laughter and noisy talk scattered over the house like the confetti of a parade.

She heard another sound coming from the yard and looked toward it. A raccoon ran into a sheet of moonlight, paused, gave a masked-eye look toward her, then scurried off. She turned and went back into her home.

In bed, she thought again of *The Grapes of Wrath,* remembering the scene of the death of Grampa, and of his burial, and how the Joads had coped with the question of reporting the old man's death, and how Tom had written of the dying on a sheet of paper torn from a Bible and of that sheet of paper being put in a jar to be buried with him, and how Granma had slept during his burial—all of it done to save the money they were using to go to California.

In many ways, her life was not much better off than that of the Joads driving away from the Oklahoma dust bowl, headed for the place called California, she thought. In California almost anything seemed possible.

She did not live in a dust bowl. She lived in a place known for the sun spreading its brightness over the land, and she had come to believe there was a quaint truth to the claim. Sometimes the sun's light seemed to swirl over the valley, giving it a soft brilliance that did not exist in other places. She had tried to explain it away, saying to herself that it was nothing more than an illusion. And maybe it was that—an illusion made from words said so often they had taken on meaning. Words were powerful. Steinbeck had painted the dust bowl with word-strokes over the canvas of book paper. She could see it clearly. Rembrandt could not have painted it more vividly.

Illusions were made of words, like a magician's singsong of abracadabra secrets.

The Valley of Light could be nothing more than some old settler's abracadabra.

Still, it was hard for the mind to ignore what the eyes had seen.

The dust bowl had certainly been real enough.

She could feel a choking when she read of the dust bowl.

And there were times when she could feel the same choking in the Valley of Light, and she wondered if it would be the same in California, or some other place.

FOUR

His parents had not been churchgoers, nor had he, not beyond the occasion of his baptism at a springtime revival visited in morning services by the higher grades of the elementary school he had attended. He had given himself to the church—Methodist—because it was expected, because he was a follower and had followed classmates sitting around him to the altar, where he had received a palm-patting of water over the thick matting of his hair and, in so doing, had had his soul coated with the protective grace of God the Father, God the Son, God the Holy Ghost. It had been an experience that seemed wondrous in the moment of its happening. The old minister bending over him, smelling of shaving oils, his warm breath having a scent of mint, saying to him in a whisper that only he could hear, "Follow me and I will make you fishers of men." Out of the metaphor—though he did not think of it as that, but as something actual and physical—there had been a single pulse of blood jolting his body, rinsing him of all sin, making him as clean as a river bath. Later, he had thought about it and had wondered if what the preacher had said about being a fisher of men was the thing that struck him, causing his blood to jump inside his chest. Wondered if the preacher knew about his fishing.

He did not know if his mother and father had ever been baptized, though he believed they had. In their youth, likely. They were familiar with the Bible, often reading it at night by lamplight, and his mother was fond of certain verses which, for her, held such truth that no argument could be made against them.

Still, they had not been churchgoers, nor had they tried to convince him or his brother, Travis, that their way was the right way, choosing to let them keep their journey in such matters private and personal. Yet, they had made a path for him and for Travis, like an animal following its own scent. On Sundays, they spent the morning in rest, often in walks around their farm, making observations they might have missed during the blindness of weekday work. In afternoons, they would do small tasks in the home, or around it, or they would accept visits from neighbors, or make visits of their own.

At his father's death in 1939, the neighbors had gathered in force at a small Baptist church near them, and a young minister who was a stranger to the community had said kind words about his father's gentle nature, taking hints from his eavesdropping of the neighbors. And that, too, had affected Noah. A man who had never met his father had issued the petition to have God the Father, God the Son, God the Holy Ghost accept his father into the society of heavenly hosts. It had been a simple ritual, as quietly conducted as the Sunday morning walk of his parents.

Noah did not know about his mother's funeral. She had died of a stroke while he was in Germany nestled against the stock of a rifle in a soggy foxhole, with gunsmoke angels floating in the air around him. He had visited the gravesite only once, bringing flowers, which he divided—half for his mother, half for his father. Side by side in the ground, dirt mounded over them like a red wool blanket, they had seemed as peaceful in death as they had in life.

• • •

He was awake early, as was his habit, and made his breakfast of grits and coffee—enough for two cups. Knowing it was Sunday, he did not think of fishing. There would be no reason. On Sunday, in the Valley of Light, no one would buy fish, but it was the same everywhere he went. Sundays were not used for buying or selling. If he fished on a Sunday, it was for himself, sometimes for pleasure, sometimes for food. Mostly, Sunday was a day for travel, for the leaving of one place and the search of another. Sometimes on his travels he passed churches with services and could hear voices singing old songs from hymnals, and he knew the people doing the singing were only holding the hymnals, not looking at them. No reason to look. The songs had been committed to memory over years of singing them. Often, he had stopped near the churches, out of sight, and listened and later would find himself humming the songs as he walked, even singing the remembered verses in a voice so quiet only he could hear it. "Just As I Am" was his favorite.

It would be a squandered day for him, one he would spend walking the valley, studying it, maybe going to the lake that Hoke Moore had called the Chatuge, maybe walking to Hayesville if he could find the right road. The eye-patch man, who had identified himself as Howard Reynolds, had invited him to services at the Church of the Resurrected Christ, telling him it was the only church in the valley, and he had said he would think about it, but had not made a binding promise. In the exchange, both men knew the invitation and the reply had been only an exercise of civility. Still, it had been a good meeting with Howard Reynolds, who had been astonished at the fish delivered to him. Howard Reynolds had said, "You stick around, boy, you'll be taking home twenty dollars from the fishing. Not a man around here could of done what you done in that short of time, not as bad as fishing's been lately. Not one, not even Littleberry Davis."

The day was sun-bright, cloudless, yet cooled by a slight breeze. By eight o'clock, he had made his camp safe from the nosy inspection of animals and had left the lake and the woods around the lake, finding himself wandering.

He discovered a road nearby and followed it for a short while and then veered off into the woods, making his way by curiosity. In a short time, he came to a large body of water that he believed to be the Chatuge. It was hard for him to imagine it was man-made, the way it was settled into the land, as natural as any lake formed of its own accord. A pretty place, he thought. A good place to fish, for fish would have a liking for the water with its washed-in food from small branches and creeks.

He turned away from the lake and made his path back toward the road. There was no purpose in the path he took. No urge. His body moved in the direction that it chose, an aimless wandering not unlike the meandering of a butterfly on a still day. If he had been forced to make a reason for the path of his walk, he would have said it was gut instinct, using the same explanation his army sergeant had used to dismiss his bewilderment over the presence of some guardian force he could not see or touch.

Above him, he heard the drone of an airplane and he raised his face to the sound. High up, he could see the plane making its slow crawl across the blue-lit dome of sky, its four engines jutting out over its wings, and he remembered watching paratroopers leaping from airplanes in the war. Little bubbles of bodies striking the wind, hurling away from the black dot of the opened door, dragging parachutes. It was like watching something being born—small, wiggling animals erupting from their mother's belly.

The airplane crawled away, taking its droning sound with it.

He could smell the faint scent of the rosemary soap he had used for his lake bath on the day before, and for washing his face that morning. In the war, he had gone days without bathing. Now, he was obsessed with being clean. The scent of the soap gave him pleasure, caused him to remember his mother's soap-making, taking lye from the drippings of a potash barrel and combining it with the fat of pig slaughterings. The rosemary soap was a good buy, he thought. Worth the money. He would get another bar before leaving the valley, he decided.

From far away, he could hear the faint sound of a church bell.

Church of the Resurrected Christ, he believed.

The bell ring was so faint it could have been something hidden in the air, something made by thin clouds bumping into one another.

He found himself leaving the woods and crossing a field of long-dead corn stalks, and he realized that he was going again in the direction of the house belonging to the woman named Eleanor Cunningham.

The field had not been plowed in a year, perhaps longer, he judged. It was weed-covered, too rocky for good farming, eroded in the middle below the washed-through break of a terrace. On the ground, there were curled, decaying cobs where left-behind nubbins of corn had been gnawed down by rats and squirrels, or pecked away by crows. He guessed it was the last crop that Eleanor Cunningham's husband had planted and harvested before taking his life.

He left the field and walked the road toward the house, slowing as he neared it. Through the windbreak of trees, he could see the car and beyond the car, Eleanor Cunningham. She was near the barn, going to a place in the pasture he could not see, and then retreating from it, going back, retreating. From where he watched, Noah believed something had happened that perplexed her, or frightened her.

He stepped from the road and walked through the trees toward her, approaching cautiously. He saw her look up in recognition.

"You got some trouble?" he asked quietly.

"Yes," Eleanor said in a voice that wanted to be brave, but trembled. "One of my cows is down. Dying, I'd guess."

"I'll take a look," he told her.

"Thank you," Eleanor replied. She paused. "You're that fisherman."

"Yes ma'am," he said. "Noah Locke."

"You were at the store."

"Yes ma'am," Noah replied. He glanced toward the pasture, said again, "I'll take a look."

"Thank you," Eleanor repeated.

The cow was dying. She lay on her side, her head on the ground, legs folded over legs. Her eyes were dry, making a glazed stare, as though seeing some place far away, too far to reach. Her breathing was labored, a foam holding in her nose.

Noah squatted close to the head of the cow, leaning his elbow on his knee. The cow's eyes floated to him and he said to the cow in words that did not carry, "I know." Then he stood and walked back to Eleanor. "You got a rifle?" he asked.

Eleanor answered with a nod.

"If you get it, I'll take care of things," Noah said.

Again, Eleanor nodded. "It needs to be shot?"

"Yes ma'am."

"I can't just leave it lying out there," Eleanor said.

"No ma'am," Noah replied. "If you want some meat from it, I can butcher it for you, but if you just want it taken off and buried, I can do that."

"Meat?" Eleanor said. She shook her head. "No, I don't want any. She's too old."

"Yes ma'am," Noah said. "I'd say so, too." He paused. Then: "If you got some trace chain and a shovel, I can drag it off with your car and bury it."

"I can't ask you to do that."

"You don't worry about it," Noah told her. "I'll find a good spot."

"She's too big to bury."

"I've done it before," Noah said. "It'll take a little time, but I can do it."

Eleanor did not watch the mercy killing of the cow. She sat at the kitchen table in her house, waiting, her body tensed for the shot. When it came—a sharp crack—she jerked involuntarily. And then she listened, letting the knowing of sounds tell her what Noah Locke was doing. The car motor. The clattering of chain pulled across the car's frame. The strain of the car dragging its weight. And then nothing. The nothing told her that Noah Locke had pulled the cow away, deep into the pasture, to a spot that would be soft enough for digging. She knew he would be working for many hours.

At one o'clock, Eleanor carried a meal of baked sweet potato, ham biscuits and iced tea in a quart sealing jar to Noah, following the trail of the car and the dragged body of the cow. The spot he had selected for the burial was in the edge of a stand of new pines, growing where older trees had been harvested for lumber mills. The ground was gray and sandy from wash-off of the mountain above it, making it surprisingly soft and free of rock, and the digging had gone well. He was almost shoulder-deep in a hole wide enough and long enough for the cow. The trace chain used for the dragging had been dropped over the side of the hole for climbing out and lowering himself back in.

He took the offered food reluctantly—in the fashion of rural manners—saying it was not necessary to feed him, but he was privately glad for it. He had not eaten well in days and the work had tired him, reminding him of a weakness in his back earned by lifting ammunition cartons into a Jeep. A pulled muscle, he had suspected, but it was more. He did not know what, but something more.

He knew being with him was awkward for Eleanor, could see it in the way she stood away from him as he sat eating, leaning against a hickory tree, letting its shade cover him. He knew it by her eyes making glances to and away from the cow. Knew it by the way she searched for words to bridge the silence between them. Knew it by the measure of his own discomfort, for he had not been alone in the presence of a woman for a long time.

Still, it was good to have a break from work and to have some company. People of the hills were often like skittish animals, staying to themselves the way they did.

The death of the cow was no surprise to her, Eleanor told him, being so old. She expected the mule to die soon, also. There had been another mule—younger, stronger—but it had been sold, since there was no longer a need for it with the farming stopped. And the calf of the milk cow had been sold also, after it got to the weaning stage, she added. Not enough food to go around for all of them.

The old mule's name was Fanny and it had been kept more as a pet than a working animal, she said. Even when it had been worked, it was too slow to be of much value.

He smiled easily, said his father had also owned a white mule named Fanny. Jittery. Fast-stepping. Given to kicking at the trace chains. He had grown up believing all white mules were spirited.

"Not my Fanny," she said; then realizing how the comment must have sounded, she turned away to hide her embarrassment.

He looked down, feeling the crimson of a blush rising over his neck. A nearby bird made a mocking chirp, almost like laughter.

She turned back after a moment, touched her face with her hand as though testing the July heat. She said, "Were you in the war, Mr. Locke?"

He drank from the jar of tea, answered, "I was."

"My late husband was, too," she said simply.

"Yes ma'am," he replied. "The man at the store told me—the storekeeper."

She let a pause build, then: "Taylor Bowers. He tell you how Boyd died?"

The question made Noah uneasy. "Yes ma'am," he said quietly. "Sorry to hear about it."

"Thank you," she said evenly, as though she had given the answer many times. She glanced back at the cow, held the gaze. "Why do you think he did that, Mr. Locke? Why would a man go through a war and come home and kill himself?"

"I don't know, ma'am."

"Nobody does," she said. She added, "I don't think he knew himself. Maybe it was because he lived and there were others from here who didn't."

"Could of been," he replied.

"Sometimes I think it was because he was at one of those camps where all the Jews were killed, and he couldn't get it out of his mind," she said.

"Yes ma'am."

"Did you know about those camps?"

"Yes ma'am," he answered. "I was at one of them."

"You were? Which one?"

"The one they called Dachau," he said.

The expression on Eleanor's face changed to curiosity. She said, "I've read about them, because of Boyd. That was one of the worst."

"I don't know," he answered honestly. "It was bad."

"You have trouble forgetting it?"

"Some," he said, keeping the answer short, not wanting to talk about it.

"I don't understand how all that could happen," she said.

"Hard to make sense of some things," he said.

"I guess I've lived long to enough to know that a lot of things don't make sense." She paused again, turning her gaze back to him. "I thank you for what you're doing, helping out. I want you to have supper at the house."

"That's all right," he said. "What you brought me will do."

"I wish you would," she said earnestly. "Maybe Taylor said something about the rumor of Boyd coming home from the war with a lot of money—and he did have some that caused some talk—but if he had any left over when he died, I don't know anything about it. It's why I'm trying to sell the place. No way of me making any money out here, but I guess there's not many people looking for a farm that's got more rocks than dirt on it."

"No ma'am, I guess not," Noah said, remembering the rocks of the cornfield he had crossed.

"The truth is, I don't have much to pay for all you're doing, but I can feed you. I'd not feel right if I didn't," she said.

"You don't owe me," he told her. "I can't take money for just helping somebody."

"Then you'll have supper," she said.

"I don't think it'd be right, ma'am," he said after a moment.

She looked at him curiously. A hint of a smile lifted in her face. "Is it because you think I live alone?"

His answer was mumbled: "Yes ma'am."

"I don't," she replied.

He looked at her quizzically.

"My husband's grandmother lives with me. I take care of her for a little money from my in-laws. I think it's their way of saying I still belong to the family." The way she said it sounded almost bitter.

"I didn't know," Noah said.

"Taylor didn't tell you?"

"No ma'am."

"Sometimes I think they forget about her," she said. "I know Arthur and Rachel do." She paused, explained, "Arthur and Rachel are Boyd's parents, and I guess I sound mean about it, but they don't come around very much."

Noah let a disapproving frown say it was sad to treat old people in such a way.

She added, "So you'd be having supper with the two of us, not just me."

"All right," he replied hesitantly, knowing there was a matter of pride to be considered and knowing also that he would be hungry again before his work was finished.

"How old are you, Mr. Locke?" she asked.

The question surprised him. "Twenty-eight," he answered.

"I'm only three years older," she said. "You don't need to call me ma'am."

He smiled, stood, handed her the empty tea jar. "I'll do that—on a trade. You don't call me mister."

"All right," she said. She looked again at the cow, then began her walk back across the pasture.

FIVE

The supper, taken at the dining room table, was abundant in food—pan-fried chicken, butter-rich creamed potatoes, snap beans, garden onions and peppers, corn bread, mint tea, a pie of fresh peaches—yet the mood of it was awkward. Boyd Cunningham's grandmother was tiny, brittle-old, her shoulders bowed, her eyes watery, her hair white and thin, her skin powdery. She seemed mindless, the way her head bobbed constantly on the hinge of her neck, the way her hands moved over her lap, like someone trying to brush away crumbs from her dress or to make a cat-in-the-cradle without the string to do it with. A bandage was on her left hand, reminding Noah of the iodine and gauze roll Eleanor had purchased in Taylor Bowers's store, but he did not ask about it. The old woman did not speak, and Noah believed she did not understand anything Eleanor said to her. She did not sit at the table but in a rocking chair Eleanor had moved into the dining room. A man's belt held her in the chair, circling her waist, buckled in the back behind two of the chair slats. She knew it looked cruel, Eleanor said of the belt, but it was done for safety.

Eleanor called the old woman Granny, but had given the name of Beatrice Cunningham to Noah in making an introduction that was one-sided since the old woman did not lift her face to acknowledge him.

"She's not feeling all that well today," Eleanor said in a kind way. "I'll give her some candy later on." Then, remembering she had bought candy on her first meeting of Noah, she added, "Hershey bars. She likes Hershey bars. Sometimes I think it's Hershey bars that keeps her alive. Maybe I should write to them and give them a testimonial."

They ate slowly, employing manners that seemed necessary to ease the discomfort each of them felt. The talk offered was mostly from Eleanor. Small talk with long gaps of silence, and though she made an attempt to have Noah say something of his life, she realized quickly he was a quiet and reluctant man.

He said only that he had been born in Elbert County, Georgia, had grown up there with his parents and his brother, helping his father sharecrop the farm where they lived. For two years after the death of his father, he had farmed the land on his own before leaving for the war. Said his mother had died while he was away, and when he returned from the war, another family was living on the farm, sharecropping. And then he had taken up fishing. When asked about his brother, he replied, "He's still in Elbert County." He did not say his brother was in jail.

What he offered was said with so few words that much of it was assumed, not spoken, leaving Eleanor to fill space with a story of her own life—born in Georgia, the third child of a three-child family. Her parents still lived near Hiawassee, she said. Her siblings—two sisters—were married, both living with their husbands in Gainesville. One was a nurse, another a teacher. Her parents were readers, a habit each of their children had acquired, which explained the long shelves of books that lined the walls of her home. She and her sisters had a kind of lending library system, swapping books after they had been read, but neither of her sisters had as many bookcases as she did.

"Boyd made them for me when he came home," she said. "It's about all he did for months—work on this house. He was doing carpentry work before the war—that and trying to farm, but he was better at building things than growing things." She paused, smiled, added, "Put in a bathroom and wired everything for electricity, which is something I didn't think we'd ever get, and then he got them to run a telephone line in with it. After that, he put in the bookcases. He just got up one morning and left and came back with all the lumber and started building." She paused. "He knew I liked to read." Another pause. "Do you?" she asked.

It was a question that had always made Noah uncomfortable. He had never read a book—not a long one—start to finish. Reading was not easy for him, the words vanishing from memory as soon as his eyes passed over them. What he knew, he had learned from listening and watching. His teachers had passed him along, grade to grade, with tiresome sighs and with whispers about him being slow-witted, and he had accepted their judgment.

"Not much," he answered. "Never been much of a reader."

"Nothing wrong with that. Not everyone is," Eleanor said. "When I was younger, just a girl, I had thoughts of becoming a writer. Books for children. But things took a different turn." She looked across the room at the shelves of books—oddly out of place in the house of a farmer—and she smiled. "A lot of words," she said. "But none of them are mine. It's the only thing I'll miss about this place when I finally find somebody to buy it—all those bookcases."

She told the story in a light voice, though it had a nervous edge, leaving Noah to believe she was not accustomed to so much talking and wanted to avoid saying anything that would sound boastful. He knew he should be responding, but he did not, not beyond nodding and a smile made out of politeness. Yet, he liked her smile, remembering what Taylor Bowers had said about it, that it was the kind of smile you could see a long time after she gave it.

When the supper was finished, he made his compliments of the meal, spoke his appreciation, then stood to leave, saying it was time he found his way back to his campsite, the day still holding some light.

"I'll drive you," Eleanor told him.

"No need for that," he said. "It's not far, where I'm going."

"Doesn't matter," she insisted, standing. "You've got to be bone tired. Where's your camp?"

"At a little lake down the road," he said.

He saw the flicker of shock on her face, in the blink of her eyes. She said in a small voice, "Oh . . ."

"It's not far," he said again. "You've got your husband's grandmother to look after."

"She'll be fine by herself," she said. "She's just sitting there, anyway. Doesn't know anything going on around her most of the time. I don't think she's said a dozen words in a week. I'll drive you. There's a pull-off on the road that'll put you maybe two hundred yards from the lake." She paused, offered a weak smile. "I know the lake well," she added quietly. "It's where my husband died."

He did not speak, did not know what to say.

"Are you using that old shack?" she asked.

"No," he answered awkwardly. "Didn't know who to ask about it, and it don't seem right using a place that belongs to somebody else."

"It's all right," she said. "Use it. Lots of people have over the years—or they used to. My late husband did. He used to go there to stay the night, just to be by himself. I think everything there—the cooking utensils, the lamp, the cots, everything—was something Boyd put there. Use anything you need, anything at all."

"I appreciate it," Noah said.

"The man who built the lake—his name was Arch Wheeler—put up the shack so he'd have a place to stay in when he wanted to go fishing at night," she added. "He died about six months after the lake filled up with water. They found him sitting in a rocking chair on the porch, facing the lake, like he was watching the sun go down and his life went down with it. They said there was a smile on his face, like he had seen something that made him so happy he couldn't let go of it. It was just after they put the fish in, and he never got to fish in it at all. His son owns it now, but his son lives in Texas somewhere. Not far from Dallas, I think. Comes back here every three or four years. Doesn't matter to him who fishes the lake, or uses the shack. Boyd's daddy helped build it and Boyd used to look after it, so I guess that makes me the person who can give permission to use it."

She paused. "Do you know the name of that lake? It's called the Lake of Grief." She paused again, watched for a reaction from Noah, saw none. "Arch Wheeler made a famous statement about it—at least famous for this community. Building the lake cost him a lot more money than he thought it would, and one day when somebody asked him about it, he said, 'If I'd known how much grief it was going to cause me, I'd never have built it.' After that, everybody called it the Lake of Grief." She looked toward the swaying head of Beatrice Cunningham. "For me I guess it's the right name," she added softly. "People around here think it's haunted. That's why no one ever goes there. You can hear all kinds of stories about it. Dogs chasing game around there and coming back out of the woods whimpering, their hair turned gray. Hunters telling of seeing lights at night moving across the lake. That sort of thing. It's the kind of talk you hear a lot of in the mountains. I've never met anyone who hasn't seen at least one ghost, and if they haven't, they know someone who has. Boyd used to laugh about it. He used to say he liked going there so he could have a conversation with Arch Wheeler's ghost. Said he and Arch were drinking buddies." She paused, looked at Noah. "It was his way of trying to scare me, I think, but it was a waste of time. I don't believe in ghosts."

The drive from the house to the pull-off of the lake was taken in silence. At the pull-off—a wedge of open land that had the faint look of a place where a house might have been—she stopped the car and turned slightly to face Noah.

"Could I ask you something?" she said.

"All right," he told her.

"When you were at Dachau, you saw a lot of children in the camp, didn't you?"

Noah dipped his head. "I did," he said quietly.

"Did you want to bring one of them home with you?"

For a moment, Noah did not answer. He looked out of the window, at the dimming light, the gathering of darkness under the trees. In his memory, he could see the hollow-eyed faces of boys standing motionless behind chain fences. Then: "I guess so. I guess everybody did, in one way or another. Not much anybody could do for them. Give them some food, things like that."

"It's not easy to talk about, is it?"

"No," he said honestly.

"My husband met a little girl at the camp his company liberated," she said. "He wrote me that he wanted to bring her to America. I didn't know what to think. It wasn't like him—not at all. He'd never had much to do with children. Even told me once that it didn't much matter to him if we had any, but it seemed like he just couldn't get her out of his mind."

"It's kind of hard to forget," he said.

"I know it must be," she said softly. Then: "I want to thank you for what you did today. I don't know what I would have done if you hadn't come along."

"Glad to help out," he said. "I appreciate the ride." He opened the door to the car and stepped out.

"I think maybe I could use some fish tomorrow night," she said suddenly, leaning across the car seat. "Catfish or bream or even some trout. Doesn't matter to me. My husband loved catfish, so I guess that's what I should cook. Three or four ought to be plenty. Unless you're moving on."

"Not for a while," he told her. "I'll be glad to bring some by."

"You know there's not any in the lake, don't you?"

"That's what they were saying at the store," he replied.

"My husband told me that one time there used to be a lot of fish in it, but they just disappeared, and nobody knows why. There's all kind of stories about it. Some say it was poisoned. Some say they all washed out through the drain. When I found Boyd's body there, everybody got it in their head that the lake was a place of dying, since it's where Arch Wheeler and Boyd were both found, and there was a lot of talk about Arch Wheeler's ghost, of course. Exactly the kind of thing you'd expect to hear when there aren't any answers that make sense. All I know is nobody even tries fishing there anymore. At least nobody I know of."

He thought of the leaping bass he had teased with his lure and of his dream, and he wondered if he should tell Eleanor of the dream and of the bass, but he did not. It would be a curious story to her, since she was one of those who believed there were no fish in the lake, and the telling of the dream of the ghost-fish might cause some fear for her. "I'll see you sometime tomorrow afternoon," he said in the muttering way he talked when he was uncertain of the right words to use. Then he closed the door.

She had said too much, she thought. It was a fault, and she knew it, and the drive back to her home was one of regret. One of her sisters—Miriam—had always teased her for being a jabbermouth and it was true. Once, she had felt good about talking, had loved the sound of words pouring from her like happy music. It was part of her nature, like the color of her hair and eyes. In school, she had easily won classroom debates because she had no fear of speaking before an audience. Teachers had called her exceptional, often saying they envied her—so naturally gifted at such a young age. Teachers had predicted remarkable things for her. Then she had met Boyd Cunningham in her history class at Young Harris College and Boyd Cunningham had stunned her with his presence, and the music of words had become the music of flesh, the language spoken between them read from fingertips of touch like the raised codes of Braille. She had married a man who overwhelmed her and she had become silent in his presence. Yet, for a reason she did not understand, her silence had ended with the appearance of a stranger who had done a good deed for her, and when the words began again, she had been unable to stop them.

A thought struck her: Did Noah Locke remind her of her husband?

No, she decided. No. Noah was quiet. He had a way of standing that made it seem as though he were about to take a backward step, but his feet never moved. Her husband had been talkative, noisy even. A braggart. She did not think Noah Locke had ever called attention to himself.

The disappeared sun had left a pale sheet of light, melon-flesh in color. On surrounding hills, trees had already pulled the dark cover of night over them.

The war, she thought. It was the war. Noah Locke had been in the war. The war was the tie between them. Only the war.

Tomorrow, given a chance, she would apologize again to him for her assault of words, for being a jabbermouth.

She would pay for the fish that he would deliver—if he did—and she would wish him well.

She thought of her fish order—three or four—and wondered why she had asked for such a large number when one would do, knowing that Boyd's grandmother would not eat fish. Maybe he thought she was hinting at inviting him for another supper.

She felt an uneasy blush on her face, thought, Why did I do that?

She pulled the car to a stop in front of her home, switched off the motor, said in a whisper, "Three or four fish." And then she smiled foolishly, a young girl's smile. She rubbed at her face with her fingers, kneading the smile. She said again, "Three or four fish." And she laughed quietly, wearily. She opened the car door and got out and walked into her house.

SIX

At the Lake of Grief, Noah moved his belongings into the shack, taking the mattress and blanket and pillow from the inside cot and putting them on the cot on the porch. Cooler sleeping outside, he reasoned. Besides, the room needed airing out, and he had raised the windows and left open the house door to let the breeze go through it. On the porch he would sleep comfortably enough and the moon would give him light through the mesh of the screen wire and the wire would keep out the mosquitoes.

He sat for a time in the rocker, watching the night turn dark-thick and moon-glazed, letting the day settle into his memory. A long day, it had been. The mercy killing of the cow and its burial, the filling supper, the stories of Eleanor Cunningham, the silent presence of the old woman who stared at her hands, her body so thin it made him think of the living skeletons at Dachau.

At Dachau, on the railroad siding running into the camp, he had seen freight cars holding bodies that had been stacked as fire-wood would be stacked, body on body, the rot of death causing them to sink into one another. A soldier with him had said,

"Bones. They ain't nothing but bones." And Noah had always thought of the cars as Bone Cars.

Inside the camp, there were more stacks of bodies placed in rows—like the rows of a woodpile lodged between posts. Some of the stacks head high, oddly neat in their arrangement. He had watched a young boy—twelve, maybe; maybe younger, being so thin it made guessing a tricky thing—walk along the rows, searching them, running his fingers delicately over the corpses, calling in his language, "Papa? Papa?" Noah did not know the language, but he knew what the words were: "Papa? Papa?"

Remembered a lieutenant, his face crimson with anger, tears streaming shamelessly, bellow to him, "Goddamn it, get that kid out of there."

He and another soldier, whose name he knew only as Makepeace—remembered it because it was an odd name for war—had gone to the boy, had tried to lead the boy away from the rows of bodies. The boy had resisted, pulled from them, making his small cry, "Papa? Papa?" He had handed his rifle to Makepeace and had picked the boy up and carried him away. Air-light, the boy. Bones beneath clothing. Like holding a bird. The boy had finally rested his head against Noah's shoulder, his call fading to a whisper: "Papa? Papa?"

He had taken the boy to a medic and left him and returned to his guard duty, where Makepeace waited with his rifle, taking deep, quick swallows of air to keep from sobbing. Makepeace had murmured, "Son of a bitch. Son of a bitch."

And they had stood, not speaking, watching. A man, mostly naked, wandered aimlessly into an electric fence, his first steps in freedom ended by electrocution. He did not cry out. Did not have the strength. His body jerked wildly, twisted once, fell. Noah believed he could hear the cracking of bones.

No one went to the man. From nearby buildings, emaciated bodies oozed through doorways. A chorus of voices made in the jabbering of many languages—Yiddish, Russian, Polish, German—hummed in the air. Celebration and eulogy made of the same words.

A man had clawed forward through the wad of bodies and approached Noah and Makepeace. He had a wide-mouthed, toothless smile. His skin, as gray as fine ash, seemed glued to his bones. He had said, in a hoarse voice, that he could speak English. Had said he would volunteer to translate if translation was needed.

The lieutenant was called for, was told what the prisoner had offered. Yes, the lieutenant said to the man. Gave the man a small amount of chocolate and his canteen. The man slipped the chocolate into his mouth, sucked on it, making tears come to his eyes. Licked the filth from his fingers that held the candy. Lifted the canteen to his mouth and drank slowly.

The lieutenant instructed him to tell the prisoners around them that they were free but needed to be patient. Soon they would receive food, medical attention, clothing.

The man turned and waved his arms frantically above his head. He began speaking in a shout—German, Noah had believed—and the close-by crowd became quiet. The man motioned to the lieutenant, made a small bow.

From the crowd, someone asked a question. Noah had not known the language, but he knew the meaning: Is it true? Are we free?

"*Ja, ja,*" the translator answered eagerly. He said again in a stronger voice, "*Ja, ja,*" as though the words were a sudden discovery. And the words were picked up among the listeners, repeated over and over, until the words became a cheer—a song, an anthem—lifted above their heads by waving hands.

From behind the crowd, a greater noise erupted, and the crowd parted, turned back. A group of men—younger, stronger than others—shoved at a German soldier who wore the insignia of the SS, bringing him into the center of the crowd, forcing him to kneel before an older man who wore a dirty rag around his head, covering his right eye. A look of horror was on the soldier's face. The crowd became silent. One of the men stepped forward, handed the older man a pistol, a luger taken from the soldier, then stepped back.

The older man stood motionless, staring at the gun. His lips moved, but did not make words. His arms struggled to lift the pistol, the barrel aimed at the soldier's head. The soldier whispered, "*Nein, nein* . . ."

"Sir," a sergeant said to the lieutenant in a voice that carried warning.

"Shut up," the lieutenant ordered.

"He's going to kill that man," the sergeant said.

"Who gives a shit?" the lieutenant growled.

"Sir, he's a prisoner," the sergeant replied. "The Geneva—"

"Look around you, soldier," the lieutenant hissed. "You think the goddamn Geneva Convention did the first goddamn thing for these people?"

"But, sir, you can't—"

"Mister, I gave you an order, didn't I?" the lieutenant snapped.

"Sir?"

"Shut up," the lieutenant said again.

A low moan began in the crowd, a shuffling of feet. The old man with the eye-rag let his face scan the crowd slowly, his head bobbing. His mouth opened and his tongue tipped tenderly over his cracked lips. He turned his face back to the man kneeling before him, glared at him bitterly, then pressed the trigger of the luger. The German soldier's left temple exploded in blood, in fragments of bone and brain, and he fell, rolled onto his back. No one moved, no one spoke. The prisoners gazed down at the fallen body, watched the last heaving of life leave his chest. Then one of the men crept forward, leaned over, spat on the soldier, and a cheer flew up around him.

The sergeant's body shivered. He swallowed hard, brought his face erect, lifted his eyes above the crowd.

"What was that about?" the lieutenant asked the translator.

"An eye for an eye," the translator replied, making a motion with his hand to his eyes. He explained that the soldier had blinded the old man for no reason more compelling than looking away when the soldier addressed him.

"Looks like he got more than an eye in exchange," the lieutenant said.

"You could kill him a hundred times and it would still not be equal," the translator said bitterly.

In the dark beside the lake called Grief, Noah moved from the rocker to the cot, stretched across it, pulled the blanket over him, resting his head on the pillow, and he tried to push the memory of Dachau away from him.

Still, something was there. Not Dachau. Something else. A sense that he was being watched.

He closed his eyes. Thought again of the man in Dachau with an eye-rag over his face, and picturing the man made him think of Howard Reynolds, who wore an eye patch to cover a dead eye. He liked Howard Reynolds, liked the boy with him, the boy with thick eyeglasses. His grandson, Howard had said, reaching out to run his hand over the boy's head, and the boy—Matthew, was his name, Noah remembered suddenly—had flashed a glad smile.

"He likes fishing," Howard had added. "Maybe before you leave, we can all go over to the Chatuge and drop a line."

"Yes sir," Noah had replied. "I'd like doing that."

Outside, he could hear the lake breathing in rest. Real as a person. Soft. Slow. He wondered if the breathing was from the lake or from Arch Wheeler's ghost. Or maybe from the ghost of Boyd Cunningham.

Whatever it was, it was not frightening.

Whatever it was, it lulled him to sleep.

Surprisingly, his sleep was a good one, a sleep earned from his day's labor of digging and from the filling supper, and he awoke realizing he could not remember dreaming. It was a good sign, he thought. During the war, and after it, he had dreamed nightly, and the dreams had often left him spent and dazed. He had expected to dream after thinking of Dachau. Not to dream was relief. Not to dream was hope.

He made a small fire in the shack's stove and boiled water for his coffee, but was not hungry, not after so much food at the supper prepared by Eleanor. Taking his coffee, he walked to the lake and stood at the water's edge watching the morning light turn the water's surface to glass, reflecting trees and mountains that surrounded it. God taking a look at himself, his mother had called it, for his mother believed God had better judgment than to take on the resemblance of man. Trees were grander, more noble. God would be a tree, if he needed to be anything at all.

The lake was a good place, as Hoke Moore had said it was. Peaceful. Hard to believe it was a place where a man had taken his life.

From the middle of the lake, he saw the water shimmer, saw a bulge, saw a ripple slide gently down the swelling.

A smile broke over his face. Mr. Fish, he thought.

Hoke Moore's fish.

Maybe he would keep his promise to the bass and catch it and give it to Eleanor Cunningham as proof there were fish in the lake.

He squatted at the water, touched it with the palm of his free hand, could feel the vibration of life that swam deep below the surface, hidden like bees in a hollow tree. He wiggled his fingers in the water, imagined the life stirring, fish darting like meteorites across the universe of the lake.

He remembered his dream of fish swimming in air, following the ghost of the bass.

Maybe the people of the valley had told their stories about the lake being a place of dying while they were there, he thought, and their words had been trapped in the tangled limbs of the trees and had stayed there to be heard in dreams. It was possible. In the war, he had heard voices of men long after they had died, had imagined their voices clinging to his uniform like grime.

Marvin Linquist.

Marvin Linquist had been like an older brother to him, guiding him along through boot camp and then in the fighting. From Kentucky. Tall. Strong. Made nervous laughter out of being scared. In quiet times, talked about his wife back home, their two children, the land he farmed, his games of baseball with a team of town boys. Bragged proudly about the long home runs he hit, about the crowd calling him Babe and how that had made him want to take everybody's turn at bat, and damn the rules that said he couldn't. Those who made the rules had never seen him hit.

Marvin Linquist had been such a yarn-spinner of stories that other soldiers found their way to him when there was a lull in the fighting. Made them smile, Marvin did. Made them write home to tell about Marvin and his stories, which was better than telling about killing and being killed.

When Marvin was shot—the bullet exploding through his spleen, his warm blood steaming in the cold air of winter—he had collapsed into Noah's arms, had turned his surprised, paling face to Noah, had said in a whisper, "I wish you was God, Noah. If you was, I'd know I was going home." And then he had nuzzled his head gently against Noah's chest, like a child wanting to nurse. He had exhaled softly, a gurgled sigh. And then he had died. For the rest of the war, Noah had seen the angel-ghost of Marvin Linquist in acid clouds of gunsmoke.

Even now, Noah realized, he could hear Marvin saying, "I wish you was God, Noah."

He stood, dried his hand across the front of his shirt. He took a sip of his coffee and let Marvin's face take focus in his memory, like a pose in a camera picture. In the picture, Marvin was grinning, his mouth fixed in the way it always was when a story was about to spring from his tongue.

He thought of the trip he had taken to Kentucky a year earlier, tugged there by a promise he had exchanged with Marvin: if one died, the other would make a visit to his grave site, just to make sure the body had made it home. In a cemetery near the town of Paris, at a grave that seemed not long dug, he had found a small tombstone giving Marvin's name and the dates marking the separation of his birth and death. Also, his service rank—*Cpl., United States Army*. A line of truth chiseled into the granite tombstone told his last story: *He Gave His Life to Keep Life from Perishing.*

It was strange remembering Marvin Linquist, seeing him so clearly. A sense of being in Marvin's presence seemed to swim around him, and he realized suddenly, with surprise, why Taylor Bowers had appeared familiar at their meeting: Taylor Bowers could have been the twin of Marvin Linquist—the way they looked, the way they talked. And that, too, was a sign, a good one.

He took his pocket watch from his pocket and looked at it. Twenty minutes after seven. He could be at Taylor Bowers's store by eight, he reasoned, and if the offer to paint the store still stood, he would take it.

SEVEN

Each morning, when she looked into the bedroom occupied by Beatrice Cunningham, Eleanor half expected to find the old woman dead, yet she was always awake, her head resting on her pillow, her open eyes gazing at the ceiling as though mesmerized by something only she could see.

Death would be better than the kind of living the old woman had, Eleanor believed. What the old woman had was not living. It was only an act of remaining, of holding on, of being there.

Still, Eleanor was always privately relieved to find the old woman alive. She did not want the guilt of wondering if she secretly wished for the surprise of death, and the wish carried enough power to make it real.

Yet, it was not a wish. Not a conscious wish. Maybe only a dream, but that, too, was bothersome. In one of her books she had read that dreams were wishes too secret to admit without sleep, and she believed there was truth in the thought. She had had many dreams that would seem foolish to anyone who knew her.

On some days, the old woman was alert and would roll her face to Eleanor on the morning peek-in. Would say she had slept well, or that she was hungry. On mornings of hunger, she always wanted pancakes with corn syrup, and as she ate—slowly, absorbing the food more than chewing it—she would tell Eleanor stories that lingered fresh and real in some lobe of her brain, memories passing over her mind like the sun passing over Earth—bright and clear, then fading into night. The stories intrigued Eleanor, and she had found it easy to make pictures of Beatrice Cunningham as a young woman, a wife, a mother. Could hear Beatrice Cunningham singing in the stories she told of singing. Could see her at quilt-making, at cooking, at field work. With each of the stories, the old woman offered smiles that held some gladness.

She did not talk of hard times. It was as though she had willed the hard times to die off, yet Eleanor knew of them from stories told by Boyd. One was of the death of Beatrice's husband, who had been found shot in the barn on the farm they owned. Like Boyd's death, it had been determined a suicide, yet there were those who believed the shooting had been done by someone else, that it was murder, or a rightful killing.

There would have been reason, the rumors said. Horace Cunningham had been a rough man, had treated his family with the kind of meanness that down-and-out men often used. It was also rumored that Arthur Cunningham, his son, had been the shooter, taking some measure of vengeance on a man who deserved it earlier than God could get to it.

"You think about that," Boyd had said to her in one of his drinking spells. "My daddy killing my granddaddy." He had smiled, had let the smile break into a laugh. "My daddy. Hell, he'd jump at his own shadow. He must of been scared to death of that old son of a bitch."

Whatever the hard times had been, they stayed locked in the brain of the old woman happy with the taste of pancakes, and Eleanor had accepted her role as caretaker. It was a role she was accustomed to. She had her own sorrows. Buried sorrows. Her own bruises coming from a brutal rage that seemed to fester in her husband. She had kept the outbursts and the bruises to herself as much as she could, though her sisters had always seemed to know something was wrong. Her sisters had begged her to leave.

When she thought of it, she imagined herself as a chameleon resting among the leaves of a tree of changing colors.

Beatrice was awake on the morning after the supper with Noah Locke. Was hungry. At breakfast, she asked Eleanor, "Who was that man?"

"What man?" Eleanor asked.

"One who was here last night."

"You remember him?" Eleanor asked with surprise, not realizing the old woman had been aware of anything, and it made her wonder what else the old woman kept locked behind her watery eyes.

"Some," Beatrice said with hesitation, as though making a regretful confession.

"He—helped out with some work yesterday," Eleanor told her, not wanting to speak of the cow, for the presence of the cow had been a pleasure to the old woman.

Beatrice did not reply. She sat, eating, her eyes wandering to the window and the early light.

"Would you like to go outside today?" Eleanor asked.

Beatrice nodded. "To the store?" she said.

"If you'd like to do that, we can."

"We can get some ice cream," Beatrice said brightly, said as a child would say it.

"That would nice," Eleanor said. "Maybe you'd like to go see Arthur and Rachel while we're out."

A frown came across Beatrice's face. She seldom saw her son and daughter-in-law and Eleanor believed she knew that her son and daughter-in-law had found great relief in sending the old woman away to live with someone else.

"I want some ice cream," Beatrice said, suddenly stubborn.

"Then that's what we'll do," Eleanor told her.

A moment of silence rested in the kitchen. The old woman held the sweetness of the pancakes and syrup in her mouth. Eleanor took coffee from the cup she had been holding.

"Where did he go?" Beatrice said at last.

"Who is that, Granny?"

"The man."

"The one who was here yesterday?"

"Him."

"He's staying down at the lake," Eleanor said. "You remember the time Boyd took you down the lake?"

Beatrice made a circling motion with her head, leaving the answer either yes or no, an answer Eleanor had learned to accept, knowing it could mean yes in part, no in part.

"He put you on his back and carried you down the hill. Do you remember that?" Eleanor asked. "You thought it was great fun."

The old woman stopped the circling of her head, let her body rock.

"The man that helped us out—his name is Noah, like Noah in the Bible—is going to stay in the shack for a few days," Eleanor explained. She added, "He's a fisherman."

Beatrice turned her face to look at Eleanor.

"Yes, that's what he does," Eleanor said patiently. "He fishes. I even said I'd buy some fish from him, since he was so good to help us. Maybe you'd like some tonight."

Beatrice again made the circling motion with her head, deciding the answer; then she said, "I want ice cream."

"And we'll get it," Eleanor replied.

"He know Boyd?" Beatrice asked.

"No, he didn't."

A look of sorrow came into the old woman's face and she sat very still for a long moment, keeping her eyes on the window. Then she said in whisper, "Boyd's dead."

"Yes," Eleanor said.

"He give me that thing when he come home from the war," the old woman said.

"The tussie mussie?" Eleanor asked, remembering the gift of the small, elaborately enameled tussie mussie that Boyd had presented to his grandmother in a show of drama, of paper torn from the box, of the pulling back of tissue.

"You put flowers in it."

"Yes ma'am. That's what it's for. Sometimes a bride uses one in her wedding."

"Where's it at?" the old woman asked in a suddenly strong voice.

"It's in your room. Do you want me to get it and put some flowers in it?"

Beatrice turned her head, pulled her hands up to her chest as though holding the tussie mussie. "He wrote me a letter one time," she said. "I still got it."

"Yes ma'am, I know."

She thought of her own collection of letters from Boyd. The first ones had been filled with boasting and bravery, with a cocksure notion that the Germans had never seen the likes of an American soldier, and the war would not last beyond a few weeks, and then, later, the letters had become little more than confessions of fear, fear so real that she could close her eyes and see the trembling in his hand as he wrote to her. Each of them had always started with the same line: *This may be the last letter you get from me . . .*

And then she had received a letter that began, *I can see an end to all of this . . .*

The letter told of the liberation of the concentration camp called Mauthausen in Austria, where he had met a young girl, almost starved, and had taken pity on her. She was Polish. Her name was Roza Solnik. Her family had all been killed by the Germans. He was thinking of bringing her to America, if he could find a way. She had written back that if he wanted to bring Roza to live with them, it would be all right with her, but he had never again mentioned it. Even when he returned home and she asked him about her, he had said nothing beyond, "You don't know how it was over there." She had let the subject drop.

"Ice cream in a cup," the old woman said.

"Yes ma'am," Eleanor told her. "In a cup."

EIGHT

The bargain to paint Taylor Bowers's store was struck by the answer of a question cheerfully asked before Noah could speak of it: "You ready to start painting, Fish Seller?"

Noah paused, glanced around the shadows of the store, thinking that Taylor's question had some tease to it for the pleasure of someone listening. He did not see anyone and realized the question was merely a greeting. "If the offer's still made," he replied.

"Well, it is. It's still on the table," Taylor said with a hint of surprise in his voice. "Fact is, knowing you like coffee, I'll throw in all the coffee you can drink. I keep it perking all day. Let's get us a cup right now and work things out."

The bargain was simple: Noah could paint at his leisure. If an order for a string of fish was given, he could take the time to catch it. "I'm not in any particular hurry about the store, and I don't believe in keeping a man away from what he wants to be doing," Taylor said easily. He smiled with satisfaction and added, "Littleberry Davis stopped by my home yesterday afternoon. He's already got the word about you being here. Looked a little worried."

"Hope it won't cause trouble," Noah said.

"Trouble? What it'll do is to put people to talking and there'll be a crowd to watch you and Littleberry go at it," Taylor countered. "By the way, Littleberry said he'd run into Howard Reynolds at church and Howard was bragging on the fish you got him, said he couldn't hardly believe you'd got them so quick, especially as many as you did. Nobody's caught a string like that in a month of Sundays. Talk gets around. You'll be getting some more orders unless I miss my guess."

There was one such order, Noah told him, without giving names. Still, he could get started on the paint job, could work until mid-afternoon.

"Fine with me," Taylor said. "Like I told you, I'm not in a rush. Rather have it done right than done fast. I don't guess it's over two or three days' work, anyhow." He paused, looked at Noah, and Noah knew he was weighing a question. "How about if we make you a little place in the back of the store?" Taylor added. "I got a cot at the house I can bring up later."

"That's all right," Noah told him. "I found me a place."

"Where's it at?" Taylor asked.

"A little shack up on a lake."

"Which lake?"

"Up the road a couple of miles," Noah answered.

"Not the big lake?"

"No," Noah said. "A few acres, I'd guess."

Taylor bobbed his head in acknowledgment. "I know the place," he said. "Some people call it the Lake of Grief." From the look in his eyes, he wanted to say something else, but did not, and Noah, guessing the unsaid thing was about Eleanor Cunningham's husband and about the ghost of Arch Wheeler, looked away, letting the pause linger between them.

"I guess you heard there's no fish in it," Taylor said.

"I did," Noah answered.

"You ready to start?" Taylor asked.

"Anytime," Noah said.

It was not a surprise to Noah to find Taylor Bowers as talkative as Marvin Linquist had been. Having made the connection of similarity between the two men, he could close his eyes and listen to Taylor and think that Marvin was with him. Yet, it was more than his voice, more than the stories made by the voice. Taylor had Marvin's mannerisms—the lanky man's casual way of moving about, his extra inches of arms and legs having a quaintly disjointed motion. Marvin had been ribbed about it, had taken the ribbing in stride, saying it was nothing but the dancer in him, and there may have been some truth to it. Clowning around on the battlefield, showing dance steps he claimed were from Kentucky, Marvin had been as graceful as a bird riding a wind-wave. Noah believed Taylor would also be a good dancer, the way he talked about his boxing days.

The scar over his eyebrow was earned in a boxing match, he explained as he helped Noah bring the paint out of storage. Took place in Hiawassee, where a traveling hawker was offering five dollars to any man who could stay two rounds with his boxer, twenty dollars to the man who could knock his fellow down. Some of his friends who knew of his boxing ability had made the trip to Bowerstown to get Taylor, saying there was considerable side money to be made on wagering.

The boxer had been a giant of a man. Fat. Mean-faced. Eyes that had the gaze of a rattlesnake. Hands the size of a stove skillet. Knuckles callused from his battles. Wore the tattoo of a Satan face on both upper arms.

"First lick he hit me opened up my eye," Taylor said. "That put me to moving around like a dog snapping at a bull. He was strong—I give him that. Never been hit by nobody that strong. But I could tell he'd get winded pretty quick, so I kept going around him in a circle, sticking out my hand now and then, just to get a measure of how far I'd have to go to get in a couple of licks on my own, and that wasn't easy, I can tell you, not with blood running down my face like somebody'd turned on a faucet."

Noah knew the event of the fight had been polished by the exaggeration of many tellings; still he enjoyed hearing the story, understanding where it would lead since it was told as Marvin Linquist would have told it—the fighter becoming dizzy, sucking for breath, and then Taylor suddenly stopping his circling and leaping forward to land a blow that sent the fat, mean-faced, tattooed fighter reeling and collapsing to the sawdust fight pit as a chorus of cheers rose in a howl from onlookers, cheers that had stayed with Taylor as permanently as his scar.

Noah even guessed the closing line of the story: "Last time I ever stepped in the ring."

It was exactly what Marvin Linquist would have said.

"Hardest twenty dollars I ever made," Taylor added.

Just as Marvin would have.

The morning passed quickly with the work of making ready to paint, the getting of ladders and buckets and brushes, the scraping of the clapboard. Taylor judged it would be best to do the work in sections. That way, he reasoned, it would keep dust from settling over the whole store once it was cleaned. Noah took the instruction as he had taken orders in the army—without comment. He had hired on for work, would do it the way Taylor wished it to be done; still he knew Taylor's decision was the right one.

It was not a busy morning at the store. Only a few shoppers appeared for whatever goods they needed, yet Taylor insisted that each meet Noah and each meeting was made with stories, with quick histories given in Taylor's way of making the person and the moment somehow extraordinary. Without knowing their names, Noah knew the people. They were the same in nature as the people he had known in the community of his birth and in his boyhood. Plain-dressed, plain-faced, the look of work resting wearily on them, a dullness carried in their eyes. They had survived the Armageddon of depression and war in their valley of isolation, and had emerged from those numbing years resigned to the toil that getting by demanded of them. The women had flickering smiles, wary, guarded glances, like nervous birds balancing on the twigs of tree limbs. The men were nodders, saying little, though word of Noah had made its way quickly through the valley and they seemed curious about him, never having met a traveling fish seller. The men talked of the school fishing contest and of Littleberry Davis, who had a reputation for being lucky—with some suspicion of being a cheat, only no one knew how a man could cheat at fishing. Some volunteered spots for fishing they knew about, telling fish tales of the places and of the catches they had made.

At noon, Taylor made sandwiches from tomatoes and carried them outside with two ice-cold Coca-Colas to share with Noah under the shade of the oaks, sitting on chairs moved from the porch. It was part of the bargain like he had promised, he told Noah. Just having the job of painting started was worth a couple of sandwiches, and, besides, if a man didn't have to take time off for making his own food, he'd have more time for work. The reasoning was made with a laugh that Marvin Linquist would have made, and with Taylor's declaration that nothing on earth was better than a tomato sandwich lathered with mayonnaise and covered in pepper and salt. He said, "I'd almost rather have me a tomato sandwich than a day off from work."

The two were finishing their sandwiches when Eleanor pulled her car to a stop near them. "Well, look at this," Taylor said in a low voice, beneath his grin. "It's Eleanor." He craned his neck for a better look, then added, "And I believe she's got old lady Cunningham with her." He paused, shook his head. "It's a miracle how that woman stays alive. She must be close to a hundred." He looked at Noah. "You remember Eleanor, don't you? She was in the store the first time you came in."

"I do," Noah said simply.

"The old woman's the grandmother of her late husband. Mean as a snake, I hear. Eleanor takes care of her," Taylor whispered.

"I met her," Noah told him.

A look of surprise flickered over Taylor's face.

"I came up on her place yesterday when I was out walking around," Noah said.

"That's—good," Taylor said. He knew intuitively there was more to the story than Noah was telling, but he also knew it would be useless to ask about it. Noah was a man who kept things to himself, and that was to be expected. A man who spent time alone would have taken on the habit of not talking, and Noah was not a talker, not more than the few words needed to keep a conversation barely alive. If the event had any meaning beyond an exchange of greetings, it would come from Eleanor, not Noah. He lifted a hand, waved toward the car, watched Eleanor open the car door and get out and walk toward them.

Both men stood.

"You look like you're enjoying the day," Taylor said in his cheerful, storekeeper way.

"I am," Eleanor replied, also cheerfully. "Granny's feeling better today. She wanted some ice cream." She looked from Taylor to Noah and Taylor believed he could see a blink of gladness in her eyes. She said, "Good afternoon."

"Hello," Noah said quietly. He dipped his head in a nod.

"I thought you'd be off fishing," Eleanor said. "You didn't forget my order did you?"

"Be getting to it in a couple of hours," Noah answered.

"I talked him into doing some painting for me," Taylor said quickly, "but he told me about needing to fill a fish order." He paused, grinned. "Just didn't say who it was for."

"Oh, you're working for Taylor?" Eleanor said with surprise.

"Hired on this morning to paint the store," Taylor replied before Noah could answer. "I've been trying to get somebody from around here, but I guess everybody's staying busy just doing nothing. From what he's already done, it's worked out to my advantage."

"Don't stop work for me, then," Eleanor insisted. "I'm not going to starve if I don't have fish."

"Don't you go worrying about that," Taylor said. "I knew he was going to take some time off this afternoon when we struck our deal. He'll have your fish, if he can catch them. If he can't, I won't take the blame."

"Really, it's not necessary," Eleanor said.

"Is to me," Taylor countered. "I can't have one of my paying-on-time customers turning on me for keeping food off the table." He laughed easily. "Might even close up and go with him."

"Maybe you should," Eleanor said.

"Maybe I will," Taylor replied, and the thought seemed a good one to him. "I've not been run over by business today, that's for sure."

"If you do, and if you catch enough fish, the two of you need to plan on having supper with us tonight," Eleanor offered. She looked at Noah. "That is if you can put up with us for two days in a row."

Noah could feel heat on his face, knew his skin was coloring. He looked down.

"Two days in a row?" Taylor asked. The question had tease in it.

"He was a great help to me yesterday," Eleanor said, and she told of the cow's death and burial—a quick story, knowing Noah was uncomfortable with the praise.

"Well, he talks a lot, as you probably know," Taylor said lightly. "Hard to get a word in edgewise, the way he goes on, but somehow he failed to mention anything about that." He smiled, looked at Noah. "You're a good man, my friend. I knew that about you the minute I saw you." Then, to Eleanor: "You got a deal. We'll bring the fish, you get the supper."

NINE

His father had taught that fish would not bite if they heard fishermen talking, and Noah believed there was truth in the warning. He had always made it a practice not to talk, or to talk only in whispers, while seriously fishing.

If Taylor Bowers knew of the not-talking theory, he ignored it. In his tug of war between fishing and talking, talking easily yanked fishing off its feet. To Taylor, words were tastier than fish, and more filling. He talked constantly, his voice skipping like flat stones over the tumbling water of the river, and if the fish heard him, they were not bothered by the noise, for the catch made by Noah was an abundant one—four fish in an hour, nine by the end of the second hour.

Maybe it had to do with the talker and not the listener, Noah reasoned. Maybe the fish only heard voices through the line of the talker, like words going over a telephone wire. Taylor's catch was laughable, though laughing would have been unkind. Two fish, only one large enough to keep, both barely lip-hooked. Noah knew the catches were by accident, probably made by fish trying to get away from the noisy hook of the talking man.

Still, it was good having Taylor Bowers with him. There was something childish about Taylor's fishing efforts—his jittery way of casting, his impatience, his exuberance in watching the cork float on his line tremble in water swirls, thinking each bob of the cork was a nibble. It was easy to tell he had not fished in a long time, and had never been good at it.

It was also entertaining to hear the stories that Taylor told with a historian's passion for events and a gossip's flair for spice. Noah was certain no one knew the Valley of Light as well as Taylor. He made a map of roads with his words, gave the roads landmark descriptions that took on images as revealing as photographs, placed people in the homes that were attached to them. The people, too, took on images. Old to young. The sick, the vigorous, the good, the mean, the suspicious, the caring, the dawdlers. The same people Noah had known as a boy. Only their names were different. The way Taylor told it, almost everyone in the valley was related in one fashion or another, by blood or by marriage, with enough suspicion to muddy the water on which relationship went with which relationship.

He confessed he had failed in his own marriage. "Took me a Methodist from down in Hiawassee," he said, "but she found more favor with a banker down in Gainesville a couple of years after we made that great walk of torture down the aisle. Left me high and dry, but, Lord, I don't guess I can blame her much. It can get a little tiresome around here."

Things had changed, though, Taylor observed. Little by little. Season by season. Year by year. Changed with death following death, changed with the building of roads, changed with the coming of the automobile, with the depression, with the construction of the Chatuge, with the war, changed with the selling of land to strangers by descendants of the settlers, the descendants having moved off to larger towns and cities. The Valley of Light had lost more men to the war than any community in North Carolina if you took the size of a place into consideration, he said. Some good men.

It was like the pruning of an old and damaged tree. The more limbs taken off, the more the tree was left with only a trunk.

His own family was an example, Taylor offered, and he told the story of the settling of the valley by his great-grandfather, who had built the first store in the community. Had fathered nine children. Once it was easy enough to find a Bowers under every rock in the county, but that had been long ago. Now there weren't enough of them left to fill a small room, and the ones still alive were a peculiar group—himself included, if you took the word of some people in the community. He had a cousin, Pete, who was a barber in Hayesville. Joe Bowers, an uncle, was in his eighties, and a man with the sour personality of a hermit. Joe's two sons, Carson and David, were both traveling salesmen, both with the con artist's shifty-eyed look. Once they found they had a liking for the road, they had seldom returned to the valley. Holidays, maybe.

Taylor paused, made a little laugh. "Don't know why I'm talking about Carson and David," he said. "Used to think about being a traveling man myself when I was growing up. Probably would have, too, except I always knew I'd have the store one day, and it didn't make a lot of sense to go off looking for something, when I had something looking for me." He paused, wiggled his fishing line in the water, shrugged, made a small sighing sound. "Listen to me. Sounds like I'm griping, don't it? And, good Lord, that's the last thing I ought to be doing, out here fishing for the first time in a thousand years, it seems like." He laughed. His voice became suddenly merry. "Fish Seller," he chortled, "why don't we go into business? Me and you. Set us up a little fish house on the side of the road going down to Hiawassee. You catch and clean and I'll cook. We'll call it Noah's Ark."

A flutter, like a twitching of muscles, struck Noah in his chest. It was the same joking offer Marvin Linquist had made during the war, during one of his rambling stories about fishing. A fish camp, he had called it. Had even suggested Noah's Ark as a name.

"Sounds good to me," Noah said.

Taylor sat hunched forward, his legs stretched out, his knees up a bit, his forearms resting on the kneecaps. His fishing pole—a bamboo cane that he found in the back of his store—dangled loosely from his fingertips.

"What did you think about Eleanor Cunningham?" he asked.

The question was one Noah had been expecting. "She's a nice lady, like you said she was," he replied.

Taylor rocked his shoulders in agreement. "Yeah, she is." He made a playful circle with the tip of his pole, causing the float to sway on the water. Then: "She was married to a man who was hard to figure, though. Everybody got along all right with him before he went off to war. He was in college a couple of years and he bragged a lot about being smart, but nobody paid him much attention. Couldn't farm a lick, but he was a good carpenter and he got a lot of work doing it. After the war, he lost some of his grin. Let his temper get the best of him at times. You always got the feeling he was up to something, and he had all that money, all in new twenties. I used to think it was counterfeit. I heard some talk from Hayesville, that he was up there a lot trying to sell some stuff he brought back from the war. Some jewelry and things like that. Mostly little stuff."

He shook his head slowly, swiped at a fly, added, "And there was this fellow that used to come up to see him from Atlanta, trying to buy his farm. At least that's what Boyd said. But that didn't make much sense. That farm's not worth much. Got a good house on it, but that's about all. Anyhow, there was some talk going around that him and Boyd had some business together that they didn't want people to know about, and there wasn't nothing to the story about buying land. But there's always some talk about everything. I never thought much about it until this fellow showed up at my store one day and bought some stuff. Paid me with a new twenty-dollar bill, just like Boyd was always doing. Started me to wondering."

"I guess it would," Noah replied in an accommodating way.

"Eleanor say much about how Boyd died?"

"Not much."

"Guess it's not something she likes talking about."

"Probably not."

"It got called a suicide, since the gun was right there beside him," Taylor said, "but there's a lot of questions that never got answered."

"That right?" Noah said.

"For one thing, the gun was a luger, that German handgun," Taylor replied. "Eleanor said she'd never seen it and didn't know Boyd had it. Nobody else had ever heard him talk about it, and he was always bragging on his guns. And there was the shack. It was pretty tore up inside. Mattress on the floor, stuff from the pie safe on the table—things like that. They put that to rest by saying Boyd must of gone a little crazy before he pulled the trigger. Said it was what happened to some people after the war."

"Could have, I guess," Noah offered. "I saw one or two men freeze up in the fighting, and they had to be shipped home."

Taylor rocked his shoulders again, wiggled his line. He said, "Well, I guess it's best nobody knows what was going on, if anything was. Let the dead rest in peace."

"You probably right," Noah said.

"That's a fine lady, though," Taylor said wistfully.

"She is," Noah agreed.

"I'm just surprised she stayed on here, but I guess that's because she had the farm," Taylor added. "Tell you the truth, she's not the kind of woman you'd expect to find in a place like this. She's got some refinement not many of us know much about. I keep expecting to see her walk in the store one day and pay off her debt and tell me she's going off to Atlanta or New York or Los Angeles or someplace like that, someplace where a woman can buy real perfume instead of that sweet water stuff I sell. Lord, that stuff could blind a man if he got too close to it."

Noah laughed quietly.

"There's some women around here who put it on so heavy, you need a gas mask just to talk to them," Taylor added. "I hear they use it to kill boll weevils down in cotton country." He was following a fox of humor and he knew it, could tell by the way Noah was grinning. "Every time they have a revival down at the church, I give the visiting preacher's wife a bottle or two," he declared. "Makes all the other women come in, wanting the same thing. It's a trick I learned from my daddy. You want to stir up women somewhere, throw the preacher's wife in the mix. They going to have some kind of reaction to her, and that's the truth."

"I never thought about it," Noah said.

Taylor lifted his pole, taking the hook out of the water to examine his bait. He made a swinging motion with the pole, dropped the hook again. "Women are hard to figure," he said. "They're the only creatures on earth that speak one language with their mouth and another one with their eyes, and most of the time what the mouth is saying has got nothing to do with what the eyes are saying, and vice versa. But I can tell you one thing, that Eleanor Cunningham is one fine lady. Yes, she is. One fine lady."

She put the flowers in a vase and placed the vase on the dining-room table. Roses cut from her own yard, and daisies. The scent of the roses seemed stronger than the scent of the food cooking in the kitchen. It had been a long time since she had placed flowers in the house.

She paused at the table, touched one of the daisies to turn its face toward her. Truth was, it had been a long time since she had planned such a supper for anyone. With Noah, it had been more of a payment than anything else. She had not cut roses or daisies. Had not put out the lace tablecloth, or set the table with her good china and silverware. Had not cleaned the house so thoroughly.

She liked the feeling of it. Liked the energy it seemed to bring to her. Liked the thought of having her life jolted by doing something that would be talked about with suspicion if anyone in the community knew of it.

The old woman could tell, she thought. The old woman had

lapsed into her world of silence, of faraway gazes, but she was not sure if the silence and the look was nothing more than a grand performance given for the attention it got her.

It did not matter. The anticipation of the supper, of having Taylor and Noah invade her life, was liberating.

She looked at her watch. It was five o'clock. She had an hour, or more. Time for a bath. She would use the scented soap her sister had given her for Christmas, and she would wear the new dress she had purchased on her last trip to Gainesville.

She wanted to feel fresh, new.

Alive.

TEN

It was almost six-thirty when Taylor pulled his Ford to a stop in front of Eleanor Cunningham's home.

"This is going to be a night to remember," he said to Noah, reaching under the seat of his car and pulling out a bottle of after-shave lotion. "I came out here one time right after Boyd got home—to bring them something, but I forget what—and he made me stay for supper. It was before his grandmother moved in. Guess he knew I hadn't had a square meal since my divorce, and that was only a few months old then. I'll never forget that night. Lord, this woman can cook." He paused, dabbed some of the lotion on his face, handed the bottle to Noah. "But I guess you know that, don't you? You're a lucky man, Noah Locke. Two nights in a row at the table of Eleanor Cunningham. Wouldn't mind that kind of duty myself." He grinned his boyish grin, opened the car door, stepped out, bellowed toward the house, "Put the lard in the pan. You got fish on the way."

The supper was festive, not strained as it had been the night before. The reason was Taylor. Taylor's stories, Taylor's hands sweeping in emphasis over the table and the food, his hands making laughter as a magician made silk handkerchiefs and flowers out of air.

The laughter was as contagious as a plague. Whatever formality had greeted the two men at their appearance—bringing twelve fish of good size, even after the cleaning—had disappeared at the table with Taylor's question to Eleanor: "You mind if I say a few words of grace?"

The question had surprised Eleanor. Saying grace had never been practiced in her home. "I—suppose not," she had answered, casting a nervous glance toward Beatrice Cunningham, who again sat silent in the rocking chair near the table.

"Well, now, I can hear from the tone of your voice that you're a little bit uneasy with that," Taylor had said, grinning.

"Oh, no, it's not that. I—"

"Here's why I want to do it," Taylor had said. "This has been one of the best days I've had in a lot of years, and I can't help but be proud of sitting at your table again. Is it all right?"

"Yes," Eleanor had said quietly.

"We don't even have to bow our heads for this one," Taylor had added, "but we got to take hands. Granny Cunningham, too."

"She's not at the table," Eleanor had said.

"That's all right," Taylor had replied. "Let's all just stand around her."

They had formed a circle of hand-holding around Beatrice Cunningham's rocking chair. The old woman had gazed dumbly at them, making a frown that seemed to ask why Taylor and Noah were holding her hands, unless they were trying to pull her up from her chair.

"Lord," Taylor had begun in a deliberate drawl, his eyes wandering comically to the ceiling, "here we are, about to have some catfish, which is one of the better objects of your whole creation, if you don't mind my saying so—especially when there's some hush puppies made with onions to go along with them.

"It's kind of a strange group you've got here, Lord, as you surely know. You've got Eleanor Cunningham, who's a good, paying-on-time customer of mine, and a refined lady who reads a lot of books. And then there's Granny Cunningham, who don't really know what's going on, but she's a grand lady from all I've ever heard, and I know you're the one who keeps her happy. And then there's Noah Locke, who's likely to lie before the supper's over about catching more of these fish than I did, but I forgive him for that, Lord, and I hope you do, too. I can say he's a fine worker with a paintbrush in his hand, even if he does talk too much. And, of course, there's me, who's always been some trouble to you, I suppose, but who's truly grateful to be in this fine company close to this loaded-down table, especially since you and I both know I'd planned on having another bologna sandwich for supper. It just goes to show how lucky I am.

"The fact is, Lord, we're all lucky. Every one of us gathered here. We've got more catfish than we can eat, hush puppies, green beans, squash, corn on the cob, ice tea, and, unless my smell has left me, a peach pie warming in the oven. That's something.

"So, Lord, we'd all appreciate it if you'd sort of give us your blessing and loosen up our tongues so we can talk about everybody we know who's not here, and forgive us beforehand for what we'll be saying about them. Amen."

Eleanor had smiled.

Taylor had said, "Now that wasn't too bad, was it?"

"No," Eleanor had answered.

Marvin Linquist, Noah had thought.

Eleanor was not sure if it was God or Taylor who loosened the tongues. God through Taylor she decided, since it was Taylor who started the talk and kept it going in a manner that was lively and fun. Watching him, she was amused by the way he had settled in at the table, rooted into his chair, keeping the food circling. It was as though he belonged to the table and to the house, and she knew he was making his pitch to her, saying it was time for her to put aside her grief and to step back into the world.

His stories were like funny gifts a man would offer a woman when hinting for a date.

He bragged about having to bait fish hooks for Noah, about teaching Noah to make a proper cast, about throwing back huge fish he had caught just to keep from embarrassing Noah.

He fake-whispered a story to Noah about needing to explain to Eleanor the meaning of certain books. Mostly foreign books that had been translated into English. His only advantage was in the fact that he had read them in their original language.

He leaned toward Beatrice Cunningham and told her he had been thinking seriously of calling on her, maybe taking her to a picture show, but was afraid she would think him too old.

The old woman's face seemed confused.

Still, Eleanor enjoyed the absurdity of Taylor's joking.

The house, too, seemed to enjoy having Taylor and Noah in it. Seemed warmer, more peaceful. Seemed filled. Since the death of her husband, the house had been more building than home, empty except for furniture and fixtures. With Taylor and Noah in it, with the sharp scent of after-shave lotion, the deep sound of the voices of men, of heavy footsteps on the floor, the house again had life.

After the supper, Taylor went to his car and got his camera and returned to the house with it, insisting on having photographs made of the occasion. Busied himself posing Eleanor and the old woman, Eleanor and Noah, Eleanor alone, Noah alone. And then he gave the camera to Eleanor and to Noah to take pictures that would include him.

"I like having pictures of happy times," he crowed.

"So do I," Eleanor said.

"I'll give you some of them," Taylor told her.

"I'd like that," she replied.

After the picture-taking, the three of them retired to the front porch to sit, leaving the old woman in her rocker, lost in the darkness of her mind.

The sun seeped into the mountain, limbs of trees drooped into sleep, night rose up from the ground, whippoorwills took up their song.

Taylor leaned back in his chair, laced his hands behind his head, smiled his comfortable smile. "Know what I was thinking a minute ago?" he said. "I was thinking I never once sat out on the porch with my wife and watched it turn dark. Maybe that was what was wrong with us. Maybe that's what she's doing right now, at this very second, with her fellow down in Gainesville." He paused. "If she is, I hope the mosquitoes are eating them up."

"Maybe she's thinking the same about you," Eleanor told him.

"Knowing her, I'd say she is," Taylor said. He rocked forward, pulled himself from the chair, stood. "All right, time to go. I'm so full, I'm going to have to wobble my way to the car." He turned to Eleanor. "I got to tell you, Eleanor, I can't remember when I liked a night as much as this one."

"Me, either," Eleanor said, standing.

"So, you think we ought to try to keep this wayfaring fisherman around for a while?" Taylor asked, making a wink.

"Don't see why not," Eleanor answered easily.

"You guess that old shack down by the lake's good enough for him?" Taylor said.

"It could probably use a good cleaning and some more furniture," Eleanor offered.

"It's fine," Noah said. There was a sound of embarrassment in his voice.

"I didn't pay you for the fish," Eleanor said.

"Didn't mean for you to," Noah told her. "I'd say I owe you, much as you fed me the last couple of days."

"But I ordered them."

"And I ate a lot of them," Noah said. "I just thank you for the meal."

"All right, enough of that," Taylor said. He tilted his head comically at Eleanor, mugged exasperation. "See what I mean about him? Talks all the time. Can't hardly get him to slow down."

Noah grinned, felt a blush on his face.

"Leave him alone, Taylor Bowers," Eleanor said. "Or next time, you won't get invited."

"Next time?" Taylor asked.

"Well, I thought we should do this again before long," Eleanor replied.

Taylor rocked on the heels of his feet. He nodded thoughtfully, said, "I like the sound of that. I like it a lot."

The moon, orange-yellow in color, two nights from being full, made its slow crawl against the dome of stars, its light coating the trees of the lake.

Noah rested under the blanket on the porch cot, his head pushed against the pillow. Watched the moon through the rusting screen wire that wrapped the porch. Watched the light sliding off leaves of the beechnut. Listened to the sounds around him. Nightsounds, his mother had called them, making it one word. Nightsounds were the best sounds in the world, his mother had said. So much singing you'd think the grass and the bushes and the flowers and the trees had taken on voices. And maybe it was that, she had added. How many times had anyone ever seen a cicada or a whippoorwill or an owl or a tree frog singing? Never, she had guessed. She hadn't. Not once. Had spent her life listening to them, but had never seen one at song. A cicada could easily have been a daffodil in hiding, a whippoorwill or an owl the high blossom of a tulip tree. Could have been. The night held many things that could not be seen, only guessed at.

If you listened carefully to nightsounds, you could hear the music that must have been playing when God made the earth and moon and stars and all the other parts of the heavens, his mother had whispered to him.

It was a good memory to Noah. Went far into his childhood, when he was still at his lap-curling age, before the birth of Travis, his brother. He wondered if it was memory from one night, or from many nights. Wondered if his mother had said the same to his brother in the same kind of cuddled moments. There were times when he could feel the warmth of his mother's breath against his face, could smell the sweet odor of tobacco smoke from his father's pipe, and he imagined the memory was from nights of sitting on the porch of their home.

An image of his mother floated up from his thinking. His mother, early in the morning, outside, kneeling in the grass, letting her hands sweep over the dew clinging to grass blades, then lifting her hands and rubbing the dew across her face, tasting it with the tip of her tongue.

He blinked and the image of his mother vanished. The night-sounds were shrill around the Lake of Grief.

He thought of Hoke Moore, how Hoke Moore had said the valley was a place to find rest and to fish. He had liked seeing the lake called the Chatuge and thought he would fish it before moving on, though, like Hoke Moore, he had always preferred small lakes or rivers, or creeks running into rivers. There were speckled trout in the creeks and the small rivers, especially where the water was cold. He liked fishing for trout, liked the taste of them. Had never used a fly rod, but wanted to try one, even if the casting seemed a mystery the way the line whipped over the water like an unraveling of the alphabet letter *S*. He had done well enough with his bait caster and with the three flies taken in trade from a fisherman somewhere in Tennessee. Three flies for two bass. He remembered the grin of the fisherman—the grin of a man who thinks he has gotten the best of a deal. "These are old," the man had said of the flies. "Don't know if there's any catch left in them, but I've had my share of luck with them." Noah had caught many trout with the used flies—letting the flies drift on top of the current like a water bug taking a water ride—and considered the trade one in his favor. Other fishermen had said to him that he couldn't catch trout the way he did, but they were wrong. He had done it and it was not luck. Maybe it was what his mother had said it was—a gift. If it was that, he was glad he had been trusted with it.

He was also glad Hoke Moore had pointed him in the direction of the valley. It had good people living in it from what he could tell. In his travels since leaving his home, he had not met people so quickly, had not been invited into their company with such ease. He knew that Taylor Bowers was the cause of it, having the same kind of friendly nature Marvin Linquist had had. If it had not been for Taylor, there wouldn't have been a second supper at the home of Eleanor Cunningham. People like Taylor always took the edge off the awkwardness that seemed to cast a spell among strangers.

Thinking of Taylor caused a smile. Taylor had his eye on Eleanor, for certain, and it seemed as though she had a fond feeling for him. Still, it had not been long since the death of her husband and she would not be disrespectful of his memory. Taylor would have to be patient—more patient than he had been as a fisherman. He had the good bait of his nature, but it would take more than being lively to attract Eleanor Cunningham's attention. She was a woman with a strong mind, a strong will.

In the war, he had listened to many stories of women, of wives and girlfriends and daughters, had watched men read letters from the women of their bragging, unashamed of tears that rolled off their faces or of the broad smiles that blinked out of their eyes from whatever words were on the folded pages of the letters. He had never received a letter from a woman, except from his mother, had never written one to any woman other than his mother.

He thought of Marvin Linquist, how Marvin Linquist would make up letters from such movie stars as Betty Grable and Ava Gardner, telling him how they were dreaming of him, how they were remembering their tender nights with him. The letters were always signed in Marvin Linquist's make-believe reading with, *Love and kisses . . .*

Marvin Linquist, being a merry fool, making laughter.

The nightsounds flew up around him.

ELEVEN

Eleanor knew she had overslept by the sun's light in her room, soft white on the walls. She rolled in her bed, lifted her head, looked at the clock on the nightstand. The time was ten minutes before eight. She let her head fall again against the pillow. It had been years since she had slept so late, she thought. Years. And it was nice. She closed her eyes, took in the feeling of comfort. From outside, she heard the singing of birds and, from the barnyard, the low mooing of the milk cow.

Not used to being milked so late, she reasoned. Udders tight with milk, the teats swollen, ready for the pull of hands. She remembered learning to milk, a quick lesson taught by Boyd before leaving for the war. Remembered being afraid of the cow and the backed-off leg tensed for kicking. Remembered the warmed water drained from the milk pail for washing dust off the teats, calming the cow with a gentle massaging. And then the milking, the steady, rhythmic squeezing. Something nice about it. Something she understood in a strangely sensuous way, though the thought of it embarrassed her.

She moved her hand lightly over her breasts, letting the touch run through her body, making heat. Thought of her husband as he had been in the early days of their marriage, before the war. His hands on her, sending electricity across her chest and arms, into her throat, pulsing through her abdomen, quivering in her thighs, leaving her body flushed with blood. Convulsions. She remembered the convulsions.

She pulled her hand to her throat, let it rest against the heartbeat she could feel with her fingertips, waited for the memory to slide away. Surely she had dreamed of her husband, she thought, having the wish for a man's touch, but she could not remember a dream. Or was it because Noah Locke and Taylor Bowers had been in her home the evening before, and the scent of their presence was still there, floating free? Or maybe it was not a scent, but a sound, still slamming against walls. There had been enough talk for it. Especially from Taylor. He had been like a performer too long away from an audience, his voice ranging from whisper to thunder, his laughter having a bell-ring to it, and the merriment he left behind had followed her to bed, lodged in a smile she could not keep from her face.

Or maybe what had followed her to bed was the soft voice of Noah, saying he had enjoyed the supper. Quiet Noah, making more words with his body than his mouth.

She rolled her body into a sitting position on the side of the bed and listened. The only sound was from outside, from birds and the cow and the drone of an airplane that had the annoying sound of a wasp. Cole Berry, she guessed. Cole had the only airplane in the county. Flew it for his own pleasure on clear days. In autumn, he would take passengers with him for a small charge, making slow circles over trees that had the look of red and orange and yellow embers from a fire slow-burning across the mountains.

Once, after the war, she had taken a ride in Cole Berry's airplane and had marveled at the colors below her. She remembered Cole shouting at her, "That's why God keeps a look on things from up here. Got a prettier view."

She slipped from the bed, took the robe she had draped over

the back of a chair in front of her dresser and put it on, then moved into the hallway separating her bedroom from the bedroom where Beatrice slept. The door to the room was open, causing her to pause in surprise. The door had never been open in the morning. She stepped quickly to the doorway and looked inside the room. The old woman was not in her bed.

She hurried into the bedroom, took a quick look at the sides of the bed, thinking Beatrice could have fallen, but did not see her. She turned, went back into the hallway, then to the bathroom. Still did not see the old woman.

She called out, "Granny." Listened. No answer.

A flutter of fear struck her. She rushed down the hallway to the living room, then into the kitchen, calling, "Granny. Where are you?"

The old woman was not in the house.

She ran outside, hurried to the barn, calling in a loud voice. The cow stood at the barnyard fence. Made a deep lowing sound from her raised head.

The old woman was not in the barn, or anywhere around it, and Eleanor thought of her own grandfather, how he had been in old age, his mind wandering aimlessly, how he had followed his mind, taking off without warning, disappearing into the woods of the mountains that were as much a part of him as his own heartbeat. Once, he was missing for two days and a search party of men had taken their dogs and tried to track him, but even in his mindless old age, he had been a better woodsman than any of them. When they finally found him, he was huddled in a gouged-out break of land where a large tree had fallen, covered in limbs that he had pulled over himself, hiding like Indians would hide, he would say later. From stories told about it, her grandfather had fought mightily against being rescued, even bringing blood to one of the rescuers.

She went back into the house, found her keys to the car, then left the farm still dressed in her robe. Instinctively, she drove south on the road.

No reason to panic, she thought. The old woman had wandered outside the house before, but never far away like her grandfather had done, never off the property. There had been times when she simply wanted to feel sunshine on her face and had found some false energy to pull herself from her chair and make her way to freedom. And always, she was annoyed with Eleanor when Eleanor tried to urge her back inside the house, always complaining in the kind of hissing, old-age temper that had the venom of a poisonous snake in it. Once, she had even tried to attack Eleanor with a stick she had found in the yard, calling her a bitch and a whore, saying she had made Boyd kill himself.

Eleanor sat up in the driver's seat, close to the steering wheel, driving slow, knowing it was possible the old woman had fallen and rolled into a gully.

Maybe she was headed toward Howard Reynolds's home, she thought. Hoped it was true. Hoped she had made it that far, yet doubted it. By the road, it was almost two miles between their homes. And if Howard or Howard's wife, Ada, had seen her, they would have taken her in and would have made a telephone call about it. They were good people, good neighbors. Often they stayed with Beatrice while she shopped, or they would have Beatrice stay at their home. They knew what it was like to watch over people who had wandering minds. Their grandson, Matthew, was thought to be slow-witted enough to need watching. Maybe she was going to the Reynolds home out of some remembered pleasure, like a homing bird taking flight.

And then she saw her.

Ambling on the roadside, still wearing her white sleeping gown, a bent-over figure, ghostly in the way she looked and in the way she moved.

Eleanor pulled the car to a stop behind her, got out, went to her. She said, "Granny, what are you doing out here?"

The old woman lifted her face to look at Eleanor. A pink flush was in her face from the labor of walking so far. "Going to the lake," she answered.

"The lake?" Eleanor said. "What for?"

"To see Boyd," the old woman said, and there was a tone of defiance in her voice.

Eleanor took her by the arm and began to lead her back to the car. Beatrice tried to pull away.

"Granny, we need to go on back home now," Eleanor told her.

"I'm going to see my grandboy," she said.

"He's not there," Eleanor replied gently.

The old woman glared at her. "You told me he was."

"No, ma'am," Eleanor said. "I said the young man who helped us out was staying down there. Noah. Do you remember his name? He and Taylor Bowers had supper with us last night."

For a moment, Beatrice did not respond. Then she said, "He looks like Boyd."

"A little," Eleanor said. "A little." Then: "Let's go have some pancakes."

"With syrup?" the old woman asked eagerly.

"With syrup," Eleanor told her.

At home, the old woman's energy faded quickly and she became irritable. She spat the pancakes from her mouth, saying they had no taste to them. Refused her cup of coffee, made with two teaspoons of sugar as she liked it. Talked in her rambling way about men being in the house and about the boy who had come to take Boyd's place. Said to Eleanor that she knew the boy had been in her bedroom during the night. Could hear them, she vowed. Said Eleanor had brought shame to the house.

Eleanor did not argue with her. She listened, talked calmly, trying to tie the fragments of the old woman's thinking together.

Yes, she said, there had been men in the house. Taylor Bowers, who ran the store where they shopped, and Noah Locke, the young man she had confused with Boyd. They had had supper and had left. And, no, the young man had not been in her bedroom. Nor Taylor. No man had ever been in her bedroom except Boyd.

Finally, the old woman gave way to sleep, sitting in her rocking chair on cushions Eleanor had made for her. Her head drooped to one side, her hands positioned in her lap, palms up. Eleanor draped a blanket over the old woman's legs to keep them warm and fastened the belt around her waist and the chair slats to keep her from tumbling out of the chair.

She took the milk pail and went to the barn and milked the cow and then returned to the house and poured a cup of coffee and carried it to the porch and sat in the swing. It was early morning and she was already exhausted from her worrisome search for her grandmother-in-law. A mix of anger and pity stirred in her. She closed her eyes and pictured the old woman strapped to her chair, her hands in her lap, palms up, like the photographs of Gypsy beggars in magazines, and the image made her think of Noah Locke, of his wandering-about life. Like Gypsies.

She reached behind her head to pull free the clasp that held her hair, letting her hair fall around her shoulders. Combed it loose with her fingers. Felt suddenly free, like the Gypsies had seemed to be on their annual trips through the region, coming over the twisting mountain road from the small town of Helen to Hiawassee, traveling in a caravan of large wagons painted in vivid colors, stopping to camp beside the river not far from the home of her parents. The Gypsies were people from a storybook, the way they dressed and the way they sounded. Dark, flashing eyes, the eyes of people from India. Her father had warned her about them, warned they might take her captive and drive off with her and then, in some faraway place, they would sell her as quickly as they would sell a chicken. She had watched them from a safe distance as they made their camps and cooked their spice-rich meals and made music and laughter. And then they would be gone as mysteriously as they had arrived, with only the wide wheels of their wagons and the watered-down ash of their campfires holding any evidence that they had been present.

Noah would be like that, she thought—without having colorful wagons, or being dressed in a colorful costume, without spice-rich meals and music and laughter. Noah would be like the

Gypsies only in his leaving. Quietly gone, with little trace of having been there.

She wondered why the old woman had accused her of having him in her bedroom.

Meanness, probably.

Or maybe the old woman could sense something that existed, ghostlike, in the house, the awkward mix of a man and a woman, both with a yearning to be Gypsies.

And maybe it had nothing to do with anything other than the existence she shared with the old woman, the monotony of day following day for both of them—the mind playing tricks, making little lives out of nothing, like a child playing with paper dolls.

TWELVE

From the ladder leaning against the store side, Noah watched cars gathering under the oaks fronting the store, and he knew the people driving them—all men—were there because the story of his fishing had made its way across the valley, as Taylor had predicted it would.

"There's talk," Taylor had said earlier, taking coffee with Noah. "When I got home last night, I got a call from the principal of the school, asking about you. He said there'd been more people bringing money by his house to get in on the fishing contest than he ever remembered, especially this soon. They usually wait to the day of the fishing."

All the talk had been caused by the number of fish Noah had caught for Howard Reynolds, Taylor said, and the principal wanted to know if it was true.

"I told him whatever he heard wasn't half the story," Taylor had added. "Told him I'd been fishing with you yesterday and I saw you do the same thing at a fishing hole where nobody's caught nothing bigger than a minnow in the last five years."

Taylor had smiled proudly, had said, "You wait and see how many people show up around here today. They got their corn laid by and there's nothing much for them to do, so they'll be here. But don't you worry about it. I'll keep them away from you until you come down to eat." He had laughed, had added, "You know the story about Tom Sawyer?"

Noah had said he did not.

"It's a book by that writer Mark Twain," Taylor had explained. "In it, this boy named Tom gets some help painting a fence. Maybe you can do the same thing with the store."

Noah did not know what Taylor meant about Tom Sawyer, or how Tom Sawyer got help for painting a fence. Whatever he had done, Noah did not think it would work for him, even if he wanted it to. But he did not want help. The painting was his job. He had started it, he would finish it.

At the noon hour, Taylor called Noah to stop his painting and to come down from the ladder to eat his sandwiches. One pimento cheese, one tomato, Taylor said.

It was Taylor's doing, leading Noah to the front porch of the store where the men had gathered—Taylor boasting about his day of fishing with Noah, saying Littleberry Davis would have thrown his rod into the water if he had seen the way Noah pulled in fish. Fast as he could drop the hook, Taylor vowed. Fish so eager to get on Noah's hook, you could see them lined up in the water like tractors in a Fourth of July parade.

Whitlow Mayfield was on the porch, sitting in the chair that seemed to belong to him, and Howard Reynolds with his grandson, Matthew, and other men whose names Noah did not know, or had forgotten if they had been introduced to him.

"What'd you do with them fish?" one of the men asked.

A blush rose in Taylor's face. "We ate them," he offered, not saying they had had supper at Eleanor Cunningham's home. He glanced at Noah and in the glance Noah knew to keep quiet. Taylor was not ready for any torment over Eleanor Cunningham.

"You sure you didn't drop a stick of dynamite over in the river to catch all them fish?" Whitlow asked in a teasing way. "What they used to do around here when they was building the dam."

"No sir," Noah told him, taking a bite out of his sandwich. And then he said, "I just got lucky," knowing it was an answer they wanted to hear.

"No such thing as that much luck," Whitlow said. "I'm guessing you got a deal with the Lord or the Devil, one or the other."

Noah smiled, did a tilt of his head, took a swallow of his Coca-Cola.

"You ever hear about George Perry, down there in Georgia?" Whitlow asked.

"Name seems familiar, but I can't place why," Noah said.

"Back in nineteen thirty-two, George Perry caught the biggest largemouth bass anybody ever has," Whitlow told him. "Weighed a little over twenty-two pounds. Got it on a little lake down there somewhere, fishing out of a bateau. I read about it lots of times." He grinned. "Know what I like about that story, more'n anything else? Old George took that fish home and filleted it and they ate it. By God, he didn't waste it by having it stuffed and hung from some wall. But I got to say, I wish I could of seen the head on that thing. It must of had a mouth you could run a elephant through."

"I've heard about it," Noah admitted. And he had. Had met men who knew George Perry. The men had described him as someone who just liked to fish and never made much over the catch. He had won some kind of contest from *Field & Stream* magazine. Got him a new rod and reel and a little money.

"You ever hook anything close to that big?" Howard asked.

"No sir," Noah answered. "Nothing like that."

"What's the biggest you guess you ever caught?"

"Twelve or fourteen pounds, maybe, if you talking about bass," Noah told him. "I got some bigger catfish, but not bass."

"He got a mess of them yesterday, I know that," Taylor said. "And all I been hearing all summer is how bad the fishing is."

"Could be they just beginning to bite," said a younger man with a stubble of a beard and a sun-brown face.

"Could be," Marshall Hawk, who had the look and heritage of an Indian, agreed, and he began the talk of how peculiar fish could be, feeding on everything from worms to dough balls to grains of corn at certain times of the year, then snubbing every kind of bait a man could offer at other times.

"Harder to figure out a fish than a woman," Marshall said.

"I wouldn't go that far," another countered. "No need to give fish a bad name."

And the men laughed the laughter of men when joking about women.

The talk drifted lazily, bringing argument about fish and bait and fishing times and certain habits of certain fishermen such as Littleberry Davis. Noah listened with amusement, having heard the debate many times, and he knew the arguments would eventually lead away from stories of fishing to topics that had the nature of jest in them. With men, it usually had something to do with women or cars or some game like baseball.

And he was right. Marshall said he needed to be leaving to go into Hayesville to buy new tires for his car, and Whitlow Mayfield suggested the reason he needed new tires was from driving too fast.

"If you drove like Howard, you could go a lifetime on a set of tires," Whitlow observed, and the men laughed, making Noah realize that Howard Reynolds had a reputation for being a slow driver.

"Beats walking," Howard said.

"Not by much, if you behind the wheel," Whitlow countered, and the men laughed again.

The talk of cars and trucks filled the store porch with noise, louder than needed. And though he was with them—bodily with them—Noah felt distant, removed, somehow suspended above them, watching. It was like the view a bird would have of things, the view he had from the ladder while painting the store. It was a sensation he had felt before, something as mysterious as tricks he had seen stars play on clear, winter nights, when stars seemed closer to Earth.

He listened, making his nods, as Taylor told of his first car—an old model-T Ford—and of running it into a creek when chased by a dog. How the dog had stopped at the creek bank, braying loudly, probably thinking it had run the biggest fox on earth to water. His father had hitched a trace chain to the car and pulled it from the creek with a pair of mules, giving an opinion that motor cars would never replace good mules. Not even good goats.

And then Whitlow told his story of having ridden in a Pierce Arrow during a visit to Atlanta, told it in a way that left his listeners knowing the truth had been lost somewhere in the distance between Atlanta and the Valley of Light. It might have been a Packard but not a Pierce Arrow.

Another story was of a moonshiner named Hugh McMillen, whose Ford had run out of gas transporting his high-quality cargo to Athens for students at the University of Georgia, and how Hugh McMillen had used a gallon of his moonshine to finish off the trip, claiming his Ford had never run as well or as fast or as far on such little fuel.

From his high, suspended place, Noah listened to the talk and the laughter. Watched himself listening. Watched the hand-waving of men making a bid for attention.

And there, in his looking-down place, he thought of his brother, thought of Travis. Once Travis had been in a car accident, had lain unconscious for days, a lung punctured, and there had been fear of his dying. He remembered his mother sitting for hours beside Travis's bed, holding his hand, making sounds that he took to be prayer, though he could not hear the words since the words were sent to her soul and not to the ears of anyone listening.

He believed his mother had made a bargain with God. He believed his mother had whispered to her soul, "Let him live and I will take his place in hell, if that is where you want to put him." Travis had lived. Had come back to health over time and, over time, had resumed his dangerous ways.

His mother's bargain had not been the only one offered for Travis.

He, too, had tried to make a deal. Not with God, but with his mother.

On the day Travis had been sentenced—twenty years at hard labor—he had gone to his mother privately, had said to her, "I want you to do something."

His mother had asked, "What is it?"

He had said, "You know the sheriff and some of the lawyers, don't you?"

"Not much," his mother had told him. "I just know them from everything that's been going on. Tell me what you getting at."

He had said, "Travis is smart, Mama. If he gets the right chance, he'll do things that'd make you proud."

"Maybe," his mother had replied. "But he's got to own up to all he's done wrong before he can get straightened out."

He had said, "The truth is, I'm never going to do nothing but get by. I wish you'd talk to the sheriff and the lawyers and let me take Travis's place."

For a long moment, his mother had not replied. She had turned away at the kitchen table, which was dimly lighted by a kerosene lamp. Still, Noah could see she was hiding a film of tears that coated her eyes. And then his mother had said in a soft, aching voice, "No, son, I can't do that. I can't let you take the punishment for something your brother's done. Even if your daddy was alive, he wouldn't let that happen."

And maybe it had worked out the way it should have, Noah thought. If he had traded places with Travis, Travis would have been in the war and the way Travis was at taking chances, most likely he would have been killed.

He had seen Travis only twice since coming home from the war. No, four times. Twice in the jail where he would be for another twelve years, and twice with a road gang, cutting johnsongrass with a sling blade. Bent to the work of the sling blade, Travis had had the look of an old man.

Looking down from his above view, he saw himself shift uncomfortably on the porch step, lean forward, elbows on his knees.

Saw himself nod to something Whitlow said to him—a question he believed. But he had no sense of the question. The memory of Travis had overpowered him.

"Fish Seller, you look like you a thousand miles away," Taylor said in his good-natured way. "You hear what Whitlow just asked you?"

The suspended Noah fell back to the porch. He said, "Sorry." He looked at Whitlow, saw a smile still fixed on his face.

"He asked you if you were going fishing today," Taylor said.

"Didn't plan on it," Noah answered.

"Well, some of these boys were thinking about going to get in some practice fishing before Saturday," Whitlow told him. "They was wondering if you'd like to go along."

"I better pass on it," Noah said. "I still got a lot of painting to do."

"Well, damn," said the younger man with the stubble of beard and the sun-brown face. "If that's what's keeping you, maybe we all ought to pick up a brush and give you a hand."

Taylor laughed.

A cooling air slid from the mountain, air that had autumn in it, though autumn was weeks away. Still, Noah could feel it, and liked it. His mother had talked about such autumn-in-summer weather, saying it was nature's way of telling squirrels to quit their frolicking and to start putting up stores for later on, saying that if people studied squirrels they would have some idea of how best to conduct their own lives.

Such things as his mother told him about weather and squirrels were easy for Noah to remember. He had never heard such things in school. In school, the teachers had talked from books opened in front of them, talked in rapid-fire words too confusing to understand. In school, he had been lost from his first day, had endured nine grades of it before reaching the age of leaving.

He sat in the porch rocker of the shack, having taken a supper of oatmeal and coffee, and he watched the moon's light spread itself across the unmoving surface of the lake. A soft color, the moon's light. Orange-red poured into yellow. The color of the sky when the sun skimmed it sometimes at sunset. Sky and water. He felt good with sky and water. Remembered as a small boy his first seeing of a globe of Earth, with the oceans colored blue, and wondering if the blue had fallen from the sky.

The owl he had seen on his first night at the lake made its call. Or maybe it was not the same owl, he reasoned, but another. Maybe the Lake of Grief was a nesting place for owls, a hunting ground of field mice skittering along dark paths made in dark grass.

Once Travis had found a young owl near the barn, its wing somehow broken, and they had tried to mend it with sticks and adhesive tape, but the owl, with its sorrowful eyes, had died during the night and the death had numbed Travis, causing him to hide himself in a cave he had gouged out of hay stored in the barn loft. It had taken long coaxing to get Travis out of his cave, he remembered. He had said, "Come on, I'll take you fishing." It was a trick that always worked. Fishing. Travis loved fishing, though he had no gift for it. Sometimes, he would switch poles with Travis when he knew a fish was about to hit his own line, would say to Travis, "Here, hold my pole. My arm's getting tired." Each time, with each catch, Travis would fidget with excitement. "Look, Noah, look, I caught me one," he would cry, dragging the fish to the creekside.

An ache swept him, thinking of Travis. A sadness heavy on his arms and shoulders and chest.

It was hard to picture his brother in prison, dressed in the stripes of prison wear. Travis was five years younger, but had become old in prison. The last time he had seen Travis—before leaving Elbert County to take up his fishing trade—Noah had felt lost. Sitting in a cold room, prison guards keeping a hard watch over them, he had been mostly silent. Travis, too. They had made small talk about the sharecroppers now working the farm of their childhood and about the death of their parents and about Noah's plan to travel and fish. It was good, going away, Travis had mumbled, nodding his head monotonously. Getting away from all the drag-down times they both had lived. Yes, that was good. Wished he could tag along, he had said, but things being as they were, he guessed he'd be too old to do much more than take up space on some porch when he finished his time.

"I wish I wasn't here," Travis had said softly.

"Wish you wasn't, either," Noah had replied.

"A man's a fool to put himself behind bars," Travis had added. "And I been fool enough for me and you and a whole lot more."

Noah had not answered him.

"Hope you come to see me when you find your way back down here," Travis had said.

"I will," Noah had promised.

"You get a chance, write me a letter sometime," Travis had said. "Since Mama died, nobody's wrote me a letter."

On his travels, Noah had written two letters to Travis. One from Alabama and one from Kentucky. Both painfully done with uneven letters, like that of a child. Both short of words. Both saying where he was, and where he thought of going. Both ending with, *I keep thinking about you.*

A trough of wind blew across the lake, making the moon's orange-yellow light shimmer on the surface of the water. Noah could hear it making a hiss against the porch wire, felt it against his face, thought of it as something sent to him by Travis.

Time to go see him, he said in his head.

And I will. Soon.

Tomorrow, I will write him another letter.

Tell him I'm headed back toward Elbert County.

He swallowed a deep, quick breath, taking in the wind, taking in the still-faint scent of paint he had tried to scrub from his hands. Taylor Bowers had praised him for the work, saying he was a natural with a paintbrush in his hands, as good with a paintbrush as with a fishing pole. Had said, "You could make some good money painting, Fish Seller. Most people don't like doing it."

Painting was all right, he reasoned. Not as mean as plowing a mule over baked-hard field dirt. Maybe he and Travis could set up a painting business when Travis got out of prison.

He would write to Travis about the painting, he decided.

A soft splash sounded against the bank of the lake. Mr. Fish, he thought. Mr. Fish wondering what had happened to him, wondering why he had not kept his promise.

"Soon enough," he said in a soft voice. "Soon enough."

Or maybe it was not the fish. Maybe it was the ghost of Arch Wheeler or Boyd Cunningham stirring up the wind. Arch Wheeler or Boyd Cunningham trying to alert him to something, like gunsmoke war angels warning him of men in hidden places, waiting to kill him.

A shiver rippled across his neck and shoulders, down his back.

THIRTEEN

On the day Boyd Cunningham drove Eleanor to the farmhouse he had purchased as a wedding surprise, he had given up a secret: once, as a boy, he had taken his pocket knife and carved his initials on one of the clapboards at the back of the house. Had carved B C for Boyd Cunningham. Not something large and easy to see. A little cut made with a blade tip, barely visible even close up to it. It was his way of branding the house, he had explained to her, determined that someday he would live there.

It was also a story Eleanor remembered with sadness, having learned the whole of it from Howard Reynolds after Boyd's death.

The house had been constructed by a man named Joe Manning, whose grandson, Isaac, had been a childhood friend to Boyd. There had been a rumor—a story shared for humor by old men who knew it to be a made-up tale—that Joe Manning had dug up some nuggets of gold when he put down the foundation for the house and that, afterward, long-dead Indians began to appear to him at night, angry over his taking of the gold and turning it into cash. The story said that no one in Joe Manning's family would ever rest peacefully in the house or would ever again find so much as a pinhead speck of gold. Yet, whoever took up the place after Joe Manning's family would find enough gold to pave a road from Hayesville to Hiawassee.

It was a story told mainly to poke fun at old Joe Manning's miserly ways, yet Boyd had let himself believe it as a boy, and in the hardening years between childhood to manhood, he had made a firm vow that he would someday own the place.

"I never told nobody about what I did back then," he had said to Eleanor, and he had taken her to the clapboard to show her his scratched-in initials, and there, as she watched, he had cut her initials in the board beside his own. E M for Eleanor Miller.

"Now all we got to do is start looking for gold, and make sure nobody else gets near the place," Boyd had declared in the happy manner that was part of him before the war. The happy manner had made her laugh with glee.

Gold, Eleanor thought. Gold.

She wondered how her husband had not known it was only a made-up story. Too good a dream, perhaps. Too good to laugh off.

She did not know why she remembered the story. It had come to her unexpectedly out of the dark pitch of night surrounding her home, the night she gazed into from the porch swing where she been sitting for more than an hour, taking a rest from the daily struggle to get Beatrice bathed and in bed.

And maybe that was what she was doing, she thought. Keeping watch without consciously knowing it. Making sure no one got near, as Boyd had warned. As it was, she seemed to be losing the place little by little. First, the dogs, both killed by some hunter or some drunk playing at hunting, and then the selling of the younger, working mule and the calf, and then the cow's death.

But the watch she kept was not for an imaginary stockpile of paving-stone gold. The gold her husband had dreamed about was joke gold. Not even fool's gold. If there was gold on old Joe Manning's farm, no one had ever found it. Enough rock to build a highway to the moon and back, but no gold. It was little wonder that Isaac Manning had sold the land to Boyd, she thought. Rock farms were useless. Isaac Manning was the one who had cashed in on the deal. Isaac Manning had moved to Nashville, Tennessee, and was turning his seed money from the sale of the land into a fortune by operating a printing business specializing in catalogues. He had got his gold out of the place, all right. Ink and paper gold.

The watch she was keeping was not for gold. It was for someone to show up with money in hand and a wish to own a rock farm.

Once, she had believed she could sell it to the man named Garland Hood, who had wanted the place and had visited often to talk to Boyd about price. Had even written a few letters addressed to Boyd, marked Confidential. "More haggling," Boyd had called the letters, and he had made a show of burning each of them in the fireplace. Yet, she had found a telephone number for Garland Hood among Boyd's belongings, and had called it. The woman who answered the call had told her that Garland Hood had been killed in a car accident only a few months after Boyd had taken his life.

And maybe it was best the way things worked out, she thought. Garland Hood had struck her as a man who could not be trusted.

She remembered the late autumn afternoon he had first appeared at their home as she worked in the front yard, pruning back a damaged rosebush. Remembered how he looked: dressed in a business suit, a smile fixed on his face like the never-changing smile found in a photograph, driving a car shining with wax. He had announced he was from Atlanta, and had been visiting in the area, looking for a place for a getaway home. He had stayed in the yard, saying he wanted to talk to Boyd in private.

She had watched from the window as they spoke—friendly at first. And then whatever was being said had seemed to agitate Garland Hood and the smile that seemed to cling to his face had vanished and his voice had become loud enough to be heard inside the house, though she had not been able to make out the words. After a few minutes, he had walked away angrily from Boyd, turning at his car door to say the only words she had been able to understand: "You're making a mistake, a big mistake."

Boyd had laughed off the meeting, had told Eleanor it had to do with wanting to buy the farm.

"He's like a politician," Boyd had said. "Wants what he wants, but wants somebody to give it to him." He had added, "He'll be back, but I don't want you talking to him. I'll take care of it. He wants this place, he'd better bring money."

Maybe she was keeping watch for the ghost of Garland Hood to drive up in his waxed car, still ready to haggle, she thought. Or maybe the watch was for anyone who showed up, the first person wandering by, out of the blue, looking as though he needed a place to own.

Maybe she would sell the farm for a dollar an acre to whoever that person was.

She had a sudden image of Noah Locke standing in Taylor Bowers's store.

Maybe Noah Locke would like to own it.

A tired smile found her face. And where would Noah Locke get the money, even at a dollar an acre? If he bought it, he'd have to pay it off in fish. Noah Locke could have been a character in *The Grapes of Wrath,* as poor as he was. Could have been Noah Joad.

The smile stayed. She closed her eyes, could see a roomful of fish and Noah Locke grinning happily, holding the deed to the land.

If Noah ever owned the place, it would be because she gave it to him. That was for sure. She doubted if Noah had the money to buy a good meal.

She opened her eyes, checked the watch she wore on her wrist. It was a few minutes before midnight, yet she was not sleepy.

She stood, took another look at the yard and the woods. At night, it was a peaceful place, the way the trees seemed to fill in with darkness, their limbs drooping in sleep. She guessed it was the thing Noah liked about his travels, seeing how peaceful places could be in sleep.

In a day or so, she would try to leave Beatrice with Ada Reynolds long enough to go to the shack and to clean it while Noah was away painting, she decided. She owed him that much.

FOURTEEN

He was at the store not long after sunrise, having spent a night of light sleep and flickering dreams that caused an ache behind his eyes. His breakfast had been coffee and more oatmeal, which he had eaten at the table while forcing his mind to think of the letter he would write to his brother, and of the trip back to Elbert County, and of the gift he would take to Travis.

In the war, at Dachau, he had found a small carving of a cow near the body of a young man who had died on the night before he would have been freed. The carving was no larger than his thumb, but perfectly done. Ears and horns and tail and udders. Its head was bent over, as though grazing from pasture grass. Its back and sides had been made smooth from rubbing. He had given the carving to Travis, keeping secret the story of where it came from, but he did not know if Travis still had it. Maybe not. Maybe he had traded it for cigarettes.

Maybe he would take a work coat to Travis, he had reasoned. Something for cold weather. A work coat with a pocket large enough to hold the carved cow—if Travis still had it.

At the store, he took the hard-bristle brush Taylor had provided and began to scrape off old paint peeling on the clapboard. If he worked hard at it, and if the weather held clear, he could finish the painting in another day or so, he believed. He would use some of the money for a bus ticket back to Elbert County, and he would put away the same amount for a return trip to the valley, if he had a notion to return. That way, he would not spend it foolishly, as he had done often with the money he kept hidden in the bottom of his knapsack. Nothing confused him as much as money. It seemed to fly out of his hand, zooming away on invisible wings. There was never enough of it. He guessed there never would be.

Taylor's surprise at finding him working so early made Noah smile from the ladder.

"If you think I'm going to get here when the rooster crows, you've got another think coming," Taylor called up to him cheerfully. "Nobody stopped by, did they?"

"Not yet," Noah told him.

"Thank the Lord," Taylor said. "They'd put a warrant out for my arrest if they saw you out this early. It's one thing to show some spirit, my friend, but it's something else entirely to make the rest of the world seem lazy." He laughed. "I'll put the coffee on," he added.

The morning and early afternoon were spent in work and talk—Noah working, Taylor talking. Shoppers drifted in and out of the store, some stopping outside to speak to Noah and to comment on the good work of his painting. Made the store look fresh, they said in praise. A few of the men who had been present the day before talked to him about fishing, some saying they had spent the afternoon at the river, trying their luck. Their catches had been small, even fishing from the same spot Noah had fished with Taylor, they admitted, and they clucked their tongues over how Noah could catch fish when they couldn't.

One of them, a man named Luther Myers, said, "You must have been born to do it, that's all I got to say," making Noah think of Hoke Moore. Hoke Moore had said much the same.

"He was," Taylor declared.

All the men vowed to see him on Saturday at the fishing contest.

In mid-afternoon two men—Peavo Teasley and Moody Deal, both dressed in overalls fitting high and tight across their stomachs, both needing a shave, both having the look of a farmer taking a day away from the fields—arrived at the store with Howard Reynolds and his grandson, Matthew, and were introduced to Noah by Taylor, who called them sorry and untrustworthy, but the put-downs came with a smile and Noah knew that Taylor was fond of them.

Both men wanted to give Noah an order for catfish.

Both said Howard Reynolds had been talking about him, about his skill as a fisherman, and Howard agreed, saying, "They getting close to calling me a liar."

"Sounds like you don't even need bait, the way Howard was talking," Moody said, and he snickered.

"Tell you what," Peavo offered, casting a squinted glance at the sun, "Howard was saying he give you a dime a fish, but if you can catch me six river cats before sundown, I'll give you fifteen cents apiece. You don't, I get to keep what you come up with for free."

"Do the same here," said Moody.

"Good Lord, boys," Howard said to them irritably, "you couldn't do that with a seine."

"He's supposed to be good at it," argued Moody. "We just trying to see how good he really is."

Noah knew it was a tease, and a test. He said, "I don't know. It's not long to sundown."

"You got your fishing rod with you?" asked Peavo .

"Yes sir," Noah said. "I brought it in."

"Well, I don't blame you for that," Peavo said. "If you can fish like Howard Reynolds says you can, you better not let that rod out of sight. Somebody'll be stealing it, saying the luck's in the rod, not the man holding it."

Moody laughed. He looked at Taylor. "Ain't nobody that good," he said.

Noah could see a flush of irritation sweep across Taylor's face. "And I tell you what," Taylor said. "He catches the order you just gave him, it'll cost you a quarter a fish. He don't, you get what he's got for free."

Moody looked at Peavo, made a little shrug. Peavo shrugged back, let his grin wiggle over his mouth.

"Sounds like a sporting offer," Moody said. "Shoot, Littleberry Davis ain't that good, and Littleberry's the best I ever saw."

"Littleberry couldn't bait Noah's hook," Taylor said defiantly. "I been fishing with him."

"I got to go along with Taylor," Howard said. "Nothing against Littleberry, but I never seen nothing like this boy." He looked at his grandson, winked. Matthew's grin flew up happily.

Noah listened to the men talk, making the same kind of harmless quarrel that small boys would make over nothing more serious than which could spit the longer distance. After a time, it would call for a showdown. It was the same with men as it was with boys. His mother had called such boasting the mule-stubborn way the male half of the race had for playing the fool. Chicken-sense, she had scoffed. Gave proof that the male brain was half the size of the female brain.

And maybe his mother had been right, Noah thought as he listened, staying out of the talk between Taylor and the two men making the bargain. Some things learned as boys were carried like souvenirs into manhood.

A side bet was made, Taylor putting up five dollars on Noah's ability to catch the orders before sundown, and Moody and Peavo putting up two-fifty each, saying he wouldn't. Howard turned down the opportunity to make his own wager. Didn't believe in gambling, he said, and he looked at his grandson and his grandson nodded agreement.

The side bet gave way to an agreement that Taylor and Moody and Peavo and Howard and his grandson would go along with Noah for the fishing.

"Just to make sure there's no shenanigans," said Peavo.

"Just to make sure you don't stand around throwing rocks in the water, or talking your heads off, scaring off the fish," said Taylor. "Way the two of you go on, they'll be trying to find their way to the ocean."

There had been other bets, other dares, in Noah's travels. Men believing he could not catch fish when the weather was odd, or when the water was too hot or too cold, too shallow or too deep, or when the moon was in the wrong phase. He had never made a wager with anyone on what he could or could not do—at fishing or anything else—but he had watched money being exchanged among others when he took fish some vowed he could not take.

Each time there had been bets, he remembered Burl and Cork.

Burl and Cork were old men when he was only a boy—sharecropper Negroes who loved to fish after a rain, when field work was stopped and the creeks of Elbert County were swollen with wash-off water. They had believed there was something wondrous about him, having watched him catch fish, and over time they had begun inviting their friends to meet them at the creeks, making sly boasts about the white boy who could make fish come to his hook just by touching the water, and the fish could not resist him. Magic, they called it. Their friends had put down their nickels and dimes against a catch, and then had stared in amazement when the fish took the hook.

He gave the bettors the fish he caught. Among themselves, they agreed with Burl and Cork: he had magic. Said it loud enough for him to hear.

On some days there had been as many as twenty gathered to watch him fish. Watching as silently as owls. Shaking their heads in disbelief.

"Told you so," Burl and Cork had said proudly. "Told you so."

FIFTEEN

At the Hiawassee River, running north out of the lake called the Chatuge, Howard Reynolds and his grandson watched Noah bait his hook as Taylor and Moody and Peavo kept their wager alive with rule-making. Sundown, they agreed, would be when the sun's light disappeared from the top of a hemlock that grew on a nearby hill. To be counted, a fish had to be seven inches long, and there was joking about how the measurement would be made—Moody saying seven inches was pretty much the length of his goober and Peavo countering that if they went by Moody's goober, they'd be keeping minnows so small and skinny you could read a newspaper through them. Had to be a river cat. No bream or bass or trout or crappie or sucker fish. Any fish that got away after being pulled in and put on the stringer still counted—even if the stringer slipped from its tie-off or if a turtle made a meal of the fish. No help from Taylor, not even to string the fish. Noah had to do it all on his own.

Howard would be the judge of any violation of the rules, Taylor suggested.

Moody agreed.

Peavo agreed.

Taylor wanted to double the wager.

Moody and Peavo chose to keep it at five dollars.

They were still arguing as Noah went to the river and kneeled and put his palm on the water. From the look of him, he seemed to be praying.

"What's he doing?" Moody whispered suspiciously, lighting a cigarette.

"Washing the worm slime off his hand," Taylor said.

"Lorda'mighty," Moody mumbled. "I never saw nobody do that."

"He likes to keep clean," Taylor told him, thinking the explanation sounded good enough. Two days before, readying to fish for the supper at Eleanor Cunningham's home, he had noticed Noah touching the water in the same manner and he, too, had wondered about it, but had said nothing. Every fisherman on earth had some quirky superstition.

He added to Peavo and Moody, "Maybe that's something you boys ought to do once in a while—wash up a little bit. From the looks of the two of you, last time you got near any water was when you was baptized."

The first catch was taken in less than a minute after Noah made his first cast.

A catfish, ten inches long by Howard's estimation.

"Goda'mighty," Moody whispered in awe.

"How about making it twenty dollars?" Taylor said boastfully to Moody and Peavo.

"That ain't but one," Peavo muttered, watching the fish thrash about on the stringer as Noah dropped it back into the water.

"I tell you one thing," Taylor said in a languid voice. "That sun's sure bright. Almost blinding, it's so bright. Looks like it's just hanging up there, don't it, boys? Yes, it does." He laughed easily.

In thirty minutes, Noah had six catfish, all keepers. Moody and Peavo sat on the bank of the river, smoking and shaking their heads in disbelief, giving each other puzzled looks, trying to find some way to wiggle out of the bet. They muttered about Noah finding a catfish hole none of them knew anything about, wondered aloud why he did not hook a crappie or a bream or a trout. Howard's grandson pranced about near Noah, excited, saying to Howard that he wanted to fish also.

"We will, later on," Howard said gently. "Right now, we just watching. You keep a good look. See what you can learn. Next time we go fishing, you can try it out."

The explanation seemed to satisfy the boy. He squatted down, turned his face to Noah, peered intensely at Noah through the thick lenses of his glasses.

"That's right," Howard said. "You keep a good look. You watching a real fisherman, now. You keep a good look and see what you learn from it."

The sunlight began to slide up the side of the hemlock chosen as the sundown tree.

Peavo and Moody began to smile.

Five minutes passed before Noah caught another fish. A large one. Three pounds, Taylor guessed.

"Looks like they about to quit biting," Peavo said.

The sunlight reached halfway to the top of the tree.

Taylor began to pace. He said, "Maybe you fished that hole clean, Noah."

Noah did not reply.

In ten minutes he caught four more fish.

"One to go," Taylor said anxiously.

The sun disappeared behind a hill. The light on the top of the hemlock began to fade. To the north, dark clouds hovered. A wind began to whip across the river, carrying the scent of far-off rain.

"Come on, Noah," Taylor urged. "We got about five minutes left."

"That sun ain't so shiny now, is it?" Moody teased. "No sir. About to be pitch dark the way them clouds look like they moving in, and we about to go home with a free mess of catfish and five of them dollar bills you got in your pocket." He cackled, lit another cigarette.

Noah did not rush. He threaded the worm onto the hook, held it up, examined it. Then he pulled the worm to his lips and kissed it lightly. It was a show-off trick he had picked up from fishing with Marvin Linquist when they could find a break in the war and a stream to fish in. Marvin playing the clown, bragging that a kissed worm caught the big ones.

"Good Lord," Moody said softly. He looked at Peavo and then at Taylor. Taylor shrugged. He had never seen anyone kiss a worm.

The cast arched high, landed with a soft thud in the middle of the pool of water, causing a ripple. The float turned, settled.

"He ain't gone make it," Peavo whispered, glancing at the pine. "Sun's about gone."

The float bobbed once, then disappeared in a violent jerk.

"My God," Taylor said in disbelief.

"He ain't got it to shore," Moody declared. He looked at the tree, chortled, "And the sun's gone."

"You blind as a bat," Taylor said. He stretched, pushing himself up on his toes. "I still see some."

"Where?" demanded Peavo.

"Right there," Taylor argued. "Right on the tip of the tree."

A high wind blew across the top of the hemlock, causing it to bend and wave. The last light of the sun slid away with the wind.

"It ain't there now, by shot," Moody said gleefully.

Taylor turned to them. "Don't matter," he growled. "He caught it when some light was still up there."

The sound of his voice caused Peavo to step back, remembering Taylor's reputation as a boxer.

"Deal was, he had to have them on the stringer," Moody argued.

"I didn't hear nothing about that," Taylor snapped. "Deal was, he had to catch them, and if that one he's got on the hook's a catfish and if it's over seven inches long, then he's done it." He turned to Howard. "Who's right?"

"I'd say you are," Howard declared. "Didn't hear nothing about having to have them on the stringer. Just caught, and that one's caught if he gets it to the bank."

The catfish was twelve inches long by Howard's declaration, with no argument from Moody or Peavo. The two men paid their wager to Taylor and then gave Noah the bargained price for the fish. Three dollars. A quarter a fish.

"Damn," Peavo said in a grumbling voice, "them fish better taste good." Then, to Noah: "Well, boy, I guess what they say about you might have been right. I know some boys that come out here yesterday, standing right where you been standing, and they didn't get a nibble. I don't know nobody else who could've done what you just did. Maybe Jesus, but that's all."

The drive from the river in Taylor's car was Taylor-noisy. He gloated in taking his five dollars from Peavo and Moody, and he crowed joyfully over witnessing what certainly was a fishing miracle worth exploring for future benefit. No reason to worry, now, he said to Noah. Peavo and Moody would be talking and the talk would spread like a flash fire in a field of dry grass, and there would be a parade of people stopping by the store for no reason other than to see Noah in person—which would slow down the painting, but that would not matter. They would feel obligated to purchase something, like buying a ticket to see a picture show with a star actor. Business would boom, but it would be small change compared to what they could make on the river. Or on the road, Taylor added, his eyes shining with the sudden thought. If they did it right—if Taylor went along with Noah to handle the business end of things, to talk up Noah's gift—they could make more money than either of them had ever seen, just by traveling around, place to place.

"Nothing gets to a man's pride faster than somebody saying they can outfish him or outhunt him," Taylor declared. "We'll have more showdowns than Wyatt Earp."

Noah listened patiently, and with amusement, and listening made him remember the story of a man in Elbert County during the depression. The man—Abel Cromer was his name—did not have a job, but he had a large family needing to be fed and clothed, and the sharecropping of a dry summer had not made ends meet. One night he had a vision-dream, the story went, and the next day he took some red clay from a gully and made a kind of dye out of it with water; then he applied it to his skin and to the skin of his wife and children, tinting them a pale red. Remembering his vision-dream, he went off in his secondhand model-T Ford to travel the South, claiming to be a descendent of Cherokee Indians. Made stops at schools along the way, announcing that for a little change and goods, he and his Indian family would give lessons about the way Indians used to live. The history he gave was lively, but made up. So were the songs and war whoops and rain dances. And the way to make arrowheads and to skin buffalo and to throw up tepees. All of it, made up. Still, a few years later he had returned to Elbert County a man of moderate means, and had purchased the farm he once worked as a sharecropper. Went by the name Indian Abel. Even had it put on his tombstone.

Too bad Indian Abel did not know Taylor Bowers, Noah thought. If Taylor had handled the business end of things, Indian Abel might have become a Cherokee chief worth writing about in history books.

The thought made Noah smile the smile that did not show.

"Tell you what," Taylor said as they neared Bowerstown Road, "why don't we drive on down to Hiawassee and get us something to eat? Treat's on me, since I got some extra money to burn. There's a little café down there that sets a good table. Got the best meat loaf I ever had."

"Maybe another time," Noah told him. "I guess I better not get caught in the rain."

Taylor craned his neck to study the clouds. "You probably right," he said. "I left some windows open at my house, and I'm in too good a mood to do any mopping, but I owe you a supper and I won't forget it. Peavo and Moody's always aggravating me over one thing or the other. This time, I got the best of them, and you were the one that did it." He laughed suddenly, happily, slapped at the steering wheel of the car with the palm of his hand. "Lord, I feel good," he chirped.

The rain lashed against the house, thrown by a hard-blowing wind, causing an uneven drumming sound over the shingled roof. It caught in the mesh of the screen wire covering the windows and the mist that blew through the wire trickled in thin, wriggling rivulets down the glass, leaving the impression of slender, wet statues that had come to life and were trying to dance themselves free of the sticky surface of the panes.

To Eleanor, seeing water dancers on the windowpanes was the same as seeing faces in clouds, or in the grainy patterns of wood. As a child, she had tried to point out the figures to her sisters and to her parents, but they had not been able to see what she could see, and it had become a gentle, laughing ceremony in her family. At each rain, someone would go to a window and say, "Look, I see . . ." And they would say they could see Santa Claus or an elf or the Lone Ranger or someone they all knew from school or church or the community.

Eleanor's faces, they had called them.

Her grandfather had seen the faces, though. One face, at least. Her grandfather had said he could see the face of Jesus. Three days before he died, during the last rain that would fall in his life, he had sent for Eleanor and he had pointed to the window and had said to her in a voice of joy, "Look, honey, there's Jesus." The smile on his face had been peaceful. "Jesus, coming for me," he had added.

And maybe what her grandfather had said was true. Maybe he had seen Jesus.

If Jesus could show himself in clouds, he could surely show himself in rivulets of rain.

The drumming of the rain had forced an early-night sleep on the old woman, giving Eleanor time for her own rest, something her body needed but her mind could not understand. Her mind was restless. Had been all day, and perhaps for several days, and she believed she had finally reached the point of change. People had said to her that it would happen. Had said she would wake up one morning and place her feet on the floor and she would realize her life had changed during the night. Magically changed. Changed as though some angel had visited and swept its healing hand over her body as she slept. It would be like coming out of a high-fever sickness, or like a butterfly escaping its cocoon, they had said. Done so suddenly it would puzzle her until she accepted the truth of it.

She believed it had happened that morning, the morning of sleeping late, of having wishes for a man's touch.

She went to the closet holding the clothing of her late husband, and to the bedroom dresser, and she took the clothing off hangers and out of drawers, and she folded and stacked them on the bed. Gathered his shaving cream and after-shave lotion, his razors, his toothbrush, his deodorant—all the things that still carried his man-scent—and she dropped them into a waste can.

Soon, she would take the clothes to churches in the area and would offer them as gifts for people needing clothes. Would do it in Boyd's name, having a sense that Boyd would go away with the clothing, like in an act of exorcism.

A flash of lightning—quick, splendid in its white heat—burned across the darkness of the clouds covering the Valley of Light and thunder exploded near the house. She went to the window and looked out. On the windowpane before her, she saw water rivulets making the outline of a man with water legs and arms, a water hat covering a water head. She thought of a caricature of Don Quixote she had seen in a book. Skinny as a skeleton, riding a swayback horse, carrying a lance with a broken tip.

Or the rivulets could have been Tom Joad. Or Noah Locke.

But not her husband. Not Boyd.

A surge of relief flowed in her.

• • •

The rain had stopped and the clouds bringing it had thinned, leaving a fluorescence of light from moon and stars. At the lake shack, Noah sat in the dark of the screened-in porch and watched the dripping of water from the roof and from tree leaves that had the look of wet wax.

The day had been long—a stretched-out day, started early. His body ached from nothing more than the hours it had endured. Still, he was not sleepy. It had been the same in the war, he thought. Long days of long marches, of wondering if there were Germans hidden along the way, ready to do their killing. Sleep had never been easy after such days. Not for him. For Marvin Linquist, yes, but not for him. Marvin had boasted he could sleep on a bed made of thorns, under a blanket of chigger briars, if given the chance. Sleep, Marvin had said, was just a matter of letting your body go limp, like shutting off the motor of a Jeep.

The rain had cooled the day's heat and over the water of the lake, a fog-sheet suspended itself, giving the lake a ghostly look. From nearby, he heard an owl—a low, soft call. The same owl as he had seen before, he guessed, making known its ownership of the lake, saying to Noah that he was freeloading in a place where he had no right to be.

He pulled himself from the chair, stretched against the tender ache of his muscles, then walked to the screen door of the porch, letting his eyes search for the owl, and in the search, he thought of Howard Reynolds's grandson, the boy called Matthew, and of the glasses Matthew wore, giving him the appearance of having large, owl-like eyes. Yet, the boy's eyes were small behind the glasses—small eyes made large, like a telescope made far-off things seem close. The boy's eyes had seemed to make words that his grandfather understood, for his grandfather had answered many questions about the fishing without Matthew's making a sound.

To Noah, the words of eyes often made better sense than the words of the tongue.

In the war, he had relied on eye-talk, since he could not understand what was being said by people who lived in the countries he had passed through, going from fight to fight. It had all been a mystery to him, though sometimes he knew the gist of what was being said by the way the speaker said it, and by the tilt of the head, by gesture, by pointing, by nodding. Mostly, he had read their eyes. If their eyes showed up fearful, he knew to take guard. If he could see some laughter, some shine of gladness, he knew the danger was not so great.

He remembered unexpectedly the deaf-and-dumb Negro man he had met in north Alabama. A tall, thin man, showing four teeth when he smiled, a scar down his right cheek that had the look of a whelp, his right leg bowed at the knee, making his walk have a wobble to it. Noah had no name for him, since the man could not say it or write it in the dirt, but the name did not matter. They had met on a road going into Tennessee, not far from the Flint River, the man ambling along in is wobble walk, carrying a large cook pot that contained a small sack of cornmeal and another of sugar, and they had walked together for a day and a half before the man veered off, waving his goodbye. The man had made talk with his hands and with his face and, mostly, with his eyes, and Noah had made awkward attempts to speak the same language. It had been a cause for laughter, two men walking along a road, one white, one black, trying to make words out of air, like two old and addled women sitting in porch chairs, knitting imaginary garments from rolls of imaginary wool. Or like two children in chase of fireflies, their hands snatching at darting dots of yellow light. Or like Beatrice Cunningham's hands moving over her lap. Not a word had been spoken between the man and Noah, yet at the break-off of their journey together, Noah knew much about him. Knew he was a farmer. Knew he had a wife and two children. Knew he had served some jail time in Alabama—Huntsville, Noah guessed—and had been set free and was heading back to his home, carrying the cook pot and cornmeal and sugar as prizes. All this he knew because the man could draw pictures of it with his fingertips and with his eyes. His fingertips were like fine paint brushes, his eyes like the screens of picture shows.

He had liked the time spent with the deaf-and-dumb man.

They had shared a campsite by a stream with a fast flow to it, and there the deaf-and-dumb man had picked the tender leaves from a patch of pokeberry stalks and had cooked them in his deep cook pot—rinsing them and recooking several times to get rid of the poison—and Noah had caught some trout and pan-fried them in a tobacco tin's worth of lard bought for a dime at a farm house nearby and had made hoecakes from a small amount of the colored man's cornmeal mixed with water and salt, and the deaf-and-dumb man had made a silent, closed-eye prayer over the food. He had said his thanks to Noah by a slow blink and a head-dip that had its pull from deep in his chest.

He wondered if the man had found his home, and if he was still there. Wondered if he had ever spoken of their time together, and, if so, wondered how the man's fingers looked when they told the tale. Or maybe the man's wife was too happy over her cook pot and corn bread and sugar to care what was said in air woods about a white man wandering from place to place, looking for a place to fish.

The owl made a sudden dive from a pine tree, its great wings flapping once; then it disappeared into a pool of night behind the tangled limbs of a mountain laurel.

No reason to think about getting up early, Noah reasoned. It would take time for the store siding to dry enough for painting. He turned his body to look at the lake. Hoke Moore's fish was there, waiting.

"You got to take your time with him," Hoke Moore had advised. *"Got to aggravate him some. Got to make him want you as much as you want him."*

Soon, Noah thought.

Soon.

SIXTEEN

He stayed late on the cot, watching the sun ease out of the trees—the trees still holding the rinse of rain—and then he went to the spring to wash the sleep from his eyes and to get water for his coffee and oatmeal. He was cleaning his dish in the wash pan when he heard his name being called from the front of the shack. He knew by the voice that it was Eleanor Cunningham.

She was carrying a basket that appeared to be filled with towels or something like towels, and she seemed surprised to find him at the shack, saying, "I thought you'd be gone already."

"I was waiting a little bit for the sun to dry out the store some," he told her.

"I can come back later," she said, and she turned to leave.

"It's all right," Noah said. "I'll be going in a few minutes, anyhow." It was a small lie, but one that seemed necessary.

She paused, looked back at him. "Are you sure?"

"Soon as I finish my coffee," he answered.

"You have enough for two cups?" she asked.

"More than enough," he replied. "I'll pour you one."

"I could use it," she told him.

The basket contained towels and bedsheets for the cot and some cleaning materials.

"I thought I'd clean up the place a little bit," she explained. "Put a sheet on the cot and leave you some towels."

"You don't need to do that," he said.

"I know I don't," Eleanor told him. "But it's something I want to do. I owe you, and it's little enough as a payback."

"You don't owe me," he said.

"In my way of thinking, I do," she replied. "Besides, I haven't been down here in a long time. I always liked it here, almost as much as my husband did."

He wondered if being at the shack bothered her, remembering her husband's death. Yet, she did not look bothered. There was a freshness about her. Her hair was not gathered in the small bun at her neck as it had been. Her face seemed to hold a faint coating of makeup. Her eyes seemed clear, bright.

"I swept up some," he said.

She glanced around the shack, her face showing pleasure. "It looks a lot better than it did when Boyd would come down here," she said. "He never swept the floor or picked up anything. I'd come down every couple of weeks and try to straighten it up, but it always seemed to get on his nerves, having me around. Especially after the war. Before, it was different. We had some nice times before he went off to war, but when he got back, he liked being by himself and this was the place that let him do that, I suppose." She smiled a smile that held memory. "One time I picked some wildflowers—ironweed, pretty little purple flowers—and put them in a vase and left it on the table, and he threw them out the minute he saw them." She turned to look at Noah. "After that, I just let him do what he wanted to with it. When he died, it was like a pigsty. One of the first things I did after the funeral was to clean this place. I don't think I've been back since."

Noah poured two cups of coffee at the table and Eleanor took a seat in one of the chairs.

"I left Granny with Howard Reynolds and his wife," she said, guiding the talk away from her husband and the shack. "Sometimes they watch after her for a few hours to give me a little break." She picked up the cup of coffee, pulled it to her face and inhaled its odor. "They're good people, the best I've met since I've been here. Their son Milton lost his wife two or three years ago and he moved back in with them, but he's away somewhere working with a road builder and they watch after the boy." She paused. "It's sad about Matthew. He's sweet as he can be, but he's not far from being retarded."

"I like him," Noah said quietly.

"So do I," she said. "When Boyd was alive, and before Granny moved in, Howard used to bring him by the house and I'd read to him. He liked stories that had rhymes in them, the kind of things you'd read to a first-grader. Sometimes, he would say the line before I could, and I'd clap for him and he'd laugh like somebody being tickled."

Noah offered a smile.

"Howard was telling me about the fishing yesterday," she said. "He said he'd never seen anything like it. Told me Matthew couldn't stop talking about it. He said he wanted to be a fisherman like you."

"I had some luck," he said, taking the chair across from Eleanor.

"Not the way Howard describes it," she said. "He said it was more than luck. He said you were the talk of the valley, especially with the school fishing contest coming up this weekend."

Noah took a sip of his coffee, but did not reply.

"How did you get your name? Noah, I mean?" she asked.

"My mama told me she liked the story of Noah and the Ark," he replied. "I guess that's were it's from."

"I'm reading a book that's got a character with the name of Noah in it," she told him.

He looked at her with surprise. It had never occurred to him that his name could be in a book other than the Bible.

"It's called *The Grapes of Wrath.* It's all about people moving out to California to get away from the dust bowl," she said. "A man named John Steinbeck wrote it. Noah's last name was Joad."

Again, Noah gave her a quizzical look.

"Rhymes with toad," she said, smiling. "I'd hate to have had a name like that. I can hear all the kids in school, saying, 'Joad the toad, Joad the toad.' " She let the smile play over her face. "It was bad enough with the nickname I had. L. Just that. The initial *L.* '*L* for Eleanor. *L* from hell,' the boys used to say, and I'd get mad and start acting like that was exactly where I was from. I guess I was something of a tomboy growing up. I had my share of fights."

Noah let his head bob in understanding, and Eleanor told a story of a fight with a boy named Hoyt Rivers. A bully, she called him. Always aggravating girls, pinching them, pulling up their skirts, shooting spitballs at them with rubber bands stretched over his fingers. One day, he had made a girl named Christina Brooks cry, and Eleanor—"*L* from hell," she said—slapped him hard enough to knock him off his feet and to send him running off in shame, ducking through the cheers of everyone watching what had happened. After that, he stuck to himself.

"He became a preacher," she said. "From what I understand, he's got a big church over in Chattanooga, Tennessee." She paused. "Who knows, maybe I helped God open his eyes."

"Sounds that way," Noah said.

She took a sip of her coffee, pronounced it tasty by the look of pleasure on her face. Then she asked, "Have you always been a good fisherman?"

"Pretty good, I guess."

"You like going from place to place?"

"It's got its drawbacks, but it's all right," he said.

"What about the wintertime? You don't fish much then, do you?"

"Not a lot. I was in Florida last winter, where it's not so cold. Winter before that I found me a job."

"What kind of job?"

"It was on a dairy farm. They had a little tenant house on the place, and that's where I stayed. It was all right."

"Don't you miss home? Your friends?"

Noah hesitated in his answer, thought about the friends he had known in his childhood. The memory of them was vague to him. He said, "I been gone a long time."

"What about your brother?" she asked.

Noah's look was puzzling.

"You told me you had a brother," she said.

He remembered the night of the first supper with Eleanor, remembered speaking of his brother. "Yes," he said.

"What's his name?"

"Travis."

"What does he do?"

Noah paused again, not wanting to give the answer, but knowing it would do no good to hide from it. He said in a quiet voice, "He's in jail."

"Jail?"

He moved his head in answer.

Eleanor leaned forward at the table. She looked at the coffee, touched the cup with her fingers. "I'm sorry to hear that," she said. "What happened?"

"He was with somebody who broke in a house and stole some money," Noah answered. "It was after our daddy died. He had a hard time with it and got in some bad company."

"I'm sorry," she said again. "I don't mean to be personal. I guess I don't get to talk to a lot of people except Granny, and most of the time that's like talking to myself. When I find somebody who lets me go on and on, I tend to say too much. One of my sisters calls me a jabbermouth, and I think she's right."

"It's all right," he told her. "I don't talk to too many people myself."

"It's one of the things I miss most about Boyd being dead," she said. "Having somebody to talk to, even if he didn't seem to hear a lot that I said."

"Some people are that way," he replied.

"Have you ever been married, Noah?" she asked casually.

He permitted a small smile, shook his head, said, "No."

"A special girlfriend?"

"No," he said again.

"Never? Never a girlfriend?"

He thought of a girl named Shelia Benson, who had lived on a farm near his parents' home. Remembered her prettiness. Dark, tight curls in long hair. Blue-green eyes. Remembered first kissing her in a game the two were playing in her father's barn on a rain day, when there was no field work to be done. He had been twelve, maybe thirteen. Shelia was older. Two years older, he believed. Also slow in school study, giving them something in common and maybe that was why the first kiss had happened. The kissing had turned to touching and the touching to undressing. In some dreams, he still saw Shelia naked in the dusty light of the barn's loft, the lean muscles of her body damp with sweat, the dark, curling hair between her legs, the erect nipples of her breasts, colored like the flesh of peaches. Over the years, until Shelia left home at age eighteen, they had met periodically to kiss and touch and undress and play at lovemaking. But they had never been boyfriend and girlfriend. They had been two people—male and female—who had had a secret that was sweet and good and worth keeping, a secret that told itself only in dreams. He had never learned the truth of what had happened to Shelia. There was a vague story that she had found her way to New Orleans and had married a policeman and was happy. He hoped it was so. Hoped their secret mattered to her.

"No," he repeated, keeping the secret.

"That's hard to believe," she said. "You're a nice-looking man."

Noah could feel a blush rising in his face. No one had ever complimented him on the way he looked.

"Boyd was my first and only real boyfriend," she said quickly, recognizing the blush. "Unless you count Lester Crain, and that goes back to when we were five or six years old. He used to tell me he was going to marry me when we grew up. I think I believed him up to the age of sixteen." She paused, smiled. "I still see him occasionally. He's married, has two children and teaches school. He always tells me he's still going to marry me when we grow up."

She took a swallow of the coffee. "Maybe I should have made Lester keep his promise," she added. "I probably would have finished school and maybe would be teaching now, like he is." She glanced at Noah. "But we live with what's given us, don't we?"

"I guess so," he replied.

She stood, picked up her cup of coffee and moved to the door leading to the porch and looked out at the lake. "I do like this place," she said quietly. "I like looking out on the lake. I wouldn't mind living here myself, if this was a house instead of a shack."

"It's a good place," Noah said, standing.

"Needs some work on it, though," she said, and she moved her foot over the sag in the flooring. "Boyd said one of the pillars had come apart. He was going to fix it, but never did."

"I'll be happy to take a look at it," Noah said.

"You don't need to do that."

"Won't be any trouble," he said. "I'll do it when I come back from the store."

"Not much reason to," she told him. "Sooner or later, it'll fall down anyway, unless Arch Wheeler's son decides to move back here, and the way he talks, he won't. He likes Texas." She turned back to Noah. "I know I must be keeping you," she said. "I'm sorry. That's what happens when you're around a jabbermouth."

"It's all right," he said uncomfortably. He turned to look through the door. "Guess I better be going on. Sun's out. The store ought to be dry enough by the time I get there."

She smiled, said, "I liked the coffee."

He could feel another blush on his face.

She stood at the screen door of the porch and watched him leave, going along the path to the edge of the woods, and then disappearing. His stride was strong, like a man wanting to be somewhere else. He did not look back.

I talked too much again, she thought. No wonder he wanted to get away so fast.

She turned and went back into the shack and stood for a moment, making decisions about what needed to be done. Not much, to be honest about it. She would broom-wash the floor and make up the cot to be more bedlike, and maybe pick up some wood for the stove. What needed doing would take only a short time, but it was time away from the routine of watching the old woman sitting with a mindless expression on her face, sitting so still it seemed she was hiding from death.

Across the room, she saw Noah's knapsack and wondered about the clothes he must have in it. Maybe he kept them washed in creeks, but they probably needed a good scrubbing in hot water and washing soap. She would not take them without permission, however. People were touchy about other people getting so personal. She reached into her dress pocket, realized she had a short pencil and a piece of tablet paper with a shopping list written on it in the pocket. She would leave a note. Ask him about it.

She wondered if he could read. He had said he did not read much, but that could have been a way of putting off her questions about books. He had seemed genuinely surprised that his name was in a book, when she told him about Noah Joad. Maybe she should have said more about Noah Joad, maybe telling him that he and Noah Joad had some similarities, especially in the way of being quiet. And then she thought of another Steinbeck novel—*Of Mice and Men*—and of the character named Lenny, who had a child's mind, much like Matthew Reynolds. Noah was not that way, not severe. Yet, there was an innocence about him—a shyness, a reserve—and she guessed he had never been good with schoolwork.

People like Noah made their way through life on tiptoes, afraid of being heard, or seen, she believed. If they had stories to tell, they told them to themselves, out of the hearing of other people, having learned the hard way about saying something out of place or ill-timed. Sometimes such people turned mean out of anger because of the ridicule they got. Sometimes they tried to vanish. Some of them did. People like Noah. It was probably the reason he had taken to the road with his fishing rod.

She felt a sudden sensation of pity for him, as she would feel pity for a motherless child.

It was a wonder he had not vanished completely, she thought.

The news of Noah's fishing against the wager placed by Peavo Teasley and Moody Deal had moved flash-quick across the Valley of Light as Taylor had predicted it would. By ten o'clock, a small crowd of men and boys—Peavo and Moody among them—had again gathered at Bowerstown Store to hear the story firsthand and to take a look at Noah.

"Boys," Taylor said to the crowd, "I know what you here for, and that's all right with me, but Noah's hired on with me to paint the store and that's what he'll be doing, so you can just listen to Peavo and Moody tell lies. When it gets too deep to wade around in, I'll stop my work and tell you the truth."

Peavo and Moody laughed, beamed. They did not care what Taylor said, or how much he protested about Noah's having to work. What they had witnessed on the day before was worth talking about, a day they would never forget, they vowed, even if it did take money out of their pocket. It was made-to-order fishing. "Lord, it could of come from Sears and Roebuck," Moody said, telling how Noah took nothing but catfish out of a river made up of everything from eels to horny heads.

"I mean, he didn't get so much as a nibble from a bream," Moody swore. "Not a nibble. I swear we could of put in a order for a shark and he would of caught it."

"That's about the truth," Peavo said. "I know one thing, I'd pay up front to see it again."

"Me and you both, and at double the price," Moody added. "If you boys think Littleberry Davis can fish, you don't know nothing. Littleberry don't know how to bait a hook if you put him up against Noah Locke, and don't get me wrong, I like Littleberry. Nothing against him. He just can't fish with that boy."

"Well, he's itching to find out," a man said. "I seen him early this morning." The man made a snickering laugh. "He acted like he didn't believe a word about all the talk he's been hearing. Said Peavo and Moody would lie about the coming of Jesus, if they thought it would make a nickel for them."

"He's scared, that's all," Peavo said happily. "He's just plain scared. I guarantee you one thing, come Saturday, Littleberry might as well give his sign-up money straight to Noah. Fact of the matter, same goes with everybody here. I'll lay down even money right now that Noah wins the take-home prize by five pounds." He paused, looked at Moody, then added, "Shoot, make it ten."

"That's a lot of fish," one of the men said.

"He could of throwed back that much yesterday if he'd fished another ten minutes," Peavo vowed.

"Goda'mighty, Peavo, nobody's that good," the man said. "Know what that sounds like? Sounds like that story old John Cassidy told about that catfish he caught over on the Chatuge. Remember that? Said it was so big he had to tie it off on a tree and go home and get his mule to pull it in."

And the crowd laughed, remembering old John Cassidy's tale, and they settled on the porch and porch steps of the store, drinking their cola drinks, talking, their merry noise wrapping around the store, making its way up the ladder to Noah. It was the kind of sound Noah liked and he half-wished he was sitting among the men and boys to hear close-up the tales they were telling. It would be uncomfortable, though, since much of the talk would be about him, and most of what was being said would be colored by Peavo and Moody trying to outdo one another.

As a boy, he had gone often with his father to cotton gins during the picking season when the wagon was packed full enough to make a bale, and there, waiting their turn for the ginning, he would sit near enough to the clustering of men to hear them talking, trading stories, yet not close enough to be teased in the way men teased boys. In such gatherings, he had learned to read the moods of people, knowing hard times by hard looks, good times by cheerful looks. And always, there was one man among them who took charge of what was being said, one man who set the mood. Not always the same man, but, still, there was always a lead talker. Always. As a boy, he had liked it when Ward Cribbs was that man. Ward Cribbs was bright-faced, wore a grin like it was a piece of his finest Sunday clothing. Loved telling stories of his travels around America as a young man seeking adventure. Noah's father had confided that Ward Cribbs was nothing more than a harmless liar. Had said Ward Cribbs had never been farther away from Elbert County than Athens, which could be reached in a wagon pulled by slow mules in only a few hours. Had said, "Ward gets all that stuff from reading, and what he don't get from reading, he just makes up." His father had let a smile grow like an unfolding flower and had added, "Good Lord, whoever heard of cutting a hole through a slab of ice to go fishing? That's what Ward said they do in some places up North. Sometimes I think that boy believes the rest of us is just a bunch of fools."

Noah had remembered his father's opinion about ice fishing when he learned the truth of it—that people did cut holes in ice to fish.

Men in the army had told him about it, had shown him photographs, making Noah wish his father were still alive. His father would have been amazed to hear the story, more amazed that Ward Cribbs, the great liar, was not lying.

From the front of the store, he heard a roar of laughter.

Peavo Teasley and Moody Deal putting tale on top of tale, he thought, like boys hand-walking a baseball bat up to the knob to choose which team would bat first.

The sound of a car caused him to twist on the ladder to see the road. The car that slowed to a stop in front of the store was one that seemed familiar and he paused in his work to watch the car door open. The man who slipped from the seat was Howard Reynolds.

Noah heard the laughter from the porch fade away.

Howard lifted a hand and waved to him. Noah gestured a reply with his right hand, the hand holding the paintbrush. He watched as Howard took his wobbling, fat-heavy walk toward the front of the store and disappear around the store's corner. He could hear the muted sound of voices, spoken too softly to carry the words clearly, but hearing the words made no difference to Noah. He knew they were an exchange of greetings. Farmer to farmer. Words so worn in their saying, they were almost never heard by anyone. Expected and said, but not heard. It was near noon. Howard was probably making a stop for something his wife needed in her cooking.

He turned back to his painting, listened to the murmur of voices and believed there was something changed in the sound of them.

In a few minutes, the side door opened and Taylor stepped out onto the stoop and called up to him, "Noah, can you come down for a minute?"

Noah placed his brush across the top of the paint bucket, which he had secured to the ladder with a piece of wire, letting it dangle from one of the rungs. He made his way down the ladder, careful not to jiggle the bucket. On the ground, he saw Howard standing beside Taylor, his body slumped under the great bulk of his weight, the black of his eye patch cutting deep into the red of his face.

"Howard's out looking for his grandson," Taylor said. "He was wondering if you might of seen him this morning on your way to the store."

"Don't know exactly when he left, but it must have been pretty early," Howard added. "Me and my wife was watching out for a neighbor, and we didn't notice he was gone. He's got too big to keep up with all the time. We figured he must of been playing out around the barn, but when I went to find him, he weren't nowhere around."

"No sir, I didn't see him," Noah said. He thought of Eleanor telling him that Beatrice Cunningham was at the Reynolds home, and he wondered if the boy could have followed Eleanor. Wondered, too, if he should say anything about Eleanor being at the shack, and decided against it. If the boy had been near the lake, he would have seen him, and maybe Eleanor did not want it known she had gone to the shack after leaving the old woman at the Reynolds home. Maybe she wanted to keep that part of her life to herself. In small places, anything could make gossip.

A look of worry clouded Howard's face. His body rocked. Perspiration beaded across his wide forehead, made a bubble line over his eye patch. "Not like the boy to just take off," he said. "He used to follow his daddy down the road when his daddy went off to work, but he always come straight back. That was before his daddy went up to Tennessee to work on a road crew."

"Maybe he went down to the school to play," Taylor suggested.

"I drove by there," Howard told him. "Didn't see nobody."

"What about the river?" Taylor asked. "He had a good time yesterday, watching Noah fish. If I remember right, he said he was going to catch a fish and give it to Noah."

Howard bobbed his head. "What Peavo and Moody said, too. But he's been told not to go off to the river without somebody being with him."

"Why don't we go down there and look," Taylor said. "We can get Peavo and Moody and some of the others to help us."

"They said they would," Howard mumbled. Then: "I guess we better." He looked away. "I sure hope it's not where he headed. He don't know how to swim."

SEVENTEEN

Noah knew there were men at Taylor's store who had been in the war. He knew by the way they gathered to make plans to search for Howard Reynolds's grandson. The men from war leaned into the talk a certain soldier's way, listened with a certain soldier's look on their faces, and he could have guessed who had been field officers and who had been privates—the officers giving opinions, the privates offering nods of agreement. What they were about to do was the kind of thing they had done in war—look for someone, hoping they would not find trouble along the way.

The gathering was brief, with give and take about the search, with the land area divided mentally among the men, starting-off points made by landmarks all of them knew. They would follow the run of the river, going first to the places that seemed most likely from what Howard could tell them of the boy's knowledge. Howard and Taylor and Noah would go back to the place of the fishing.

"If he's gone to the river, that's where he'd likely be," Howard said.

"He have a fishing pole with him?" asked Moody.

Howard did not know the answer, said he hadn't thought to look, but it was possible. At the boy's last birthday, Howard had given him a rod and reel, and had worked to show the boy how to make a cast.

"Hard for him to do," Howard said softly, and the men around him made nodding motions, knowing the boy's problems.

Peavo offered encouragement: "He's all right, Howard. Maybe he just wandered off playing and got turned around. We'll find him, and it don't matter how long it takes."

The men muttered agreement, and then they left. At sunset they would meet at Howard's home.

"He may even be back by himself by then," Taylor said, and he tried to ease the worry Howard carried as heavily as his weight. "I remember running off one time when I was little, but I didn't know that's what it was. I just got to walking and kept on going, chasing after some dog that showed up, I think. It took my mama and daddy half the afternoon to find me."

Noah could see Howard's good eye blink, and he knew the blink dismissed Taylor's story. There was a painful difference between Taylor and his grandson.

There were times when memories came to Noah without reason, like unannounced, drop-by visitors, making him wonder if something, or someone, far removed from him had control of what entered his thinking. He could be pondering something, having it clearly fixed in his mind, and suddenly it would vanish, as though snatched away, and there would be a memory taking its place. Sometimes the memories were like eye blinks the quick way they came and left. Still, they came, and he would find himself wondering about them later, letting his mind make a full picture of what had been nothing but a blur.

He remembered Jack Purvis while driving to the river with Taylor—a memory blowing so quickly through him that at first he had trouble thinking of Jack's name. When the name did come to him, he frowned a puzzled frown, wondering why Jack Purvis had made his fleeting, ghostly appearance at such a strange time.

Jack Purvis had tormented him in childhood. Had taken pleasure in causing shame and embarrassment. Had called him a dummy. Had said he couldn't read with a first-grader even when he was in the sixth grade. Would take third-graders and put them against him in doing simple mathematics, always making certain there was a crowd gathered for the contest. Always led the jeering, his laugh hanging in the air like the crowing of a rooster.

Once, Jack Purvis and some of his friends had pulled him away at school recess and had stripped him of his clothes behind a hedgerow that grew between the school and a cotton field, forcing him to walk home naked, and then Jack and his friends had lied about it, saying he took off his clothes on his own because he had peed in his pants and was ashamed. Had even said he was the one who had thrown his clothes down the hole in the outhouse.

Jack Purvis had died at age fifteen in a car wreck, showing off for some of his friends. He remembered sensing relief, or maybe gladness, over Jack's death. Remembered going to the cemetery alone and standing beside Jack's grave and wondering if Jack had gone to heaven or to hell. Hell, he guessed; heaven, he hoped.

Sitting in the car seat beside Taylor, half-listening to Taylor's stories about the weakness of Matthew Reynolds's thinking, Noah thought again of the day he had been stripped of his clothes by Jack Purvis and his friends. Thought of the long walk home, of his mother's sadness and of his father's anger. His father had left the home in long strides, his voice bellowing vows of justice, and he had returned later with Travis, his body slumped, his spirit broken, telling the story of lies given by Jack and his friends, saying to his wife, "They put it all on our boy." For the rest of the school year, he and Travis had stayed at home.

And then it came to him: he had remembered Jack Purvis because of Matthew—the way Matthew must be treated by other boys his age.

A shiver made its way across his shoulders.

"I sure hope that boy's all right," Taylor said gravely. "It'd kill Howard if anything happened to him. About all he does these days is watch over that boy."

In front of them, Howard Reynolds drove his old car at his slow pace, easing over the off-road that took them to the river.

There was no sign of Matthew at the place where Noah had fished the day before, no answer to the calling of his name.

A look of relief settled on Howard's face. "Maybe he's back home by now," he offered.

"Tell you what," Taylor said to him, "why don't you go on back there. Me and Noah can follow the river for a little piece, just to make sure he's not down here."

It was a suggestion answered with a rocking nod of Howard's body. "Hate to put you to all this trouble, Taylor," he said.

"No trouble," Taylor told him.

"It's costing you some business, I know that," Howard replied.

"Anybody that wants something from me, they'll come back," Taylor said. "If I can close down to go fishing, I can close down to help out a friend."

Howard turned his head to look at the river, stared for a moment at the deep-moving water, at the swirls, then he touched his eye patch with his fingers. He said, "I appreciate it," and he began his slow ambling to his car. He added, "I guess I better try to find out where his daddy's working and see if I can't give him a call. It's going to scare him to death."

Noah and Taylor watched him leave.

"I got a bad feeling about this," Taylor said solemnly. Then: "Why don't you go the way the river's running for a little bit and I'll go back the other way, toward the dam." He pulled his watch from his pocket and looked at it. "Let's give it thirty minutes and then turn around and meet back here."

"All right," Noah said.

For Noah, it was an odd sensation following the river, with the water running north the way it did, and he made his way up a hill to take a better look. A whirlwind, like a baby tornado, rose up in front of him, lifting dead leaves of hardwoods, spinning them in a twisting funnel, and the sudden noise of leaves scraping against leaves caused a rabbit to jump up from its hiding and scurry away, its white tail making a flash in a streak of sunlight that found its way through tree limbs. He watched the rabbit disappear, then leaned over at his waist to check for a rabbit path. Remembered teaching Travis about rabbit paths when they were putting out their rabbit boxes in winter. Hard to see, unless you knew what you were looking for. A shine on fallen leaves. A narrow ribbon of pushed-down pine needles, wiggling across the ground. Here and there, rabbit droppings. A fluff of fur caught on a stick. All signs.

It would be good to again get up early on a winter morning and check rabbit boxes with Travis, he thought. The sense of cold on his skin, the smell of dead leaves, the crunching sound of footsteps over hoarfrost. And maybe finding a rabbit for his mother to cook for breakfast along with the thin, sweet taste of rabbit gravy, or to sell for twenty-five cents to Ben Wiggins at Wiggins Store.

He had liked those days.

From far off, he heard Taylor's faint calling: "Matthew, Matthew . . ."

He pulled his watch from his pocket and looked at it. Twenty minutes had passed since he and Taylor had separated.

He looked down the hill, through the cover of trees, and found himself higher above the river than he thought he was. He stood quietly, listening, the way he had learned to listen in war, picking out sounds that were natural to the woods. Birds. The chatter of squirrels and the scratching of their claws on tree bark. The buzzing of wings from insects. The dull, scurrying noise of bugs playing in leaves. He did not hear anything he had not expected to hear.

He let his mind count the time he had been in the valley, going back to the Friday of his arrival. Six days, one day short of a week.

He could not remember staying a week at any place during his wandering, or having been caught up so much in all that was going on around him. It would have been different if he had not taken on the painting job, if he had stayed with the fishing and left the painting to some other hire, or to Taylor himself.

He was close to being finished with the painting, he judged. If the weather held and if he could keep at it without stopping to fill orders for fish, he could have it done in a half-day—a full day at the most. But there had been many interruptions. The fishing. The rain. Now the search for Howard Reynolds's grandson, though it was something he did not mind, for he liked the boy and the boy's grandfather. And there would be the school fishing contest on Saturday. Another day lost. Still, he could have the painting finished by the next Monday, he believed, and when it was done he would leave for Elbert County. He would walk into Hiawassee and wait for the early bus, going wherever it went, and, from there, he would find his way back to Elberton. From the earnings of his fishing and from the wage Taylor would pay him, he reasoned he would have enough money for a ticket and a small gift for Travis, and if he won the fishing contest, there would be twenty dollars more. The gift was more important than the ticket, though. If necessary, he could hitch rides to Elberton.

He thought of the surprised look he would get from Travis, and the thought made him smile. Maybe it was time he quit his wandering and settled down in Elbert County, staying near Travis. It would give him time to visit, even if there would be little to say between them. Maybe the guards would let him take cigarettes to Travis.

He had an image of Travis holding a new package of cigarettes, turning them in his hands like a child holding a prize, and he became suddenly sorrowful. He rolled his shoulders, as though shaking the sorrow from his skin. The last time he had seen Travis, there was a dull, weary look in Travis's eyes. He remembered the mumbling voice Travis had used in talking, as though talking drained him of energy. Remembered the way Travis had looked down when telling about not going to the funeral of their mother. "They said I could go, but I'll have to have a deputy with me and I'd be wearing chains," Travis had said. "I couldn't do that, Noah. I just couldn't. Couldn't shame Mama like that. I ever get out, first thing I'm going to do is go out there to her grave—hers and Daddy's. Tell them I'm sorry about things."

He could hear Travis's voice, as though Travis was speaking from inside his mind.

Maybe he would ask Taylor to help him make a telephone call to the jail in Elbert County, he thought. Maybe it would do some good for Travis to know he had called.

He pushed his watch back into his pocket and began to work his way down the hill to the river.

Again, he heard the far-off call of Taylor: "Matthew, Matthew . . ."

In late day, nearing sundown, the men who had spent the afternoon searching for Matthew met at Howard Reynolds's home, each trusting that someone else had found the boy.

No one had.

Ada Reynolds sat in a rocker on her porch, her head tucked, a soft moan mixed with her breathing. Like her husband, she was heavyset, and the fear over her missing grandson caused her to slump like someone carrying an invisible weight. Eleanor was with her. She had taken Beatrice Cunningham into Hiawassee to stay with Boyd's parents after learning of Matthew's disappearance, she said privately to Taylor and Noah.

"It's the least I can do after all Howard and Ada have done for me," she explained. "Besides, it's time she spent some time with them. It's been since February since they've had her for more than a day. I told them I'd get her on Sunday, but I may let them keep her a little longer. They're not working, or anything."

The men who had been searching for Matthew gave accounts of where they had been, and by their accounts the river had been covered over a distance that was greater than any of them could have walked in a strong stride. It was not possible for Matthew to have wandered farther.

"I'd say he didn't go to the river, then," Taylor said.

"He took his fishing rod," Howard said solemnly. "I looked."

"Maybe he went down to John's Creek," Moody said. "That's not far away."

The men mumbled agreement.

"Maybe we better call Whitlow and see if he can't bring his bloodhounds over," said Taylor.

"I talked to him a little while ago," Howard told him. "He said he'd head on over soon as he could find the dogs. Said they was out running."

"That'll help," Taylor said.

"I hope he don't fool around," Peavo mumbled, rolling the burning tip out of his smoked-down cigarette, then stepping on the tip. He examined the sky. "We still got a little light left. Why don't me and Moody go down to the creek and look around. I got a flashlight if we need it. Everybody else can wait here for the dogs. That's when they'll be needed."

"I'd appreciate it," Howard said in a tired voice.

"You get Milton on the phone?" asked Taylor.

"Not yet. I left word for him to call me," Howard answered.

"We'll find him before too long," Peavo said, trying to sound confident. He did not. He sounded jittery.

Some of the men used Howard's telephone to call their homes, reporting on their whereabouts and the reason they were out. Their wives gave them messages of sympathy to pass on to Ada and Howard Reynolds, adding that they would put together food and bring it over, and would call other neighbors to have the men join in the search.

In the wait for the dogs, the men sat on the porch of Howard Reynolds's home, drinking iced tea and coffee made by Eleanor, talking of where they had been, making quiet guesses of where Matthew could be. There was concern in their talk, in the way they wagged their heads, smoked their cigarettes, paced the yard near the porch. Soon their wives began to arrive, carrying trays of food they had prepared for their own suppers.

It was a practice Noah knew well from his own boyhood and from war—women appearing out of nowhere, or what seemed to be nowhere, food in their hands, looks of worry on their faces, their presence filling space that seemed empty without them.

The way the women were at Howard Reynolds's home caused Noah to remember a girl in a small, bomb-damaged café in some German village he did not remember by name, though he knew it was where his unit had been a few days after the surrender. The girl had seemed to appear from shadows and to fade back into them as she served the table—her head kept down, her eyes never looking at anyone. Some of the men with him had made remarks to her about being German and probably a Nazi, telling her she could make up for things by coming around to their camp at night. Laughing the way they did, reaching to grope her, but missing as she dodged their hands, had caused anger to leap in him that he had never felt—before or since—and he had slapped the palm of his hand on the table and said in a hard voice, "Leave her alone," and the men, surprised by his outburst, had stopped their toying with the girl. Later, one of them had told him, "You looked like you was ready to kill us. Nobody ever saw you like that."

An image of the girl came back to Noah's mind. Tall. Pretty. Reddish hair. Pale skin. He remembered a bandage on her right arm. He had seen her one other time—a day later, as his unit was leaving the village. She had been standing in the doorway of the café, watching the vehicles moving slowly on the street. When she recognized him, she lifted her hand shyly and waved. He had waved back. Later, he had dreamed about her several times—dreams from sleep and dreams that came to him when he was wide awake, but with a drifting mind. In the dreams, he had seen himself with the girl, the girl being his wife, making him warm with the way she smiled and with her body and with the gentle way she talked to him.

It was a dream worth remembering.

Whitlow Mayfield arrived as the day was losing the last of its light. He had with him two droopy-skin bloodhounds and lanterns, and was told of the area covered by the searchers. "Not much reason to look at them places again," he said. "Not to start with at least." There was a tone of fret in his voice. The natural smile he wore was missing, replaced by a furrow across his forehead and a tremor in his hands.

"Peavo and Moody went down to John's Creek," Taylor added.

"That's a good place to look," Whitlow agreed. "There's a couple of good fishing spots on it." He asked for some of Matthew's clothing and Howard went into the house and returned with a shirt. "He had it on yesterday," Howard said. "Ada hadn't got around to washing it."

"That'll do," Whitlow told him, and he took the shirt and pushed it against the faces of the dogs, encouraging them with the kind of whisper that men made with dogs, "All right, girls, get a smell. Come on, now." The dogs rubbed their noses against the shirt, made deep-chested sounds, pranced, strained against their leashes.

"They got it," Whitlow said. "Let's go down by the road. No reason to turn them loose here, since the boy's smell is all over the place."

At the road, Whitlow let the dogs explore the ground until one of them paused, sniffed, gave a short bark that had the sound of a word if a dog could make words.

"She's got it," Whitlow said excitedly, and he released the leash around the dog's collar, and then did the same with the other dog.

"Go on, girl, find it, find it," Whitlow urged.

The dogs began to circle, their noses skimming the ground,

and then one of them begin to sprint away and the other followed.

"Let's go, boys," Whitlow called, fast-walking after the dogs. "Somebody bring them lanterns."

The men followed in a pack, holding lanterns and flashlights in front of them

On the porch of the house, Ada and Howard Reynolds watched with Eleanor and the other women. The lights of the lanterns and flashlights had the look of fireflies fading into the murky gathering of night.

EIGHTEEN

The trail the dogs followed led along the road until it veered into a pasture and then into woods. It was a wandering, zigzag trail and the dogs seemed, at times, confused by it, pausing in their lumbering trot, their heads swiveling to keep track of the scent of Matthew Reynolds.

Whitlow was not sure the dogs had the scent at all.

"It don't make sense," he complained. "I never seen them running around so much, like they chasing their own tail. That boy must of been all over this place."

The men agreed.

"Looks to me like they could be headed down toward John's Creek," one of them said.

"Could be," Whitlow judged, "but they going the long way around if they are."

The moon, fading from its night of being full, made pools of light in patches where trees had been cleared or had fallen from storms, and the men talked of how tricky night light could be, even for people knowing the land and the shape of the hills that cupped the valley. They told stories of how they had been fooled by night light while night hunting, not knowing north from south or east from west.

It would be easy for a boy like Matthew to get so turned around he could be down in Georgia, thinking he was headed to his grandfather's house, they said.

Noah heard the talk—the almost-mumbled talk—and he knew the men were right. In his travels, he had followed many roads on nights when the moon gave enough light for walking, only to be surprised the next morning by where he was. He hoped that what the men said of Matthew was true, that in the morning Matthew would find a house and go to it and tell the people who lived there who he was and who his grandfather was. Hoped it would be that simple.

"What's that?" one of the men said suddenly.

"Where?" Whitlow asked.

"Coming out the woods down there," the man answered.

Whitlow peered into the night at a wobbling dot of light. "Looks like a flashlight," he said.

A voice called from the direction of the light.

"It's Peavo and Moody," Taylor said.

They had not found Matthew, but they had found where he had been, Peavo said. Or so they thought. At John's Creek—at one of the fishing places—they had found a tin can that still had live worms in it.

"It could of been somebody else's," Moody warned, "but the footprints down there looked like they was made by a boy, not a man."

"You see which way they were going?" asked Whitlow.

"Just saw them at the creek," Peavo said. "Didn't see nothing anywhere else."

"Wonder why he left the bait can?" one of the men said.

"Probably just forgot it," Moody offered. "You got to remember the boy's got a problem."

"Let's take the dogs on down there," Whitlow said. "See if they can't pick up which way he went."

At John's Creek, in the place where Peavo and Moody had found the can of worms, the dogs picked up the scent quickly, making braying sounds of announcement. In ten minutes of chase, they lost it, and Whitlow did not know why.

"It's like they picked up on something else," he said, and he called the dogs to him and put their leashes back on their collars and led them in a wide circle, coaxing them to find the scent. They could not. "Whatever they picked up, that's what they looking for," he added. "Wish I'd of brought the boy's shirt with me."

"One of us can go get it," suggested Moody.

Whitlow stood, studying the woods, the moon. After a pause, he said, "Probably be better if we start back in the morning with the dogs. They'll do better in the daytime, when the sun's put some heat on the ground. Best thing to do now is to go back to the cars and drive the roads. My guess is, if he found a road, he'd be on it, trying to get home."

It was a suggestion that made sense and the men started their walk back to Howard Reynolds's home, forming plans among themselves about the roads to drive and who would take which road. None of them seemed tired, Noah thought. One of their own was missing, one who could not fend well for himself. Rest could wait.

The people of the valley were as Hoke Moore said they were.

"You need a hand, they'll give it," Hoke Moore had said.

At Howard Reynolds's home, Taylor went to the porch to tell Howard and Ada what had happened, and about the plans to keep looking along the roads and to bring the dogs back at first light to try and find Matthew's trail. Eleanor was with them, sitting close to Ada. She said, "I can take my car and look for him, too."

"No need," Taylor told her. "I think we got enough cars to cover every road in the valley."

"I can go," Howard said.

"Maybe you better stay here with Ada," Taylor said gently.

Howard glanced at his wife, saw the exhausted, troubled look in her face. Nodded.

"I'll be here tonight," Eleanor said.

"That's good," Taylor said.

"What about Noah?" she asked. "Is he going with you?"

"I guess so," Taylor replied. "We'll drive down around the store, and up toward your place. If we don't see nothing, I'll take him to the turnoff for the lake and let him get some rest."

"You don't think Matthew went to the lake, do you?"

Taylor shook his head. "I wouldn't think so. It's in the opposite direction to the creek."

"He wouldn't of gone down there," Howard said. "We talked to him about staying away from there. His daddy told him there was a ghost there, just to keep him away from it."

"I didn't see any sign of him when I went up to my house a little while ago to milk the cow, but he might have come there after I left," Eleanor said. "Boyd made him a swing one time, and he liked swinging in it."

"We'll look it over," Taylor promised.

As they drove the road leading to his store, Taylor talked, giving Noah the history of Matthew and of Matthew's father, Milton, and of Milton's dead wife, Sarah.

In his youth, Milton had been hard to handle—a roughneck, Taylor called him—and Howard had spent much of his money paying off the troubles that Milton caused. It was how Howard had lost his eye, Taylor said. Tried to stop a fight between Milton and a man named Hootie Magill over a squabble about the trade of a hunting dog. In the fight, Milton had accidentally struck his father in the eye, blinding him.

"It cost Howard an eye, but it changed Milton, knowing what his daddy had done for him and what he had done to his daddy,"

Taylor said. "I guess you could say it was a trade—one closed eye, two opened ones. After that, Milton started doing what he could to make up for it. Started going to church and took to religion. Oddest part of it all, he started dating Hootie Magill's youngest daughter, who was a big churchgoer, and I swear to you, Noah, the prettiest and sweetest girl you ever saw. That was Sarah. They got married when she was eighteen or nineteen, and then Matthew came along. Didn't take long to know he had some problems, and Milton got it in his mind that it was God's way of punishing him for all the wrong he'd done."

Sarah had died of a fever that struck suddenly on her thirty-third birthday, Taylor added.

"Woke up feeling a little weak and the fever started and she was dead before sundown," he said. "Nobody knows what it was. It just happened." He paused. A look of memory covered his face. "I never saw a funeral like it. More people outside the church than was in it. Had to be more flowers there than there was in the Garden of Eden. Not a dry eye in the valley, that's how much people thought about her. Anyhow, Milton moved back in with his folks after that and took a job working with a road-building company. He's gone most of the time, but when he's here, you couldn't pry him away from that boy of his with a crowbar. He's a good daddy. If anything's happened to the boy, it'll tear him apart."

Taylor drove slowly, sitting upright behind the steering wheel of the car, keeping his head moving on lookout for Matthew, motioning at shadows to Noah

They saw two deer and a wandering, half-starved dog. Nothing else.

"If we don't find him tonight, Whitlow will in the morning," Taylor said. "A lot of people have fun with Whitlow over his running for sheriff every time there's an election, but he does it mostly for sport. Truth is, he knows the woods better than anybody around here. I'll give him that, and those dogs of his are better than they acted tonight. He's always getting calls from one of the sheriff's offices around here about using his dogs for some escaped convict, or some fool from Atlanta that gets himself lost up in the mountains. That's probably another reason he keeps running for sheriff. He's got those bloodhounds. Always has had some. He swears they're the best dogs on earth."

At the store, Taylor stopped the car and got out and stood beside the opened door. He called in a loud voice, "Matthew, Matthew." Waited for a reply that he knew would not come. Then he slipped back into the car, said, "Let's drive up to Eleanor's place."

The rope-and-plank swing that Boyd Cunningham had erected for Matthew Reynolds on the limb of an oak tree in the side yard of his home moved gently in a slight breeze that blew up from the open pasture behind it. It had the look of a swing coming to rest after a child had rocketed from it at the end of its long pendulum, leaving squeals over his, or her, tumbling fall to earth.

"Looks strange, don't it?" Taylor said quietly.

Nearby, a whippoorwill sang merrily. Across from the singing, but far away, another whippoorwill answered. Song and chorus.

"You remember me telling you about that old woman that makes soap up in the hills?" asked Taylor.

"I do," Noah answered.

"Around here, people think of her as the ghost lady."

"Why's that?" Noah said.

"She's always seeing ghosts, or says she does. Claims she can talk to them. There's always somebody going up there to see her, wanting her to talk to somebody that's dead," Taylor told him. "She says all you got to learn to do is look for signs, and that's where you'll find the dead." He reached to catch the rope of the swing, stopping its sway. "Wonder if she'd see anything in this swing swinging by itself."

Noah thought of the gunsmoke angels of war.

"I'm about to spook myself," Taylor said, and his body gave off a shiver, like a muscle twitch. He turned to Noah. A nervous smile flicked across his face. "It's nothing but the wind. Come on, we might as well call it a night." He looked back at the swing, saw it begin to sway again. "Maybe somebody's found him already. I sure hope so." He began his walk back to the car, with Noah following. "One thing about this place," he added, "Boyd did a lot of work on it. Not a house in the valley as good as this one. I got to give him his due: he was a good carpenter. Couldn't farm a lick, like I told you, but he could work a hammer." He laughed easily. "Fact is, this piece of land is almost worthless, it's got so much rock on it. Eleanor's going to have a hard time getting rid of it."

More than anything, Eleanor was exhausted. Muscle and soul exhausted. The day's tension was still with her, and the house of Howard and Ada Reynolds, filled with the muted sound of anguish only a short time earlier, was eerily quiet. The men searching for Matthew had returned, had reported no sighting of him, and then they had gone away to their own homes, pledging to return at sunrise. She had persuaded Howard and Ada to go to bed, though she knew they would not sleep. They would lie awake and try to bring a quilt of silence over them, but they would not sleep.

She sat at the kitchen table with a cup of coffee in front of her, the lights off, the room taking in moonspill from its windows, and she wondered if she had made a mistake insisting on staying with Howard and Ada. Maybe they would feel better being alone. Yet, neither of them was well enough to do the things that needed to be done—preparing the food, keeping the house clean and presentable for the parade of people who would fill it the following day.

Still, she realized there was nothing to be done at such a late hour, since the other women had been there for the supper and for the cleanup afterward, but it did not seem right to leave Howard and Ada to worry about anything other than Matthew. And Milton. Their concern over Milton was great. A message had been left for him. No one knew when he would get it, but everyone knew he would be on his way home as soon as he did. Milton could show up the middle of the night, panicked, and that panic could make the grief even greater for Howard and Ada. Being there if Milton appeared was important, she believed.

The clock on the kitchen counter was in moonlight from the window above it, easy to see. It was close to one.

I need to get some sleep, Eleanor thought.

She got up from the table and went quietly through the house to the front door. Opened it, stepped onto the porch and stood, letting her gaze wander over the strange landscape of another person's home.

She was less than two miles from her own house, yet she had the sensation of being in another country, far away from the Valley of Light. Someplace she had read about in one of her books. Ireland, maybe. Or the Swiss Alps. Or the Italian countryside. Or Egypt. Someplace old and beautiful. Someplace ghosted by history soaked into the soil—soil mixed with blood and relics of battles so ancient they had been siphoned up by trees and plants and could be tasted in figs and grapes and pomegranates and olives and other fruits.

One day, she wanted to see such places, to eat the fruits of history off the trees that carried them. She wanted to sit late at night—as it now was—and listen to the slumbering of time.

She had asked Boyd to tell her about the places he had seen in war, but he had refused to talk about them, saying there was nothing pretty about any of them, saying he had seen nothing but rubble and beat-down people and never again wanted to be reminded of it. If she wanted to go to Europe to look at castles and fig orchards and grape vines and olive trees, she would have to make the trip by herself, he had told her.

She remembered the look on his face. A scowl. Meanness.

"That's what you want, you go do it," he had said.

I will, she thought, watching the moon hover over the nearby mountains. She was free of Boyd, and she knew it. One day, she would go to the places that had beckoned to her from books—Paris, London, Rome, Dublin, Vienna, Edinburgh. She would go and she would hold the air of each stop in her lungs until it turned to heat in her body.

She stepped to the edge of the porch and gazed at the road in front of the house. Something seemed out of place, but it was only a guess, since it was not her home, or her land. She paused, moved back a step, looked again. At the turnoff leading to the house, parked under a tree, she saw the shadowed silhouette of a truck, and she did not remember it being there earlier.

She moved from the porch to the yard, walked hesitantly toward the truck, wondering if it had been left by one of the men who had caught a ride home with a neighbor. She did not see anyone.

And then she heard a sharp bark from near the truck and she stopped and stepped back. A man's figure rose up from the truck body, and she heard a voice say, "Quiet down, girl."

It was Whitlow Mayfield.

The dog barked again and Whitlow pulled himself up in the truck body. "You see something, girl?" he asked anxiously, hopefully.

Eleanor walked toward him. "It's just me, Whitlow," she said. She saw Whitlow shift his body toward her. "I didn't know you were down here."

Whitlow climbed over the tailgate of the truck to the ground. He said, "You up late."

"I know," Eleanor replied. "I thought you left with everybody else."

"I did," he told her, "but I decided to come on back here in case the boy showed up somewhere nearby. Thought maybe my dogs might catch the smell of him. Thought that's what they'd done when you come up."

"Can you get any sleep out here?"

Whitlow nodded. "I got me a quilt I keep in the truck. Use it sometimes if I'm out hunting at night. It's good enough."

"You think he's all right, Whitlow?"

For a moment, Whitlow did not answer. He ducked his head and shifted his weight on the ground. Then he said softly, "I'm worried about it. We had a lot of people out looking—people that know the places around here pretty good—and it bothers me not to find nothing."

"You found his tracks down by the creek."

"Lost them, too," Whitlow said. "Maybe they was a few days old. Hard to tell."

"Well, I pray he's just lost, and he's all right," Eleanor said. "If anything's happened to him, I don't know what Ada and Howard will do."

"It'll leave its mark, I know that," Whitlow whispered. He looked away.

A rush of regret flooded Eleanor. She had forgotten momentarily about Whitlow's son being killed in the war. "I know you do," she said gently. Then: "You better try and get some sleep. I'll have some breakfast for you in the morning."

"That's all right," he said.

"I won't take no for an answer," she said.

"I appreciate it," he replied.

"You need anything now?"

He shook his head. Then he said, "You had any takers on your place?"

"No," she answered.

"I was just wondering," he said.

"You know anybody looking for a place?" she asked.

He shifted his feet awkwardly, pulled at his shirtsleeve with his hand, looked away. "Don't think so," he told her.

She stepped toward him. "Did Boyd ever talk to you about wanting to sell it?"

He started to shake his head, then stopped. "He mentioned it once or twice."

"There was a man who asked about it, but I never thought Boyd would sell it," she said.

"Uh-huh," Whitlow mumbled. He shifted his feet again.

"I better get some sleep, too," she said.

"Uh-huh, me too," he said.

"See you in the morning."

"Good night," he said.

She turned and walked back toward the house and the regret of her comment stayed with her. Whitlow Mayfield was an odd man, she thought. A happy-seeming person, ready with a smile and a loud story, even after the death of his wife and his son, David. Liked by the people of the valley. Still, she knew the death of his son haunted him. She had heard from others how he had disappeared after the war notice about his son missing in action and then the follow-up about his death. Had gone off into the woods for days. And then he had returned, wearing his smile. Had talked of his pride in his son, offering up his life as he had, saying he had accepted it because he knew his son and his wife were in heaven together, and that was enough for him. Son and mother resting in paradise.

It was not surprising that Whitlow had stayed in his truck, she thought. Someone else's son was missing, a boy whose mother was waiting for him in heaven.

The way he awoke—sudden, startled—made Noah roll from the cot. He sat, breathing hard, his skin damp with perspiration. Wondered what it was that had snapped him out of sleep.

He stood and walked to the screened door of the porch and let his eyes search the night. Saw nothing.

He thought of Eleanor Cunningham. Could almost sense her.

She had kept her promise to him about cleaning the shack, had even washed down the floors with something that left a scent of wood-air after a rain, and he had found a stack of towels and two washcloths on one of the chairs. On the table, she had left a small bouquet of wildflowers—purple ironweed—in a drinking glass, causing him to remember what she had said about her husband throwing away the same flowers. The wood box for the stove had been filled with broken twigs and limbs. She had also left a note on the table, beside the wildflowers. The note read: *I'll be glad to wash your clothes for you.*

The note had made him uncomfortable. He had never had any woman volunteer to wash his clothes—other than his mother—and it made him wonder why she would make such an offer. Marvin Linquist would have said she had snaring him in mind and was doing nothing more than pinning back the claws on the trap. It was impossible to know why women did anything, Marvin had declared, and there'd never been a man to figure it out. "The harder you try, boys, the wronger you bound to be. Most of the time, you do just the opposite of what you'd do if you was by yourself, and you'll get by." The men who heard him had all laughed, had all agreed. "It's not their fault," Marvin had added, faking a wise look on his face. "It's just the way the Lord made them. They's only so much you can do with a short rib." And the men had laughed even more gleefully.

He wondered why he had thought of Eleanor Cunningham, without reason, out of a dead sleep.

It was almost as though she had left something of her presence in the shack, and had decided to remind him she had been there by jarring him awake. Marvin Linquist had said he could always tell when his wife, or one of his children, had their mind on him. Said it was like a spark made by a spark plug in a new car. Said he could be sleeping, or resting, or just moving ahead on a march, and he would feel a spark strike at his chest and he knew that, back in Kentucky, his wife or one of his children had fixed on a moment with him in it, and had thrown that moment at him with dead aim across thousands of miles of land and ocean.

Noah wondered if Eleanor was awake in Howard Reynolds's home, thinking of him, throwing him a moment that had some meaning to her.

It could be. Could be.

There were a lot of things he did not understand, but believed there was some sense in them.

He turned and went back to the cot and got on it, between the sheets Eleanor had used to make a bed of it, and stared at the tin covering the porch. Wished for rain. Rain on tin made good sleeping.

He thought of Matthew, knowing Matthew must be scared, being lost, being alone. It would be hard for him to know what to do without his grandfather to guide him along.

Outside, nightsounds rang across the lake.

He heard a thrashing in the water.

Hoke Moore's fish, he thought.

Waiting. Aggravated.

NINETEEN

It was still dark when Noah awoke, though the coloring of night in the east had purple in it. First color from the sun, long before the sun pitched in its yellow and red.

He got out of his cot and pulled the covers over it to make it look made up, the way Eleanor had left it, and then he took the water pail to the spring and drew out water and went back into the shack with it. He lit the kerosene lamp and started a fire in the stove, thinking the fire felt good in the morning's chill. Made ready his coffee and the water for his oatmeal. A good helping of oatmeal, since he knew it could be a long day and if he had any food it would be from the offering of someone else. Or maybe Eleanor would bake a sweet potato and give it to him to carry along—one for him, one for Taylor. She would think of such things, he believed. Baked sweet potatoes, even cold, were filling. Every man who had ever plowed a field some distance from his house knew about baked sweet potatoes.

His mother had always said men would starve if women did not make food for them. A man could kill any animal on earth and gut it and peel off its hide, but not many of them knew the first thing about making food out of the meat. Give a man a slaughtered pig and he could put it over a pit for cooking, and if he thought about it, he might turn it once or twice, but in the long run it would be either scorched or raw when he served it up. Having a man in a kitchen was about the same as having a donkey at a dance, his mother had declared.

There were times in the army when Noah believed his mother. Some of the food had to be swallowed, not chewed. Maybe you could fool your stomach into believing that what it had in it was all right, but if you left it long enough on your taste buds, it was a different matter altogether.

He was glad his mother had taught him how to make oatmeal and corn bread and how to fry fish, though he often cooked fish over the coals of a fire. With a little salt sprinkled over it, it was not bad cooked that way.

He wondered if Eleanor felt the same as his mother about men in the kitchen. Probably. She had seemed annoyed with Taylor over the way he hovered around her on the night of their supper together, telling him to stay away from the simmering pots and to stop poking at the fish sizzling from the grease in the fry pan.

He poured his first cup of coffee. Outside, a crow cawed, causing him to look toward the porch. Early for a crow to be making noise, he thought. A rooster, maybe, but not a crow, unless the crow had been hatched near a farm and had taken on the habits of a rooster. He took his coffee to the porch and looked out. The purpling of the sky was turning pale, like a garment washed too many times. He had promised Taylor he would be at the pull-off above the lake by sunrise, and he did not want to be late. He knew there would be men at Howard Reynolds's home at first light—more men than the day before. Calls would have gone out, and even those men with some thought of work on their farms would be there. It was their way. If the need was great enough, nothing else mattered. He had seen it in Elbert County when a crop was in danger of being lost to weather, or a neighbor had been injured in taking up hay or in threshing grain. Men gathering, doing what needed to be done, with no expectation of pay, knowing the same would be done for them in the same circumstance.

And he had seen it in war. A soldier missing, and how the other soldiers had banded together to look for him, and how rank never seemed to matter.

The chaplain had called it a fellowship of men, a thing God had put into Adam that was like a secret heart. When it started pumping, men could do things that seemed impossible.

In his own community, he knew of a man who picked up the back of a car after he accidentally ran over his wife. Later, three men, all larger, had tried to lift the car, but had failed.

God's doing, the people of his community said. God's doing.

And it was, Noah believed.

He turned and went back into the shack and made his oatmeal, sprinkling it with brown sugar, and sat at the table and ate it. It was hot and pasty-tasting, even with the brown sugar. It needed butter, but he had got used to eating it the way he cooked it. If nothing else, it was filling.

At the stove, he poured enough hot water into his bowl to clean it and then poured the water into the wash basin, wiping the bowl with a washcloth Eleanor had left. He would wash the coffee cup later, he decided, since there was still some coffee in it.

He dug around in his knapsack and pulled out a shirt that had been worn thin, but was clean, and he changed into it, making sure he pushed his dirty shirt back into the knapsack in case Eleanor got it in her mind that she would do a washing for him, whether he wanted it or not. She would not go into his knapsack, he thought. He would do his own washing later.

He checked the fire in the stove, saw that it had died to embers and was safe enough to leave. It was a fear for him—having a fire break out in the shack, burning it to the ground. To some, it would not be a great loss, but it would be a loss of his doing, and he did not want the memory of it hanging over his head.

He finished his coffee, putting the empty cup on the table, and left the shack.

Outside, he saw a possum rushing away from beneath the house, scurrying over the ground, its head down, its fat body waddling on short legs, comic in the way it tried to be fast, but wasn't. The possum disappeared into a growing of weed grass near the water, making the top of the grass wiggle.

He looked at the lake, at the morning stillness of it. Glassy on top. Fog over the glass. Already making reflections out of the paling purple, like a mirror in a dark room.

And then he saw something odd.

Hanging on a limb of one of the trash trees near the lake, but close to the shack, he saw what looked to be a single small fish.

The chill of warning struck him, raced over his back, across his shoulders, down his arms. He thought of his dream, of the bass hanging from a limb of the beechnut.

He walked cautiously toward the fish. It was hanging by a piece of binder twine, three or four feet long, he judged. Tied in a loop like a person would tie a shoe. Chest high on him. He reached to touch it, saw it was covered with flies, and he knew it had been dead a long time.

He stepped back, stood, wondered: How did it get there?

And then he thought of Matthew Reynolds.

Matthew had said he wanted to catch a fish and give it to him.

He turned and began to rush-walk along the lakeside, looking in the dark waters.

At the east end of the dam, in the place he had made his cast for Hoke Moore's fish, he saw a fishing rod lying in the edge of the water. He leaned to it, picked it up, shook the water from it, pulled on it. The line gave easily and he turned the reel, bringing the line in. On the hook was a withered grasshopper.

He put the rod down and stepped closer to the water, peering under the trash trees, and there he saw it—a body floating face-down in the water, snuggled under an overhanging limb. A shiver shot through him like electricity. He stepped into the water and made his way to the body, the water rising up around his waist.

He leaned, touched it, turned it gently.

It was Matthew, his glasses still set on his face. Behind his glasses, his small eyes were staring up, surprise still holding in them.

TWENTY

By nine o'clock, the sun was over the trees, bright, building heat. The body of Matthew Reynolds had been carried from the lake, shouldered by strong men taking turns up the incline to the pull-off, and what would be known about Matthew's death—the guesswork of it—was being talked about by those who had returned to the lake to make their judgments.

Matthew had caught his fish at John's Creek, the guessing said, and had rushed away with it, taking only his rod and the fish, and somehow had found his way to the shack in search of Noah. Had tied the fish to a tree at the shack and had believed he would catch another in the lake, forgetting the tales about the lake having no fish. Somehow, he had got in the water, maybe out of excitement, and not knowing how to swim, had stepped off over his head and drowned.

It was the only sensible answer, the guessing said, and the men who gathered at the lake offered agreement, adding they had been wrong in spending all their time searching the river. Should have thought about the creek earlier, since it was closer to Howard's house. Should have called Whitlow to bring in his dogs sooner than they did, but there had been so many of them out looking it hadn't seemed necessary.

"I wish you would of," Whitlow said softly. "I surely wish you would of." He had a tired, old look etched into his face as he scanned the lake. "Ought to blow this dam up," he added. "Too much dying down here. Too much of it."

"Last place I ever thought he'd come was down here," Moody said, "since nobody comes down here no more, not with all them tales about ghosts. Guess we should of thought about it, though, since he said he wanted to catch a fish to give to Noah. I guess he must of heard Howard or somebody say this was where Noah was staying."

"Lord, God, I feel bad about this," Peavo whispered. "If we'd just fanned out more, maybe we could of found him before he got here." He looked at Noah. "Hope you don't go putting no blame on yourself," he added. "Nobody here thinks you was at fault."

Noah did not respond. The talk meant nothing to him. He knew he was the reason Matthew was dead.

He also knew something the other men did not know: he knew about Hoke Moore's fish, and in his mind he had watched pictures of Matthew at the lake, mind-pictures so clear it was like seeing them take place on the silver-pale screen of a movie theater.

Matthew coming up to the shack with the fish he had caught in the creek, happy over it. Calling out. No answer to his calls. Tying his fish to the trash tree. Walking the lakeside, studying the water and seeing in it the rolling of the fish. Finding a grasshopper and piercing it on the hook and then going to the dam, to the place for fishing, and throwing the line out into the water. Doing little dance steps of joy as he waited for a catch.

The fish coming to the water's edge, bold in its aggravation, making its sudden leap, causing Matthew to drop the rod and to slip on the slick shore mud, throwing him into the water, causing him to thrash about, trying to get his footing, the water pulling at him, the soft slush on the lake's bottom grabbing him like quicksand. And then his body disappearing under the water.

All of it Noah could see in mind-pictures, and he could not push aside the thought that lodged in his chest: if he had caught the fish earlier, Matthew might still be alive.

He stood gazing at the place in the water where he had found Matthew's body.

I will catch you, he said silently to the fish. I will catch you.

"Peavo's right," Taylor said, standing close to Noah. "Not your fault. I guess the boy was always headed for something like this. It just happened, that's all." He put his hand on Noah's shoulder. "Howard wants you to come up to his house," he added. "Wants you to tell them about it."

Noah nodded numbly.

"Has Milton come home yet?" someone asked.

"He's on his way," Whitlow said. Then: "He don't know about this yet."

"It'll near kill him," Moody mumbled. "Losing his wife like he did, and now his boy."

For a moment, no one spoke, and then Whitlow whispered, "He's with his mama now. That's enough to know."

It was a statement the men would carry with them from the lake to Howard Reynolds's home, would pass it along to Howard and to the women who were there doing housework for Ada. They would say it again and again, and in each saying they would find some peace from the truth of it.

"He's with his mama now."

"He's with his mama now."

"He's with his mama now."

There was no wailing in Howard Reynolds's home. Only near-silence. In the living room, sitting heavily in two chairs, Howard and Ada seemed barely aware of the coming and going of people—of the helping-out women and the helpless men. They sat as though they were alone in the room where they had always found some comfort, the room holding some telling of their lives together. Photographs of people smiling for the shutter stroke of the camera, forever leaving that particular moment of merriment to be looked at and wondered about. A side table to the side of the sofa. A coffee table in front of it. The chairs. A rolltop desk against one wall. On it, a radio. A heating stove with a short piece of stovepipe going into a covering over the fireplace. It was a room they had made for their own fit and purpose and only they belonged wholly to it.

Ada had a framed photograph of Matthew in her lap, letting her fingers rest on the glass that covered his face. Eleanor sat in a straight-back chair near her, holding a church fan that she used to fan the air across Ada's face when the air seemed to fill up with heat. The church fan had a picture of Jesus knocking at a door that did not have a latch on it. Howard kept his hands resting on his legs, as though someone had posed them there and he was afraid to move them.

They listened without expression to the story told by Noah. The part-story. He did not tell them of the bass or of the mind-pictures he had about Matthew's dying.

The telling was brief, said in only a few words, ending with Noah mumbling, "I'm sure sorry about it." He paused, added, "I feel like I'm the cause of it."

No one in the room moved or spoke.

"I'm sure sorry," Noah said again.

Howard lifted his face to Noah. "Weren't your fault. Me and my wife know it. The boy had a good time knowing you. You can't fault a man for things he can't help."

Noah bowed his head.

"Why don't we go get a cup of coffee?" Taylor said gently to Noah.

"There's some biscuits and sausage in the kitchen," Eleanor said. "You need to eat something."

"We will," Taylor told her. He leaned toward Howard. "Howard, we'll be around here if you need us."

Howard dipped his head once, looked at his hands resting on

his thighs. He did not seem to have the power to move them. He said, "Where's Whitlow? I wanted to thank him for bringing over his dogs."

"He went on home," Taylor answered. "He didn't sleep much last night, and he was pretty tired."

Again, Howard dipped his head. "I expect he's got some memories of his own to deal with."

"I'd say you're right," Taylor said.

In the yard, where Taylor and Noah took their coffee and biscuits and where the men gathered, the low-spoken talk replayed the search for Matthew Reynolds and his drowning in the Lake of Grief. Maybe Whitlow Mayfield was right, some of the men concluded. Maybe they should take some sticks of dynamite and blow the dam. If they did, it would at least prevent another drowning. But there was a quarrelsome problem with taking such matters into their own hands, they admitted: the land and the lake did not belong to any of them, and it would not be fair to Arch Wheeler's boy, even if he had traded in his farm clothes for cowboy boots and a Texas Stetson. Someday, the boy would sell the place, the men guessed, and the lake was the best part of it.

Wasn't like there was a curse put on the lake, the men added, even if three people had died there—Arch in his sleep, Boyd Cunningham by his own hand, and now Matthew Reynolds, who was mostly helpless—and even if there were stories about ghosts. Nobody had ever seen one for certain. It was mostly talk.

There were other places nearby that had had as many deaths, even more, and nobody had got queasy over the thought that any of those places had been cursed.

Farther up in the mountains, a half-dozen people had fallen to their death over the years by taking chances mountain-hiking. At least a half-dozen, maybe more.

And there was the Cater place above Hayesville. One winter, five people from the same family had died in five weeks, died one after the other. Got so bad, people couldn't remember the name of the dead when they went to the funerals, and the gravediggers complained they were running out of room in the family plot.

The lake didn't cause dying, the men concluded. It just seemed that way. Had to do with the name, they offered. Lake of Grief. Good Lord, if Arch Wheeler had said building the place made him laugh, they might have called it Laughing Lake, and then what would people be saying? You could bet there wouldn't be any talk of ghosts. Talk of angels singing sweet church music, maybe, but not of ghosts.

They talked of Arch Wheeler.

Lord, Arch Wheeler had deserved his little lake. Pity how quick he died, just when he had everything lined up to do nothing with his life but fish and ramble around the valley showing off his new Nash car and talking politics. Lord, he loved talking politics, and if you didn't mention Roosevelt, he would, being a Roosevelt man. If he had been around during the war, he would have been stealing plow points for scrap metal, just to help Roosevelt make more guns.

Same couldn't be said of Boyd Cunningham, the men agreed, throwing fidgety glances toward the house to make sure Eleanor was not in earshot of their talk.

Boyd had come back from the war a changed man, they said. Touchy. Quick to anger. Acting funny at times. Spending more money than any soldier had the right to have, but dodging friendly questions about it.

One of the men said, "I asked him one time, said, 'Where'd you get all them twenty-dollar bills, Boyd?' and he said it weren't none of my goddamn business and if I kept on about it, he'd show me what war was all about. I never saw a man get so hot under the collar so fast."

Another said, almost in whisper, "I heard some talk about him having a woman in Germany, and it got to weighing heavy on him, and that's maybe why he shot hisself."

"That's just talk," said another—the man with the stubble of beard and sun-brown face. "I was over there. They was women everywhere, some of them easy enough for the taking. A candy bar would do it, or some cigarettes. But I didn't see nobody wanting to bring one back home with him." He turned to look at Noah. "You was there, weren't you? Whitlow said you was."

"I was," Noah answered.

"You see anybody wanting to stay over there because of a woman?"

"Can't say that I did," Noah replied.

"It's all just talk," the man repeated. He glanced again toward the house, added, "He had him a fine woman waiting at home."

The men nodded in agreement.

"What's anybody heard about the fishing tomorrow?" one of the men asked.

"I heard Howard wanted it to go on," Moody answered. "He was guessing they'd bury Matthew on Sunday, but they got to wait for Milton."

"Any guess on when he's coming in?"

"Early this afternoon is what Howard was saying."

"It'll hit him hard."

"It will."

"Maybe they ought to put off the fishing until next week."

"What the principal said. He was by here a little earlier, right after they'd brought the boy's body up and sent it on to the funeral parlor. Howard said no. Said they was too much already done for it, too many people coming in from other places."

"He's got a point."

"Maybe it'd be a help to everybody to go on and do it. Take their mind off things."

"That's right."

Taylor watched Noah during the talk of the fishing, saw him looking away, knew the talk made him uncomfortable.

"I was thinking we might be a help to Howard if some of us could cut the grass in his yard," Taylor said to change the direction of the talk. "He can't do it, and there's bound to be a lot of people coming by when word gets out about Matthew."

The men eagerly agreed, made offers of equipment and time. Worked it out among themselves to cut the grass and clean up around the barn and to wash and wax Howard's car.

"He'll need it clean for the funeral," Moody said.

"We better check out his oil and battery," Peavo added. "That old car can't hardly get up enough power to run down a hill, much less up one. It don't need to be stopping on the road during the funeral drive."

"Lord, I feel for them," one of the men said in a sigh. "That boy was pretty much their life."

"Yes, he was," another said. "Yes, he was."

TWENTY-ONE

He walked in an easy stride, making his way up a hill that led away from Howard Reynolds's home, going in the direction of the Chatuge, and with each step he felt the freedom of being alone.

The feeling was good.

He had been in the Valley of Light for one week, exactly. And in that week, he had been pulled into the goings-on of more people than he had ever met in his travels. It was like a leaf floating on water, being caught suddenly in the swirl of a suck-hole and being snatched beneath the surface. Still, he could not blame the people. The people had been friendly, going out of their way to make him feel welcome. What had happened was of his own doing.

It was time to leave, he thought, stopping for a moment to rest near a small stand of sassafras trees. His body knew it. His body tugged at him, quarreled with him, saying to him that he had spent more time than he needed to spend in the Valley of Light, and he knew his body was right. Still, he could not go, things being the way they were. He had made a bargain with Taylor Bowers to paint his store. And leaving so soon after the drowning of Matthew Reynolds would make it appear he did not care about the death.

He had offered to go to the store and start on the painting, but Taylor had decided against it, saying it would not look right after what had happened, and he had agreed. Start back on Monday, Taylor had said, or if he wanted to do some early morning work on Saturday, before the fishing, he could do so. The store wouldn't be open, but that wouldn't matter. Noah knew where the paint was and there was a key to the store hidden under the steps of the side porch, Taylor had said, though why he considered it hidden was a joke; half the people in the valley knew about it. And then he had offered to drive Noah back to the pull-off leading to the lake, but Noah had declined, saying he felt the need for a walk.

"You go get some rest," Taylor had advised, "and don't start to thinking you're to blame for what happened. You're not. It just happened."

He had left without speaking again to Howard and Ada Reynolds, or to Eleanor, and he did not know if he would see any of them again.

He had decided he would not fish in the fishing contest. It did not seem right, no matter what the men had said to him about it, telling him they were looking forward to watching him take on Littleberry Davis. There was a pall over the fishing, and if he had not caused it, he was part of it.

He reached to pull a leaf from the sassafras, rolled it in his fingers and held it under his nose. It had the scent of vanilla and he thought of a story about Indians using ground-up sassafras roots to drug fish in small pools of water. Many times, he had taken a root of the tree and washed it and boiled it in water for the strong taste of it. Sassafras tea. His mother had liked it better than the tea a person could buy in a store. In autumn, the leaves of the tree turned yellow, deepening to orange, then blood red. His mother had said no tree was more beautiful. Next to a maple, that is. A maple in autumn was about as grand as a tree could ever want to be. Soon, the colors would come again. The sassafras and the maple, the bright red of sumac, the gold of hickory. So much color it would look like spilled paint.

He walked for a long time, into the middle of the afternoon. Walked to the dam of the Chatuge and watched a boater in a sailboat skimming the waters, the sail having the look of a cloth napkin he had once seen in a restaurant, the napkin folded upright and placed on a plate. Sailing was not a thing he wanted to do. The boats always looked as though they were about to tip over. Watching them from shore was pleasing, though, a little like watching a horse run free in a large pasture.

He was sorry he had not fished the Chatuge. It had the look of a place where bass would thrive, and maybe on the way out, he would spend a few minutes throwing out his hookless lure, just to say he had been there if he ever again ran into Hoke Moore.

First, there was another bass waiting for him.

In a smaller place.

Hoke Moore's bass.

He turned to walk back toward the valley, thinking of the bass. He would not try for it until he was certain he was alone, and he knew there would be people making their way to the lake throughout the day, wanting to see the place where the boy had drowned. It was one of the reasons he had decided on his walk. To stay away. When people had had their view—all knowing it was an event they would be talking about for years, all gathering some sighting that would belong only to them, some fact that would make them part of the day and part of the telling of the day—they would no longer go to the lake. It seemed a strange thing to do, going to a place where someone had died, but it was the nature of people. He had done much the same himself a few times, coming upon car wrecks on the side of roads, standing around long enough to see what had happened and if somebody had been hurt or killed. Once, while riding with his mother and father, he had seen a wreck where a number of cars had pulled off the road to take a close look even though the sheriff's car was already there, and his mother had scoffed that it looked like a flock of buzzards hovering over a roadkill. Not the same, his father had corrected, and his mother had said, "Why not?" His father had looked at her with a small smile perched on his lips and he had replied, "They ain't eating nothing." His mother had made a little toss of her head and had said, as a last word, "Give them time."

By late day, he judged, the people who were curious enough to walk the distance from the pull-off to the lake would be gone, and he would have the lake and the shack to himself, but he would take no chances. He would not try for the fish until early morning. The wait would make the fish restless, would aggravate it, as Hoke Moore had said, would make it eager to show its strength. What Hoke Moore had said was something he had always known: fish were a lot like most men. Work on their nerves and they would make mistakes.

He had wandered more toward the south than he thought and he came out of the woods near the church—Church of the Resurrected Christ—and he stopped to study it. It could have been the Methodist church of his boyhood, where he took his own baptism. White-painted frame building, high in its main body where the sanctuary was, fanned on the back end by a collection of small rooms for Sunday school classes. A bell steeple rose over the front of it, with a bell rope dropped inside, too high for the reaching hands of children. Tall, plain windows lined the sides—four windows to each side. A stovepipe made an elbow turn out of one wall, and the white planking around it was soot-stained. A coal stove would be inside, Noah thought, and in winter it would be fired hot enough to turn the iron as red as the workings of a blacksmith's forge, and those who sat near it would blister and those who sat away from it would shiver.

He remembered the story of a blacksmith from Elbert County who vowed he couldn't go to church in wintertime, that every time he looked at the hot-red belly of a church stove, it made him think of work that needed doing and his mind would wander to it, and that wandering naturally caused Jesus to fly out of his thinking, no matter how hard he fought against it. Said church in wintertime was just a waste to him.

Around the church was a cemetery, with tombstones sticking out of the ground like stone stumps. Some of the stones had a crumbling look to them, and Noah knew they marked the burial of people so long dead, only the faint chiseling of their names gave any proof they had ever lived.

He approached the church slowly, curiously. It had been a long time since he had been inside one. He had no argument with churches, but he had never felt at ease in them, and he guessed it was a sense that had been bred into him by his parents. About the only time he had ever felt in accord with a church had been on the day of his baptism, and that had been short-lived. No one in the congregation had said anything to him, and the preacher who had patted him with water had not invited him to come back. It had taken years for him to realize that being baptized with classmates from school was not much different from being handed a Christmas treat by a dressed-up Santa Claus in the school auditorium. Maybe even less, in the long run. With Santa Claus, he at least had something to hold on to for a while—a comb, a piece of candy, some raisins on the stem.

Yet, there was one thing he could never forget about his baptism. He had felt something when the preacher put his damp hand on his head. Something.

No one was at the church and there was no sign of traffic coming or going on the road, and he took the steps to the door and tried it. It was not locked and he pushed it open and stepped inside and closed the door behind him. He stood for a moment, listening. The inside of the church was as quiet as his breathing, the air clean and oddly cool, though the day had been hot and sweat-sticky.

He walked hesitantly into the sanctuary and stood, looking. There was a center aisle covered in red carpet, with pews on both sides. At the front of the sanctuary, the pulpit was set on a riser in the exact center of the aisle, and against the wall behind the pulpit was a cross that he judged to be made of sweet gum. It was hand-hewed, not cut from a sawmill, and the ax that trimmed it had left it with a rough look. It dominated the wall and the sanctuary, calling eyes to stare at it, and Noah believed that the man who had cut the wood and had notched it and bolted it together wanted the presence of it to shout out that Jesus was stronger than wood or steel. Large nails—larger than any he had ever seen—had been driven into the wood in the places where the hands and feet of the crucified Christ would have been, and the sap of the wood had made stains around the nails, or if not sap, then drops of oil had been put there to look like stains and to tell tales of the blood of Jesus. The cross had the hard look of power, and Noah believed it was made that way on purpose—the cross empty of Jesus, yet holding his pain.

He remembered his father's funeral. The casket holding his father's body down front, at the foot of the pulpit. The young preacher, his hair shining with hair tonic, his eyes flashing joy or maybe sadness, his voice shrill and tinny, still more boy than man. Remembered the music that came up from those who were in attendance. *Yes, we will gather at the river . . .* Remembered his mother's face, pale, yet lifted, showing the kind of bravery expected of her. Remembered Travis sitting next to her, a string of tears rolling out of his blinking eyes.

The beautiful, beautiful river . . .

He turned quickly and left the church and walked rapidly away from it, not looking back to see if he had closed the door.

In his mind, he could hear the preacher whispering near his ear, *"Follow me and I will make you fishers of men."* And he could feel the single drop of baptismal water that had dripped from his hair to run down his face like the warm blood of Jesus.

TWENTY-TWO

Eleanor let her body lean back against the tub, and the water, carrying a film of soap, covered her, rising up over her shoulders, tickling at her chin. The water was hot, as hot as her skin could bear it, and the steam from it licked across her face.

It was not often she gave in to such luxury. Her husband had considered a filled tub a waste of water and a drain on the water heater, and believed that any person wanting to soak idly while the water cooled had too much time on his or her hands. A tub was for scrubbing off dirt, not for pleasure, had been her husband's view of bathing.

But her husband was not there to disapprove. And the old woman was not there to be nosy about why she was so long in the bathroom. She was alone, tired, and on her drive from the Reynolds home, she had imagined the pleasure of a soaking bath in a filled tub, had become almost obsessed with the thought of it.

Now, in the water, her back and shoulders slick against the hard enamel of the tub, her muscles began to relax. She closed her eyes, opened her mouth slightly, sucked in the steam air—warm in her mouth, in her lungs.

She thought of Ada Reynolds, still numbed by news that did not seem possible to her—would never seem possible, probably. She had barely moved from her chair the entire day, had not released the photograph of Matthew from her grip. It was as though she had finally faced a problem she could not handle and had surrendered, which was like a dying in itself. It was Howard who had faced the crowds of people gathered to offer sympathy and food and work, telling them in a low voice that he was grateful—that both of them were grateful. Saying he always knew he lived in the best place on earth and the people, showing their kindness, proved it. It was Howard who met his son at the door when Milton arrived soon after the noon hour, Howard who gave him the news of Matthew, Howard who had offered the same words Whitlow Mayfield had whispered to the men at the lake: "He's with his mama."

She had heard all of it, had watched Milton's face go pale, his eyes springing tears, and then he had gone to his mother and kneeled at her chair and placed his head in her lap. Ada had not spoken to him. She had lifted her hand and put it on his head and gently stroked his hair, and Milton had repeated what his father had said: "He's with his mama."

The words had seemed to be a healing, as they had been with everyone who had said them or heard them during the day. There was no better place for Matthew than being with his mother.

An image of Sarah Magill Reynolds came to her mind. A laughing woman, startlingly pretty. An aura was on her, something radiant. She had never pitied herself over Matthew. He was her son, and her son was beautiful. It was told in the community that, on her deathbed, she had said, "Bring my son to me." And she had died holding his hand against her face.

Now her son was with her again, and to the people of the Valley of Light who had gathered at the home of Howard and Ada Reynolds, that was reason to celebrate, not mourn, for all of them remembered the aura of Sarah, the God-touch of radiance that she wore like a garment made of sun-glow.

Eleanor raised her arm in the water, let it float. She watched a wisp of steam rising from her skin. The steam could have been her own aura.

She arched her body, and the water made a cushion under her back and lifted it up through the soapy surface. She closed her eyes, leaned her head back, let her body rock gently in the water, let the water lick softly at her skin.

She made a small gasp—involuntarily—and let her body sink again into the water. Lifted her hands and combed her fingers through her hair, leaving wet rows.

She thought of Noah.

Taylor had said he had gone for a walk.

Had said also that Noah blamed himself, even when everybody had assured him that what happened was not his fault.

"I'm not sure he'll be coming back," Taylor had added.

She took the bath cloth and soaped it and ran it over her body and then rinsed the soap by cupping her hand and pulling the water over her. She stood in the tub, reached for a towel and dried her face and arms and shoulders and breasts, then wrapped the towel around her and stepped from the tub.

The skin of her body was pink from the heat, pink as the color of a new child.

She, too, needed to walk, she thought.

There was still enough light for it.

A walk would feel good.

He had approached the lake through the woods, under the cover of hemlocks, avoiding the path from the pull-off at the road, thinking there still might be people going to and from the lake, though he had doubts about it. It was late afternoon. Those who wanted to see the spot where Matthew had been found would likely have done so earlier.

He had not seen anyone.

At the shack, he had taken a sponge bath with springwater heated on the stove, using the rosemary soap, and had shaved his growth of whiskers. It was not the bath he wanted—not the lake bath—but it was better than being seen by a late visitor satisfying curiosity. And then he had made coffee and a small amount of grits and had taken his meal at the table, with the door of the shack open to the porch. From his place at the table, he had watched the sun seep into the trees on the western hill overlooking the lake, throwing shadows across the water.

He was making a bundle of his clothes for washing—those he had changed out of after going into the lake for Matthew—when he heard Eleanor's voice from near the porch, calling his name.

She had with her two pieces of fried chicken and three biscuits wrapped in a cloth napkin. The chicken and biscuits had come from the overheaped table at Ada Reynolds's home, she said. So much food, it was being shared by the helpers and she had taken some for herself, but had already eaten more than she wanted. She was that way with food, she told him. If she was around it for any length of time, she lost her taste for it, and she had spent the day with the other women of the valley keeping the serving table full.

"I don't know why I brought any of it home, to be honest," she said, "but I did, and then I got to thinking that you got away without having anything to eat at all, and you'd probably wind up with some crackers, or something, so I thought I'd force some of this off on you."

She knew she was talking in chatter, in a river of words, but could not help it. She had caught him again by surprise and had seen in his bewildered expression a kind of trapped look. Talking, and being busy, kept the look cornered.

"Anyway, I needed to get out," she continued, taking a plate from the pie safe and putting the food on it and handing it to him. "Just to walk off some of the strain of the day, I think." She looked at him, flashed a smile. "I can smell coffee. Do you have enough for an extra cup?"

"I do," he answered softly, holding the plate, wondering if he should tell her he had already had grits.

"Then I'm going to impose on you again," she said. "Why don't you sit down and eat. I'll get it. Where's your cup?"

He glanced at the table, to the cup.

"Oh, I see it," she said. "Do you need some?"

"No," he said. "I just poured it."

"Sit," she said again. "Eat."

He sat at the table, watched her go to the pie safe and take a cup and then cross to the stove and pour coffee into it, talking as she moved about.

"You know, it's really not that far from the house to here," she said. "I've walked it before, but it's been a long time. I usually just drove the car to the pull-off and came in from there, but there's a shortcut coming out on the road near the house, and I took it, but I'll take the path to the pull-off going back, since it'll be dark before long." She paused. "I brought along a flashlight—it's on the porch step—but I think there'll be enough moonlight without it." She moved to the table and sat across from him.

Noah could feel her words sticking to his clothing like beggar's-lice. So many words, they seemed to be waiting in line to get into his hearing.

"I'm sorry," she said after a moment. "I told you I was a jabbermouth." She smiled. "I know it when I'm doing it, but I just can't seem to stop. It's like I've got a mouth full of Mexican jumping beans and they're popping out all over the place."

"It's all right," he said.

"Sometimes, it's worse than others."

"I don't mind it," he told her, biting into the chicken, thankful for the taste of it.

She breathed in the aroma of the coffee, took a sip from the rim of the cup. "I'll bet your mother was a good cook," she said.

"She was," he replied.

"I can tell because you make good coffee. I read something

about it once, in one of those magazine articles about how women can judge if the man of their life learned anything from his mother. It said that if a man made good coffee, he had been taught to make it by a good cook, and would probably be a good cook himself."

"I don't know about that," he said. "I usually make coffee just by boiling some water and putting in some grounds and letting it set a little bit. But I been using the coffeepot here."

"It's good, believe me," she said, taking another sip and smiling over it. Then she asked, "Are you all right, Noah?"

He nodded. "I'm fine."

"Taylor was a little worried about you."

"No reason to be."

"He said he thought you were blaming yourself for what happened to Matthew."

He made a little shrug.

"I could say the same thing for myself," she said. "I thought about it. Did he come down here when I was here, and if he did, how did he do it without me seeing him? I was here for an hour after you left, probably, and when I got back to Howard's house, they were already looking for him. I might have missed him by a few minutes."

"I guess he didn't come down that early," he said. "Probably in the afternoon, when everybody was looking on the river."

"It wasn't your fault," she said. "You've got to understand that. I guess everybody in this valley has always known something like that might happen to him, even Howard and Ada and Milton. They'd all been living on hope, waiting on some kind of miracle, but they also knew it was hope that rested on quicksand."

He took a drink of his coffee, but said nothing. He thought of the fish, had another vision of Matthew slipping into the water.

"If I told the truth of it, I'd have to say I wake up just about every morning wanting to be somewhere else," she said. "The only thing that keeps me here is the farm, and I don't know why

I'm so stubborn about that. I really don't. I'm like a fish out of water in this place." She smiled at the expression, added, "And I guess you know how that is better than anybody, as much fishing as you do."

"I guess so," he said.

"When I first came here, I didn't know anything about this kind of life," she continued. "I was just a spoiled town girl who was so much in love, it used to take my breath just thinking about it. Do you know what I did the first six months, Noah? I cooked. I barely knew how to boil eggs, so I decided I would become the best cook in the valley. I got cookbooks from everywhere, went to people like Ada Reynolds and other ladies, and stood beside them at their stoves. Boyd gained thirty pounds the first year we were married." She shook her head, gave a sigh that had the sound of resignation. "I didn't know anything about the farm—about chickens, or cows, or mules, or anything. But I learned. I learned because I wanted to be the kind of wife Boyd needed, and all the time, there was something inside me that kept wanting to get in the car and go home, because I knew I could never fit in. I wanted to be back in college. I wanted to go places and see things that would thrill me so much I would be lost for words to describe them. That something is still in me, and since Boyd's death, I think about it all the time. Every single day, I think about it. "

She laughed sadly, offered another sigh. "But just when I decide I'm going to go crazy living here, something happens like today, and I know I'll probably never find the same kind of people anywhere else," she said. "I think it's just the way country people are, though. They leave you alone until it bores you to death, and then when somebody needs them, they pop up out of the woodwork." She paused, touched her hair in a way that made it seem like a nervous habit. "When Boyd died, I didn't think many people would even show up at his funeral—dying the way he did, I mean—but I was wrong. The day after I found him, there were so many people at my house, I actually had a dream they were there to take everything away from me. I even checked my silverware after they left."

She looked at him. "It goes to show you, doesn't it?"

"It does," he said, and he remembered the death of his father, remembered the gathering of people crowding inside and outside the tenant house where they had lived.

"Do you ever think about the war, Noah?" she said, leaning forward over the table.

The question surprised him. "Sometimes," he answered.

"I do," she said. "I think about it a lot, or I wonder about it. I think it must have been something that everybody who had to fight in it will never be able to put aside."

"Maybe not," he said.

"I came here a few times after Boyd died," she said quietly, "thinking I might be able to have some sense of him, of what made him take his own life, but nothing ever happened. Nothing. I had no sense of him at all, and then I got to thinking it was because the man I married was not the man who came back to me after the war."

She paused, turned her face to gaze out of the door. "He had a kind of—of meanness about him when he came back, especially if he'd been drinking, and that's something he seldom did before the army. I don't know what it was, or what caused it, but it was there." She paused again, offered a small smile that had a quiver in it. "Oh, he could be sweet when he wanted to be. Like the bookcases in the house. That was sweet. He didn't have to do that, but he did." She turned her face back to Noah. "There just weren't enough bookcases to make the difference, I suppose. But I guess I should have known that from the start. My sisters told me. My sisters said I was jumping into a marriage that would be shaky at best, and I have to admit they were right. Everybody talks about the good and bad of marriage, like it was something lived on a seesaw, but they forget to tell you that sometimes the bad of it weighs more than the good of it and the seesaw stays in one place." She took a deep breath, exhaled slowly, shook her head.

"I'm sorry. I guess I'm just feeling sorry for myself. I did have good moments with Boyd, especially at the beginning."

Outside, cicadas began to sing. A whippoorwill made its first call. A frog gave a sound like an objection to the bird. The soup of night began to thicken. Noah stood to light the kerosene lamp on the table, then sat again.

"Do you mind if I talk about the war?" she said.

"No," he replied after a moment of hesitation.

"I've never really talked about it very much at all. To Boyd, some, but not very much. He told me not to do it. He said people didn't like remembering it."

"It's all right," he said.

"Did you ever kill anyone?" she asked.

"I don't know," he said. "I guess. I was never close enough to know if it was me or somebody else that made the shot."

"But you saw soldiers fall?"

"Yes."

Eleanor let her fingers touch the handle of the coffee cup. She gazed at it, and Noah knew she was weighing a thought that bothered her.

"Did you ever steal anything while you were over there?" she asked.

"No," he said. He thought of the carving of the cow found in Dachau—the cow he had given to Travis—and considered telling her about it, but knew it would sound foolish. The kind of stealing she was talking about would not include a carving no larger than his thumb.

In the war, soldiers he knew had taken many things from the towns and villages of their battles—jewelry and silverware and paintings and money. Many things. Spoils of war, they had called it, saying if they didn't take it some officer would and it would be an even bet that the officer was someone who had not been within shouting distance of the battle. The taking had bothered Noah, knowing it was much the same as stealing at gunpoint, the crime that had sent Travis to jail for twenty years. In Elbert

County, it had caused people to snort about evil being on the loose. In war, no one seemed to care.

"I sometimes think Boyd did," she said calmly. "I don't know where else all the money could have come from. He said it was from some rich family in New York, paying him for saving their son's life. I didn't believe him. He never gave me a name and he never told me what happened. I think he just made it up." She paused, tilted her head. "He gave me a necklace when he got back. It had diamonds in it. Lots of diamonds. But he didn't want me to wear it. He said it would cause talk, and there was enough of that already. He told me he found it. He said he was in one of the towns that had been bombed and he saw it on the ground and he just picked it up and put it in his pocket."

"Could have," Noah said. "Some of those places were pretty much blown up by bombers. You could see things everywhere."

She pulled her hand back from the cup. "Maybe he was right, then." She looked at Noah, forced a smile. The dim, peach-colored light from the lamp flickered over her face. "I've been packing the things that belonged to him—his clothes, that sort of thing. I'm going to give it all away, or throw it away. It's time to put all of that behind me." She touched her throat with her fingers. "I'll probably sell the necklace. I sure could use the money. I just hope it's worth something."

Noah moved his head in acknowledgement, but he did not speak.

"See? Jabbermouth at work," she said in a suddenly light voice. "I'm sorry. Boyd said I should never talk about the war—but I already said that, didn't I?"

"I don't mind," he told her.

She sat looking at him for a moment, her eyes locked on his face, and he thought she wanted to say something, but could not decide if she should. Then she stood in a movement that seemed sudden to Noah. "You're kind to listen," she said. She moved from the table to the door and looked out at the porch. "Do you like sleeping out here?" she asked.

"Yes, I do," he answered. "It's cool at night."

"Sometimes when it's too hot to sleep, I get up and go to the porch and sit in the swing," she said. "I think if it had a screen on it, I'd do the same thing you're doing. I'd put a cot out there and let the bugs sing me to sleep." She moved from the room to the cot on the porch, sat on it as though testing the softness of it, and then she turned her body to lie across it, her head resting on the pillow, facing the lake. "Yes," she said softly. "I like this."

Noah sat at the table numbly watching her through the door of the shack. He did not know if he should say something to her, or if he should leave her alone. Wondered what Taylor would say, what Taylor would do. Wondered if Taylor would be as helpless. Maybe if he did nothing more than sit near her, it would be enough, he reasoned, and he left the table and went to the porch, to the rocker, and sat and waited for her to say something. In the moon's light—a faint lemon color—he could not see her eyes, did not know what words could be in them. Waited. Listened to her breathing, as even and as soft as the purring sound of a cat. Waited. Minutes passed. Long minutes. Silent minutes. And then she pushed up from the cot, stood, looked at him, smiled nervously.

"I'm glad I know you, Noah Locke," she whispered. "I'm glad you came to the valley."

He swallowed. He had no words to offer.

"I know you're ready to leave," she added. "I think I'm going to miss you not being here."

She stepped to him, reached to touch his face with her fingers, let her fingers linger on his skin for a moment, turned and left the porch. He watched her disappear into the darkness and then he slowly rocked forward out of the chair and went to the cot and lay down in the place where she had been. The warmth of her body was still on the blanket—or so it seemed to be—and a faint scent of her cologne lingered in the pillow. He slept a pleasing, restful sleep, one that did not have the dreams he expected to have—dreams of Matthew.

TWENTY-THREE

Lamar Gathers knew the day would be one of many moods. He knew it because he knew the people of the Valley of Light better than anyone—an outsider who had been among them long enough to be considered an acceptable insider.

He knew it because he was a teacher and teachers had the advantage of vision through the eyes of students who saw things as they were, not as they were covered up by their parents, twisting the truth for the sake of looking good.

He knew it because teachers—good teachers—were always learning.

He was a good teacher.

He knew it also because he had seen the moods of the valley close-up and had survived them.

He had been principal of Bowerstown Junior High School for thirty years, having spent his entire career in the school that had hired him two months after his graduation from the University of North Carolina. His marriage to Arlene Weathers had caused controversy because Arlene had been a ninth-grade student during his first year of teaching. It had to be suspicious, the gossip declared. A teacher marrying one of his students, and it did not matter that the marriage had occurred during Arlene's senior year at the University of Georgia, or that she was she was only eight years younger than Lamar.

It didn't seem right, the talkers had whispered busily among themselves, their faces coated in irritation so visible it had the look of a rash. It simply didn't seem right.

The talk had been stopped by a woman named Elsie Wade at a school board meeting held to discuss the issue. She had said simply, "How many people here remember George Gurley?" The answer to the question was the answer to the foolish quarreling about Lamar Gathers marrying Arlene Weathers.

George Gurley, a widower in a childless marriage, had married Pretty Bowers when he was forty-one and she was fourteen.

Pretty had mothered six children from the union.

The land for the school had been donated to the community by George. He had been the school's superintendent for twenty years.

And Elsie Wade, whose maiden name had been Elsie Gurley, had been the first child born to George and Pretty.

The troubling gossip over Lamar and Arlene had ended as quickly as it had started.

In the years following their marriage, Lamar and Arlene Gathers had gained a reputation as fine, unorthodox teachers and even better citizens. In the Valley of Light, they were thought of as givers and leaders. They were high class, as Whitlow Mayfield had once described them. Yet there was nothing uppity about them, nothing at all. People respected them and behaved with civility in their presence, the way they would behave around a preacher.

It had been Lamar who thought of sponsoring a fishing contest as a fund-raiser for the school, the idea coming to him from a truant student named Kenny Overmeyer, a boy so stocky he had the look of someone who had grown tall, but had been hammered short. Kenny loved fishing. Next to fishing, school was as bothersome as a hornet, and he had no sense of guilt in playing hooky. Hooky, to Kenny, had more meaning than missing school. Hooky had the word *hook* in it, and that was cause enough to find the river on any day that cried to him to avoid the closed-in quarters of a classroom. There had been many such days for Kenny.

Lamar's resolution of the problem was still a story traded for idle talk at Taylor's store. Lamar had said, "Well, Kenny, if you won't come to us, I guess we'll just have to come to you," and one day the entire class had shown up at the river, catching Kenny by surprise. A spelling bee was conducted as Kenny pulled in catfish. Kenny, who was smart enough by nature to eventually own a car dealership in Knoxville, had won third place. Lamar had said, "This looks like so much fun, we ought to get everybody in on it."

And the thought had become an added-on suggestion by Lamar at the next school board meeting, and the suggestion had perked the attention of the men in attendance, causing them to sit up in their chairs. When a vote was taken, it was approved without objection, and the men had spent another hour of back-and-forth talk, making rules. The fishing would be done on the Hiawassee River, which ran through the northeast corner of the valley, and the winner would be decided not by number of fish, but by total weight. Any kind of bait could be used—live or artificial—but no seining would be allowed, and no explosives and no electric devices. Anybody caught cramming rocks or shotgun pellets into a fish to increase its weight would be disallowed and not permitted to ever again participate in the event. People could arrive as early as seven o'clock and mark their fishing spot with a stick having their name on it. Rowdy behavior would not be tolerated. No drinking of any liquid containing alcohol. Judges would be members of the school board. All proceeds would go to the school, after the prize money had been taken out for the winner.

To the men, it was simple, and they had left the school board meeting in high spirits. Lamar would later tell his wife that more words had been exchanged about the fishing than about all the issues of education he had ever presented.

"You finally found something they understand," his wife had replied gently.

The contest was in its twenty-third year, and the reputation of it had become an annual attraction for the Valley of Light and for Clay County, with some fishermen coming out of Georgia and Tennessee and from a good driving distance in North Carolina. On Fishing Day, as it was advertised, more than fifty people were certain to appear at the Hiawassee River, fishing gear in hand, and later their families would appear at the school for a money-making supper of fish and hush puppies and coleslaw.

The death of Matthew Reynolds had left Lamar with an uneasy feeling about Fishing Day. He would have preferred putting it off, but Howard had insisted that it go on as scheduled, and there was substance to his argument. A lot of people had made plans around the date, and it would be impossible to get out a notice about a date change to those not living in the valley. Besides, having something to bring them together after tragedy was, in all likelihood, a good thing.

Also, there was the matter of the fish seller. In a week's time, he had become almost legendary. By count, Lamar already had sixty-one fishermen pay their two dollars, and usually the sign-up to fish did not take place until the day of the contest. He guessed there could be a hundred people competing for the twenty dollars that most of them would have reluctantly conceded to Littleberry Davis before the unexpected appearance of Noah Locke.

"I hope he shows up," Lamar said to his wife at their early breakfast. "Something tells me he won't, not after what happened to Matthew. I heard Taylor Bowers talking about it. He said the boy felt responsible for Matthew's drowning."

"That's sad," Arlene said. "He couldn't do anything about it."

"I know," said her husband. "We'll see. We'll see."

He sat at the kitchen table and watched his wife cutting cabbage at the kitchen counter. She would be at the work all morning, making gallons of coleslaw she would keep cooled in an old icebox they had kept after getting their refrigerator. His wife called herself the Coleslaw Queen on Fishing Day, and it was a title she had well earned. No woman in the valley could match her recipe of it. Yet, she had never complained about the work, and Lamar had privately suspected it was because the work kept her occupied and away from the fishing.

On this day, he envied her.

There would be melancholy among the fishermen because of the death of Matthew Reynolds and because Howard was so well liked. The death, happening as it had, would be tangled in the cobweb of talk made on the riverbank. There would be those who would call it a tragedy, and those saying it was an act of providence since the boy would never have been able to manage on his own. Some of the listeners would be boys who had made fun of Matthew in the few days he would spend in school each year, treating him like a mutant, and he knew those same boys would try to ward off the feeling of guilt by telling stories of something Matthew had done in their presence, something that had caused them to yowl in glee. There would be uncomfortable grins mixed with their stories.

On the river, someone would say something that would find its way back to Howard, bringing with it pain and sorrow, Lamar feared.

It would be a day with a slow ticking to it, he thought. A long day. And there would be many moods settling on it. Many moods.

By sunrise, Noah had left the shack and the lake, leaving behind his fishing rod. By ten o'clock, when the fishing began on the Hiawassee River with a pistol shot fired by Lamar Gathers, he was hidden in a ridge of hemlocks that had a distant view of the river, and there he rested and watched.

The first Fishing Day that Eleanor attended had been in her first year of marriage. It had been, for her, a festive, laughing event, staying with her husband as he fished from a shade-covered spot on the riverbank. He had caught eight fish weighing ten pounds, not close to the seventeen pounds of a man named Adel Jury. The memory of it, of seeing so many people together having fun, remained joyful for her, and she had returned each year for the starting of the contest. There was a giddiness about the starting. It was like a horse race, with horses bolting from behind the gates of slender stalls, the sounds of their hooves making thunder and the shrill shouting of people rising high in the air. At the fishing, it was the explosion of Lamar Gathers's pistol shot and the sight of fishing lines whipping out over the river, flashing like cobwebs in the sun, arching, falling, splattering on the water. And always—always—there would be someone bellowing, "I got me one," as soon as the hook struck the surface. It was as though Lamar Gathers had written a script that would start with comedy, for there would be a ripple of laughter along the riverbank.

She had chosen to stay near Taylor for the starting, though she had kept a watch for Noah, hoping he would appear at the last moment, yet sensing he would not. She had known it the night before, being with him. Not by anything he had said, for he had said little, but by the look he had carried on his face, and by the way his face had felt when she touched it. She had wondered if that was the reason he had stayed away—the touch. Wondered if it had frightened him. Probably. It had frightened her. Not when she did it, but later, walking home, remembering it. The touch had been natural, something offered without thinking, a woman's touch of a man. Yet, she had gone too far with it. Women did not do such things with men they barely knew, and she had spent much of the night awake, regretting what she had done, wondering if it had happened because of the place—the lake, the shack. There was something strangely physical about the place. Once she had made love to Boyd on the same cot she had rested on the night before, with Noah sitting near her. On a clear, warm night, with moonlight skating across the lake on sharp blades of a blowing summer wind, she had made love with such power it had left her trembling with awe.

Being with Noah had caused the memory of that night to flame, burn brightly, die away, yet she believed the memory was one of the reasons she watched for Noah at the fishing.

Or maybe it was nothing more than hearing his name said so often, by so many. Everyone who had appeared at the registration place—a tent at a picnic spot near the river—had asked about him.

"Haven't seen him, yet," Lamar had said in a cheerful voice, letting his answer hold some hope that Noah would arrive in time.

"Sure hope he does," Peavo Teasley had muttered.

"Me, too," Moody Deal had added.

The men had gone to Taylor, asking if Taylor had seen him, and Taylor had answered, "Not this morning. I halfway expected him to be at the store, getting in a couple of hours of painting, but he wasn't there when I drove by. Tell you the truth, I don't think he'll be here. He was pretty upset about Howard's grandboy. Thinks it wouldn't of happened if he hadn't shown up."

"Not his fault," the men had said, sounding slightly put off, sounding as though something had been taken out of the day for them. Yet, each knew the death of Matthew would have weighed heavily on them also, given the same circumstance of finding the boy's body that Noah had experienced, and the talk among them had carried forgiveness: "Maybe I would of done the same thing."

The first fish caught was by Littleberry Davis, eight minutes into the contest.

"Damn," Moody mumbled, watching Littleberry wrestle the catfish to the bank. A large one. Two pounds or more by the look of it.

"It'd of been ten pounds if Noah had caught it," Peavo grumbled.

"Damn," Moody said again.

Littleberry held the fish up, presented it to the fishermen around him. Grinned.

From the hemlocks, far away, Noah watched the fishing. He could tell by the way the small, faraway figures acted when a fish was caught, could almost hear the whooping from it. He wished he were closer. He would have liked seeing how Peavo and Moody and Taylor were faring, and he wondered if the man called Littleberry was there, and how many fish he was catching. If he was as good as people said he was, he would have found his fishing spot early and put a claim on it, and he would know there were fish in it. Could have been sneaking to the spot for a week or longer, throwing food in it, Noah thought. He had known people to do such things. Once, in Alabama, he had met a man who had a small catfish pond and every few days the man would take a bucket of pellet-size dough balls to the pond and cast them into the water off a dock, and the fish would come to them like cows in a dry pasture stampeding to a feeding of lespedeza hay. The man had vowed he could catch fish with his hand by lying, belly-down, on the dock and scooping his hand into the churning foam when the fish were feeding. "I been finned many a time, doing it," he had said seriously.

Near noon, he ate the two biscuits and one piece of chicken he had left over from the food Eleanor had brought to him.

He wondered if Eleanor was at the fishing.

Probably not, he reasoned. From stories he had heard of it, the fishing was a contest for men, like baseball was a man's game, and the women kept themselves away from it. If any of them were there, they were likely girlfriends of younger, unmarried men, urging their men on with girlish enthusiasm, while their men flexed muscles and posed for the clicks of cameras. The women who stayed away would take the fish caught and cleaned by the men, and they would cook the fish and serve the men, making the same kind of balance that worked in their everyday life. And, among themselves, the women would complain about having to do all the real work, while the men played.

The women would be right, of course, Noah thought. More than once, he had heard his mother make the same complaint, saying her husband and her sons had no idea—not in the least—of what she had to put up with. His father had accepted the grumbling in silence and had advised Noah and Travis to do the same. "Boys, that's one tree you don't never want to climb," he had said. "Believe me, it's got thorns all over it."

Eleanor would be one of the women doing the cooking in the deep-fry pots, rolling the fish in a mix of cornmeal and flour and slipping them gently into the hot grease of melted lard. If she ate with a man, it would likely be Taylor, and even then it would be an acted-out thing—Taylor saying in his kidding way, "You look like you need a place to sit," and Eleanor replying, "Only if I don't have to get up and get you second helpings." The people around them would laugh, would make jesting remarks to Taylor.

He remembered Eleanor on the cot, her head resting on the pillow, looking out at the lake with eyes he could not see from the shadows over her face. On the cot, curled as she was, she had seemed like a young girl, not a woman, and he remembered that Shelia Benson had often behaved the same. Curled in a nest of hay, not speaking, a look of daydreaming on her face. With Shelia, he had thought of it as flying away in her mind, going places she had never been, leaving her body behind. He wondered if that was what Eleanor had done, if she had flown away to some memory of her dead husband, and if the trip to the memory and the trip back from it could be taken only in silence. It was possible. He had taken such trips.

He pulled his watch from his pocket and looked at it. It was ten minutes after twelve. The fishing would last until seven and then the feeding would begin. He stood, pushed his watch back into his pocket. He could finish the painting before seven, and then he would be able to leave the valley. He thought of Travis, and the yearning to see him returned in a jolt to his chest.

• • •

At one o'clock, Eleanor returned to Howard Reynolds's home to check on Ada. Only Joyce Magill was there, keeping watch. Joyce was the older sister of Sarah, a woman of striking prettiness as Sarah had been. Yet, unlike Sarah, Joyce was aggressive and high-spirited. She had never married because, as she proudly and often announced, she had never met a man worthy of the trouble. She had been Matthew's favorite relative, and he had stayed with her many nights after the death of his mother, being spoiled by her cookie making and her storytelling. In the Valley of Light, Joyce Magill was considered a woman worth pursuing by men—if they had the nerve to do so and if they could withstand her moods when she decided to speak her mind. Whatever she believed in, she believed in it with passion, and would have locked horns with God and Satan both—in the same place and at the same time—to make her point. If she had been Job when God and Satan got to making side bets over the patience of mankind, she would have taken both of them to the woodshed.

Joyce said that Ada and Howard and Milton had gone to the funeral home with the preacher. To pin down the arrangements for Sunday's burial, she added.

Only a few people had been by the home.

"I think it's a shame, the way people just drop off the edge of the earth when there's something going on like the fishing," she said in her bothered way. "They ought to be here, visiting with Ada and Howard and Milton."

There was no reason to argue with Joyce. Her mind was set, and it did not matter that Howard and Ada and Milton had all urged Lamar Gathers to go on with Fishing Day.

"They can all go fishing in hell, is what I think," Joyce added, and a spew of tears flowed from her eyes. "Lord, Jesus, I miss that boy, Eleanor, just like he came out of me rather than Sarah."

"I know you must," Eleanor told her.

"Every time I was with him, I could feel Sarah right there,

watching over us," Joyce whispered. "I swear to Jesus, there were times I could hear her talking, just like she was in the next room, and once in a while, Matthew would kind of turn his head toward a door or a window and listen and then he'd smile, and I'd know Sarah had said something to him. I miss both of them so much it feels like there's a fire in my chest. Only thing that keeps it from burning me alive is knowing they're back together again."

"It helps knowing that," Eleanor replied.

The two women sat on the porch of the Reynolds home and gazed at the day, and the day seemed as quiet and as calm as the cloud-puffs that made lazy crawls across the blue of sky, doing slow somersaults on cushions of air.

"I'm glad you came by," Joyce said after a long silence. "I guess they got you lined up to help with the cooking."

"They do."

"I'm so tired of that fishing, it makes me want to scream," Joyce said. "Bunch of men acting like boys, having the time of their life and the women waiting on them hand and foot. You won't catch me doing it."

"At least the school makes a little money from it," Eleanor said.

"I know it," Joyce replied irritably. And then she gave a sigh. "And that's the part about it I can't stand. Can't even complain too much, and I guess you know I hate being in that predicament." She let a smile come to her face. "But I'm still working on it," she added.

"Boyd used to like it," Eleanor said. "He never caught very much, but he liked being with the men all day."

"I saw that man everybody's talking about yesterday—that fish seller," Joyce said. "Is he down there?"

"No," Eleanor told her. "Not when I was there."

"Good," Joyce said. "Nobody's blaming him for what happened, but if he hadn't come along, Matthew would still be alive." She turned to Eleanor. "I believe that, Eleanor. I do. I hope he's moved on someplace else. Men like that, trouble puts them on the road in the first place and follows them every step they make. I took one look at him and knew that's the kind of man he was."

Eleanor could feel a stir of resentment rising in her. "Oh, I don't believe that at all, Joyce. I've been around him. He's one of the nicest men I've ever met. Taylor was talking about him this morning, what a good worker he was."

"Still, you can't change what happened," Joyce said stubbornly.

"And you can't just say he brought trouble in here with him," Eleanor replied.

Joyce twisted her body in the chair, leaned toward Eleanor. "You sound like you got an interest in him. Is that it? You got yourself all caught up in that rough-edged look he's got?"

"What are you talking about?" Eleanor said.

"You know damn well what I'm talking about, Eleanor," Joyce replied. "Some men got a look about them that gets inside a woman like a fever. I'd guess he's one of them. You get to feeling feverish when you're around him?"

"Not at all," Eleanor said quickly, feeling the rise of a blush. "I just don't believe in running somebody down because it's the easy thing to do."

Joyce settled back in her chair. Few people ever argued with her. She liked the spunk Eleanor was offering. "You're right," she said after a moment. "I guess I'm just looking to put the blame on somebody, and he's got that look of being a blame-taker." She paused, looked at Eleanor. "You still sound like you got an interest in him."

Taylor had caught only three fish the entire day—two catfish and a bream—and he had again surrendered any chance of winning the twenty-dollar prize to the report that Littleberry Davis had caught twelve, all having some weight to them. It was a shame that Noah had stayed away, he said to Moody Deal and Peavo Teasley.

"You can't hardly blame him," Moody said, sitting between Taylor and Peavo, watching his bobber floating on a small backturn of water that cupped behind a sandbar, leaving the water still, as though it had decided to pause for a rest in the river. Moody had caught four fish, judging their total weight to be five pounds. Peavo had caught five, but none of any size.

"I guess not," Peavo said. "Not after finding that fish the boy left hanging there for him."

"Yeah," Moody mumbled. He made a little up-and-down motion with his cane fishing pole, causing the line to skim across the water and the bobber to jiggle.

"That a bite?" asked Peavo.

"Naw."

"You still got some bait?"

Moody raised his line from the water. "Yeah," he answered.

"I swear this is the last year I'm doing this," Peavo grumbled.

"What you said last year," Taylor said.

"Well, this time I mean it."

"And the year before that," Moody added.

"What you talking about?" Peavo said irritably.

"Best I can remember, you been saying this was the last year for ten years now, maybe longer," Moody told him.

"Kiss my butt, Moody."

"Would, if it didn't bear such a strong resemblance to your face," Moody said dryly, lighting a cigarette.

Taylor laughed easily at the familiar exchange between the two of them and made a lazy swipe at a gnat that buzzed near his face. He looked across the river at the line of fishermen who had rooted themselves to the bank, most sitting in chairs from throw-away furniture they had repaired for the occasion. Peavo was there year after year for the same reason everyone else was there, he thought: because it was the thing to do. Along the river, on both sides, men and boys defended their wisdom, or their stupidity, in the fishing spot they had staked, and they were all close enough to spend as much time talking to one another as fishing.

And maybe he was there for the talk more than the fishing, Taylor reasoned. Over the years he had heard enough fish stories to fill a book, or a shelf of books.

Catfish that could wiggle out of the water and walk on fins across an acre of plowed field just to get to another stream.

Eels that would put a jolt of electricity in you, or jump-start your car if the battery was dead.

Salmon coming out of the ocean and swimming hundreds of miles upriver just to turn red and spawn and then die—so many salmon a man could walk across the water on their backs and bear would sit in the shallow water with bibs around their necks and forks in their hands.

Fish that could fly like a bird on flapping side fins.

Whales swallowing small boats like a man eating a peanut.

Flatfish with both eyes on one side of their head, looking a lot like old lady Gwendolyn Pilcher, who had taught school in the valley for fifty years and gave ugly a bad name.

Fish that could shoot needles of poison like little arrows, and, yes, by shot, they were in the Hiawassee River, and if you were a boy or a tomboy girl too little to swim and too dumb to stay out of the water, you would feel the sting of those arrows.

Taylor had heard all of the stories, had offered some version of them in his own turn of talking.

Still, none of them equaled what he had seen from Noah Locke, catching catfish—only catfish—like a man in a circus pulling rabbits out of a tall silk hat.

He had spent hours thinking about it since watching it happen.

It was as though the fish had been looking for Noah, rather than Noah looking for the fish, and he could not shake from his mind the sight of Noah squatting down to touch the water with his spread-open palm. It was like he was giving the fish a scent, telling them he had finally come for them. Like Whitlow's bloodhounds taking the scent of Howard Reynolds's grandboy from a dirty shirt.

It was something he would never see again.

Never.

He wondered where Noah was, wondered if he had packed up and left. Hoped not, and his hope had nothing to do with finishing the painting. It was a few hours' work. He could do it himself. And it had nothing to do with owing Noah money for the work already done. He would put the money aside and hold it in case Noah returned one day, or he would call the Elbert County jail and ask about Noah's brother and make arrangements for Noah to get the money when he showed up for a visit. It wasn't the money. Getting the money to Noah would be done. More than anything, it had to do with Noah, himself. It had been a long time since he had met anybody with Noah's nature. A long time.

"You gonna tell us about Eleanor Cunningham?" Moody asked in a voice that stayed among the three of them.

"What about her?" Taylor answered.

Moody and Peavo made glances at one another, the glances carried on grins.

"Well, good Lord, Taylor, she didn't come down here at the start to see how me and Moody was doing," Peavo said.

"Wasn't down here for me neither," Taylor said defensively.

"Looked that way to me," Peavo said with teasing.

"Did me, too," Moody agreed. He snickered like a boy.

"Well, you seeing things," Taylor argued. "I saw her walking up and down the river all morning, and she seemed to be talking to a lot of people."

"You gonna make a great ghost when you die," Moody said.

"Why's that?" Taylor asked.

"You so easy to see through," Moody told him.

Taylor shook his head, but did not respond, and the three men fished in silence, gazing at the water. The sleepy heat of the day swam around them, clung to their clothes, made their eyes heavy. Even in the shade, where Peavo had staked their fishing spot, the air was thick and still.

And in the silence, Taylor wondered if Eleanor could be using the day to announce that her mourning was over. It had seemed that way earlier. Not by her dress or by the look she wore, other than something being different about her hair. She had seemed tired, and he knew she was, spending so much time at the Reynolds home. Yet, there had been something relaxed about her, something that seemed to say she had finally made her peace with Boyd's death.

Or, maybe he was just seeing something he had a wish for.

Fooling himself.

It took time to get over the loss of someone, even if that person had not died. His divorce was proof of it. He had mourned the leaving of his wife for almost two years before he could make little jokes about it, and even now there were times when he had the need to call her name about something concerning the house they had shared.

"You got a bite," Peavo said suddenly.

Taylor watched his bobber swim over the surface of the water, saw it dive out of sight.

The fish was a bream, a large one. From mouth-tip to tail, eight or nine inches, he judged. A full, round body.

"I swear, that's the biggest fish I ever saw you catch," Moody said.

"Where's Littleberry?" Peavo asked with a hoot.

In mid-afternoon, Eleanor went to the school to help prepare for the cooking. Unlike Joyce Magill, it was a task she enjoyed. A break in the monotony of days tripping over days. And there were other women to talk to—or to listen to. She liked the listening more than the talking, for she knew she would hear stories that could have been set in type and sealed between the hard covers of a book. Somewhere she had read that great stories were those begun with a single, dark seed of gossip, planted in the hotbed of a moist tongue, sprouted to life in whispers that had been fertilized by imagination.

There was some truth to the thought, she believed. At the school, preparing for the fish fry, she had always heard stories of downtrodden men and women living such sorry lives they were a blight on the community and an abomination to God. Drunks and thieves and liars and wife beaters and whores and whore chasers. None of them worth the gunpowder it would take to send them to the gates of hell. And it wasn't just the lowlife who earned the talk. Some were among the high and mighty, taking advantage of anybody they could just to line their pockets with dollar bills earned from the sweat of somebody else's labor—bankers taking over land hard-worked by farmers needing credit, lawyers sending the sheriff for an old car one payment away from ownership, elected officials being bought on the sly by big business with an interest at stake in some law that had more twists and turns in it than a snake slithering through the woods.

The only people immune from the gossip of the ladies preparing for the fish fry were the ladies preparing for the fish fry.

It was one reason so many ladies volunteered, Eleanor believed.

The first person she saw when she parked her car near the school was Whitlow Mayfield.

He was nailing a sign to a utility pole.

The sign, hand-painted by Whitlow, read:

FISHING DAY, 1948
IN MEMORY OF
MATTHEW REYNOLDS

"Anybody touches that sign, they'll answer, by God, to me," Whitlow said to her with anger in his voice.

"Nobody's going to touch it," she said gently.

"They better not," he replied. And then his body began to quake and he slid down in a sitting position against the pole like a man who has suddenly lost his strength to stand. He pulled his knees up to his chest and cradled his head on them and he began to weep.

Eleanor kneeled beside him. She asked, "Can I get you something, Whitlow?"

He shook his head over his knees, looked up at her. His eyes were red from fatigue and worry and tears. "I want to talk to you, Eleanor," he said.

"All right," she said.

From the window of the lunchroom, Lamar Gathers watched Eleanor kneeling near Whitlow, talking to him. Whitlow seemed to be wiping his eyes with the sleeve of his shirt.

Many moods, Lamar thought.

Many moods.

TWENTY-FOUR

It was a few minutes after six o'clock when he finished painting the store and put away the paint cans. He had done the painting faster than he thought he would and guessed it was because he was alone and not slowed down by Taylor or by customers who wanted to talk. He had seen two or three cars driving past in mid-afternoon, but did not believe any of the cars' occupants had seen him, hidden as he was by the oak trees hovering over the store's front. One car had slowed as he was washing the paintbrush at the spigot near the side steps, and he had seen a hand lifted in a wave, but he had not recognized the car or the person in it.

He walked the railroad track until it made a right turn and crossed the river, and then he followed the road to the pull-off leading to the lake. The sun was still high against the trees and the day's heat was still thick in the air, even in the woods.

It would be a hot night, he thought, as windless as the day had been, and he believed the next day would be the same. Not a good day for traveling, but it did not matter. He had finished with the painting and there was nothing else to keep him in the valley except for Hoke Moore's fish and in the morning, before leaving, he would catch the fish. For Hoke Moore and for Matthew Reynolds and for himself, he would catch the fish. Yet, it was not the fish that had stayed in his thinking during the day. Travis had. Travis. It was like a voice that had been calling out to him for a long time, but had not been able to reach him because of the winding about he had been doing for almost two years.

Maybe the voice had found him because he had stayed for a week and a day in the Valley of Light.

And he remembered something once said by his mother to his father: "I told you about that yesterday. You just now hearing it?" And his father, looking puzzled, had answered, "They must of been slow words."

There was a shine across the surface of the lake. The water was as still as water in a cup.

He knew the bass was deep down in the stream bed, where the water was cool. Deep down, moving as little as possible. Waiting out the day. He stood for a moment at the lakeside and watched for movement, but saw none, and he wondered if the day's heat had cut down on the catches at the fishing contest. Some, he reasoned. Mostly because the fishermen would not be patient enough to let their lines stay in one place. They would be like jittery children, yanking up their hooks, dropping them again a few inches away, hoping the new place would be better. Sometimes he wondered if people knew that fish could swim.

He went into the shack, stepping without thinking on the sag at the doorsill, and the flooring made a little creaking cry.

The cry made him remember that he had said he would look at the pillar under the shack.

Eleanor had said it was not necessary, but he had given his word—or at least enough of it to matter—and he went back outside the shack and kneeled and peered underneath the porch. There was still enough light to see easily and he started a slow crawl toward the area of the sag, deliberately making enough noise to chase off any snakes or rats or spiders that might have decided to rest in the fine, cool sand that rain always left under houses. It was a natural fear for him, crawling in close spaces. The same kind of fear some people had for heights or for fast driving or for knives—for anything, he suspected. Travis was different, though. Travis had loved crawling under the house, or into burrowed-out caves of hay in the barn loft, or into sunken holes where trees had fallen in the woods. Once Travis had hidden a stuffed animal under the house, a gift from his first-grade schoolteacher. The animal was a brown bear with soft thread eyes. Travis had said he threw it away into the creek because other boys had teased him about it, but Noah had watched him from a hidden place behind one of the pillars and knew the truth. Travis would take the bear and hold it and stare at it and touch it with his fingertips, and then he would put it away again, wrapping it in a fertilizer sack.

He wondered if the bear was still under the house, or if some dog had carried it off or if the new sharecroppers had found it and thrown it away.

He made his way to the middle of the porch and saw the place where the pillar had fallen, and he knew immediately it was a repair he could not do without the right tools and without help from another man. He could prop it up with a log, maybe, but that would not hold for long.

He inched forward, studying the bowed floor joist. From what he could make of it, it did not seem cracked, only twisted, probably from the falling of the rock in the pillar. And then something caught his eye—a crowbar leaning against one of the rocks—and he guessed that someone—maybe Boyd Cunningham—had tried to force a rock back into place and all of them had broken loose of the cement holding them together.

Then he saw something else.

Tucked into the pillar, in a place where a rock had been, he saw a metal ammunition box from the war. It had been painted gray to match the rocks, yet Noah knew instantly what it was, knew that once it had carried 30-caliber cartridges.

He slipped closer to the fallen pillar, reached for the box and pulled on it gently. The box slid away with ease and he took its handle and began to back-crawl, dragging it with him. Out from under the porch, he turned the front of the box to him, slipped the pin from its lid and opened it. Inside the box, he saw a large envelope and beneath it, a bundle wrapped in newspaper. He removed the envelope and seeing it was not sealed, he opened it and pulled out its contents. Three photographs. Two were of a young woman smiling prettily into the eye of the camera—one a close-up of her face, the other of her full body, sitting at an angle on what appeared to be a bed covered in a quilt. She was wearing an open robe, showing the flesh of her breasts—small, but arched, tipped with dark nipples—and the smooth thigh of one leg.

The third photograph was of the woman and a man that Noah recognized as Boyd Cunningham, having seen his likeness in a framed photograph in Eleanor's home. They were sitting in a café or a bar or someplace like a bar. Sitting close, her face against his chin, her arm curled around his neck. On the back of the photograph were the words, *Roza and Boyd*.

He remembered the whispered talk he had heard at Howard Reynolds's home about Boyd Cunningham having a girl in Germany.

He put the photographs back into the envelope and pulled out the bundle wrapped in newspaper. Opened it. Inside was a large stack of new twenty-dollar bills and another envelope addressed to Boyd Cunningham. The word *Confidential* had been printed at the left-side bottom of the envelope. He held it for a moment, turned it in his hand, saw that it had been sliced open. He knew that whatever was in the envelope had nothing to do with him and he had no business reading it. Yet, he wondered about it. Wondered if the letter inside it had something to do with the money.

He fingered it open, took out a single sheet of paper, read:

I'm tired of waiting. I want my money. You play around with me and you'll be sorry you did. You think I won't put out the *word on you, you got another think coming. I guess a lot of people would like to know about all that stuff you took in the war. I know you sold it all. You got $3,000 dollars of mine and I'm coming up there to get it and this time I'm not putting on about buying that nothing farm you got. You never would have got that stuff back here without me covering for you. You have my money ready for me and I mean it.*

The letter was signed *Garland.*

Noah folded the sheet quickly and slipped it back into the envelope. He looked at the postmark, saw the date as August 3, 1947. And then he put the envelope back into the ammunition box.

TWENTY-FIVE

According to Peavo, the greatest gift God had ever given mankind, other than Jesus, was the fish fry.

His reasoning was simple: it filled the soul as well as the belly.

"A man that don't feel better after a plateful of fried fish and hush puppies and coleslaw, ought to be talking to the undertaker," Peavo declared in a voice loud enough to carry beyond his table in the school dining room, and then, realizing he had mentioned an undertaker on a day that carried sorrow in it, he sputtered, "Well, maybe not that, but he ought to be worried."

His correction earned some smiles and a whisper from Moody: "Put some pepper on your toes, Peavo. That'll keep your feet out of your mouth."

Peavo bent to his plate, feeling the sting of embarrassment.

It was now late, night coming fast, and the smell of fried fish coated the air of the school lunchroom. At the table next to Peavo and Moody and their families, Lamar and Arlene Gathers sat with Taylor and Eleanor and Whitlow and Grant Webster and his wife, Reba. Grant Webster was the minister of the Church of the Resurrected Christ. He had given the blessing of the food—a blessing far shorter than his Sunday morning prayers—thanking God for the day and for the fellowship of those who had caught the fish and for the gifts of those who had prepared it. He had also asked God to comfort Howard and Ada and Milton Reynolds, saying, "Give them the peace of knowing you are holding young Matthew against your bosom and have graced him with all-knowing."

The prayer had ended with a mumbled round of amens.

It was, Lamar Gathers had announced in his short speech, the largest turnout in the history of Fishing Day, and the school had profited enough to buy some playground equipment, maybe even field a softball team.

He had congratulated Littleberry Davis for his seventh consecutive year of winning the prize money, though Littleberry was not around to hear the praise. He had taken his fish plate and left, someone had reported.

"Guess maybe he's tired after hauling in all them fish," another voice from the audience had suggested, and the people had laughed wearily, though all of them thought Littleberry's behavior was strange. He had loved gloating as much as winning the money.

No one spoke of Noah. The fishing was over. There was no need to dwell on whether or not Noah could have taken the prize from Littleberry. Someone had said to Taylor—though he could not remember who it was—that he had seen Noah at the store, washing paintbrushes at the spigot. Had said the store looked finished, and Taylor had taken the news with a nod. He would find Noah on Sunday and pay him—if Noah was still around. Intuitively, he believed Noah had already left, forgetting the money.

After the supper and the cleanup, and while music from a band made up of fiddlers and guitar and banjo players rose up in the air on the school playground, Eleanor slipped away without making a show of it, telling Taylor she was tired, agreeing to see him on

Sunday afternoon for the funeral services of Matthew Reynolds. He had tried to persuade her to stay, saying in a put-on voice of merriment, "They just started the music. You mean you're going to pass up a chance to dance with me?" And she had answered, "I don't even remember what dancing is like, it's been so long since I've done it. I'd probably break your feet." Taylor had laughed, had replied, "Be the other way around, I'd guess."

She had with her a covered plate of fish and hush puppies and coleslaw, and she drove to the pull-off at the lake and parked her car under the low, covering limb of a hemlock, out of sight from the road. The night was dim, but she had a flashlight, making the walk to the shack an easy one.

She found Noah sitting on the porch.

"I know you must think I've got the worst manners in the world, showing up out of the blue like this, but I thought you might be hungry," she said to him. "We had so many fish left, it'd be a shame just to throw them away."

He thanked her, saying he had already eaten, though he had not, not more than a candy bar he had taken from the store, leaving his money for it on the counter.

"Well, you can always find room for some fish," she replied lightly. "Do you want to eat it now, or later?"

"I guess later," he said.

"I'll put it on the table," she told him and she went into the shack with the plate, then returned to the porch and sat on the cot. Noah sat in the rocker.

"It's still hot outside," she said.

"It is," he replied.

"A lot of people were asking about you today," she said.

He made a nod, letting it say whatever needed to be said.

"We had a good turnout," she continued, her voice in singsong. "Biggest ever, the principal said. He's even talking about buying some equipment for a softball team. I hope he does. We had a softball team at my school when I was girl. Everybody always went to the games. I wanted to play, but it was just for boys."

He made a sound that was wordlike, but not a word.

"Whitlow Mayfield made a sign and put it up on a light pole," she said. "It was in memory of Matthew."

"That's—good," he said.

"I guess you know about his own son getting killed in the war," she added.

"I heard about it," he replied.

"I had a long talk with him this afternoon," she said. "He told me something I didn't know. He said Boyd wanted to go back to Germany." She paused, smiled an uncertain smile. "Boyd never said anything to me about it. In fact, he always said he'd never go back over there. I used to tell him there were some places I wanted to see—places like Paris and Rome—and he said if I wanted to go, I'd have to go by myself. I asked Whitlow how he knew, and he said Boyd had talked about it one time when he'd been drinking, and it just came out."

Another pause. "He and Whitlow were close after the war. Whitlow's boy, David, and Boyd were in the same unit. They saw each other all the time. David was a few years younger, so they didn't know each other that much before the war. Just names, I guess. Whitlow used to come by the house to talk to Boyd, but I never listened to what they said. I just assumed it had to do with the war and with Whitlow trying to make some sense of his son's death. Boyd told me one time that Whitlow was the only man in the valley he felt he could talk to, but two or three months before Boyd took his life, Whitlow stopped coming around and Boyd never said anything else about him." She paused again, long enough for Noah to wonder if he should say something. Then: "I don't know why Whitlow decided to say what he did about Boyd today. He just did. It was like it was something he'd been holding inside him for as long as he could, and he had to say it. It's been a long time since Boyd died. A year ago in August."

Noah thought of the ammunition box and the envelope of photographs and the stack of twenty-dollar bills and the letter bearing the postmark of August 3. The ammunition box was inside the shack, under the pie safe. He wondered what to say about it, or if he should say anything at all.

"He told me something else," she said. "He said the man who had been trying to buy the farm had also been in the army with Boyd, but Boyd never mentioned that to me. He acted like he'd never seen him before."

"Maybe Mr. Mayfield was wrong," he said.

"I don't think so. He said Boyd told him all about it, that the two of them had been all the way through the war together. He wanted to know if David had ever mentioned the man in his letters. He also said Boyd was bragging about pulling the wool over the man's eyes to up the price of the farm. Said Boyd had come up with a story about a granite company looking at the property to open a quarry."

She touched her hair in the way that made her seem nervous; then she added, "It sounds so much like Boyd, I don't doubt the story at all. I told you he'd changed when he came back from the war, but he was always a dreamer and a little bit of a con artist, I'm sorry to say. It's something I learned after we were married. He liked coming up with little stories that sounded like the truth, but had no truth at all in them. Conning people. That's all it was. He thought it was funny. Sad thing is, he was the one who was always getting conned." She laughed softly, a hollow laugh. "He bought our farm because he believed it had gold on it."

"Gold?" he said.

"It's an old story, but that's all it was—just a story. Boyd wanted it to be true, that's all."

Noah offered a puzzled look.

"But it did start me thinking about Boyd's death," she said. "The man who wanted the farm was here, talking to him, the same day he killed himself."

"He was?" Noah said.

"Yes," she answered. "He showed up early in the morning, right after breakfast. Boyd was mad about it. They talked outside for a little while and the man left and Boyd said that was the last we'd see of him." She turned on the cot to face him. "I'd forgotten all about that until Whitlow told me the story about a quarry."

Noah made a small movement with his head, shifted in his chair.

"I've been thinking about it all afternoon," she said. "I always wondered about the way Boyd died. It wasn't like him to take his own life. Not at all. Maybe Garland Hood had something to do with it."

Noah looked up, surprised. "Who did you say?"

"Garland Hood," she answered. "That was the man's name. Maybe he thought if Boyd wasn't around, I'd be glad to sell just to get away from everything."

"Maybe," he said. He thought of the letter in the ammunition box, signed by a man named Garland. The letter told a different story about everything.

"And maybe it's just my imagination taking over," she said, "but I'll never know the answer. Garland Hood was killed in a car wreck a few months after Boyd died. I found his name and phone number on a piece of paper Boyd had, and I called to see if he was still interested in the place. Whoever it was that answered the phone—his wife, I guess—told me about the accident. She said she'd never heard of Boyd, and she'd never heard her husband talk about buying any land, but it could have been possible. He was a traveling insurance man, she said, and she only saw him on weekends most of the time."

She turned her shoulders to him. Her face was in the mix of shadow and moonlight. "Do you remember when I told you about the girl Boyd met over there, the one at the concentration camp?"

"Yes," he said.

"He must have wanted to go back to Germany and find her and bring her back here," she said. "I can't think of any other reason he'd want to go back."

Again, he thought of the photographs, of the woman and Boyd Cunningham sitting together, laughing for the camera. "Maybe so," he said.

"It would have been all right with me," she told him. "I've seen pictures of some of those children. They need all the help they can get. But I guess you know that, since you were there."

He let a nod speak his agreement.

"It's one good thing I can hold on to about Boyd," she said gently. "That he cared about somebody else. I just wish I knew how to get in touch with the girl. I'd like her to know how he felt about her."

He ran his hand over the armrest of the chair, trying to think of something to say. He wondered if he should tell her about the photographs. Thought: No. Nothing helpful could come of it. She needed a good memory of her husband and she had found it, even if it was a lie. Some lies served a purpose.

Eleanor slipped from the cot and went to the screen and looked out at the lake. After a moment, she said, without looking at him, "You're getting ready to leave, aren't you?"

"Yes," he answered.

"Tomorrow?"

"I guess so."

"Taylor told me you'd finished the store. Somebody saw you and told him."

"That's right. This afternoon."

She stood gazing at the lake and the thickening of night, her body making a dim silhouette against the meshed wire of the screen. Cicadas sang. The lake's water made blinks of light from the reflection of stars.

"You think you'll ever come back this way?" she asked.

"I don't know. Maybe," he said.

She turned to face him. He saw a smile dimple over the shadow of her face. "If you do and you want to grow rocks, I've got a farm for sale."

He returned the smile.

"Oh, I want to show you something," she said. She reached into the pocket of her dress and removed a photograph and handed it to Noah. It was the picture that Taylor had taken of the two of them on the night of the supper.

"Taylor had them developed," she said. "He gave me a few of them. I thought you'd like to see this one."

It was a clear photograph, and a telling one. The two of them looking into the camera, a smile—almost a laugh—on her face, a weak grin on his, a look of being out of place.

"It's—good," he mumbled. He handed the picture back to her and she slipped it back into her pocket.

"You've done a lot for me, Noah Locke," she said.

He started to speak, but she lifted her hand to stop his words.

"I mean it. And I'm not just talking about helping with the cow, or anything like that. I think I've got some of my spirit back, and you're the reason for it, or a big part of it, at least. And don't ask me why I think that. I don't know that I could tell you. I just know it's true."

She smiled again, hugged her arms to her abdomen, looked at him as though searching to find something hidden in his face. "Maybe it's because you made me start talking again," she said, "and when I started talking to other people, I started listening to myself. The men around here can say all they want to about you having a gift for fishing. I think you've got a gift for making people take a look at themselves. That's why I'd like to be a teacher. I'd like to be able to do that, too. Maybe I will, one day. Maybe I'll leave this place and go back to college and become a teacher." She looked away, at the lake, then turned her face back to him. "Maybe," she said.

She uncrossed her arms and stepped to him and reached to take his hands from the armrests of the chair.

"I want to do something I shouldn't do, and I know it," she said softly. "I want to hug you."

He did not move, did not speak.

She tugged at him gently and he stood.

She folded her arms around him. He let his hands go to her back in a loose embrace. Her body rested easily against him, her face fitting the curve of his neck, her shoulders nestled into his chest.

"I'm going back to Ada's house early in the morning, and I

don't think I'll see you before you leave," she whispered. "But I hope you come back someday."

Still, he did not speak.

She released her embrace, moved back from him, near the cot. Took his hands. Her eyes held on his face for a moment; then she lifted his hands and looked at them, pulled them to her face, touched her face against them. She sat on the cot, still holding his hands. The hard striking of a bloodrush trembled across her chest; her throat filled with moisture. She released his hands and turned her body to lie on the cot, her head against the pillow. He sat on the cot's edge.

"Will you hold me?" she asked.

He moved to lie down against her, slipped his arm around the pillow, cradling her head. She lifted her face to him, kissed him softly on his lips, held the touch to feel his breath in her mouth.

"Will you come back, Noah?" she asked again in whisper.

He did not answer.

"Will you remember me?" she said.

He dipped his head in a nod.

She smiled, turned on the cot, letting her back curl against his chest. He could smell a faint vanilla scent of cologne from her neck, a sweet, warm scent. In time, he could hear sleep come to her breathing and soon he, too, slept.

When he awoke, she was gone.

On the table inside the shack, he found the photograph of the two of them.

TWENTY-SIX

He sat at the table and tried to count the money, but got confused over it. Three thousand dollars he guessed, though he was unsure if he had come up with the figure by counting or had it in his mind from the letter. The man named Garland had said he was owed three thousand dollars, and it seemed close to that amount. Whatever the total was, it was more money than Noah had ever seen at one time.

Outside, it was still dark and the light of the table lamp inside the shack gave off a dull, yellowish glow. He had tried to go back to sleep after awakening to find Eleanor gone, but had not been able to.

He wrapped the money in the newspaper and put it back into the ammunition box. Before he left, he would take it to Eleanor's home and leave it on the porch, he thought, or he would leave it in the shack for her to find when she came back to get the bedding and the towels.

It would be best to take it to her home, he decided. No telling who might show up at the lake, still curious to see the spot where Matthew had died. She had said she would go back to Howard and Ada Reynolds's home in the morning. It would be easy enough to hide out in the tree line until she left, and then he could put the ammunition box on the porch where she would find it.

He took a school tablet and a broken-point pencil he used for writing to Travis from his knapsack. Trimmed the pencil sharp with his knife, and sat at the table and labored to write a note to leave with the money.

The note said:

> *I found this under the house where the pillar broke. I didn't take none of the money.*

He signed it *Noah.*

He placed the note on top of the wrapped bundle of money and closed the box, and then he made a small fire in the stove and burned the photographs and the letter from Garland Hood. He had thought of finding Taylor and giving the photographs and the letter to him, but had decided against it. There was no reason. What had happened was over, except for the talk—the guessing about the money and the rumors of a girl in Germany waiting for Boyd—and the talk would never end. It was better to keep the talk as it was, without adding to it. Let Eleanor have her good thoughts about her husband, even if the truth of it was different.

He remembered the kiss she had given him, could still sense it. Wondered if she had kissed him again as he slept, before leaving him.

Maybe.

The thought of it was good.

He made coffee and took a cup to the lake, near the dam, and watched the light of morning ease its way into the trees. It was his favorite time of day, or night-day. Color coming out of dark. Nightsounds fading. The air cool and sweet. Smell of trees and grass and, from the lake, water.

A mockingbird made a stolen song.

He would miss the lake and the shack, he thought.

The mockingbird changed songs.

He turned to look at the shack, imagined himself living there. With Travis, maybe. Travis would like the valley.

A tightness came to his throat, thinking of Travis, and a wave of heat ran through his body. It was time to leave. He turned his cup to empty the rest of his coffee, then began his walk back to the shack. At the lake's edge, he paused. Near the dam, beneath the overhang of limbs where he had found Matthew's body, he saw a swaying of water, and he knew the fish was there, restlessly waiting.

"Got to make him want you, much as you want him," Hoke Moore had said.

The water moved again.

All right, he thought. I will catch you now.

He turned and went to the shack and took his fishing rod and pulled the line from the eye tip and attached a lure that had the body of a small slender fish, colored like a flashing silver minnow. A large hook dangled from the lure like a tail fin.

He had caught many bass with the lure, had made a name for it: Lucky. The naming of lures was from one of Marvin Linquist's stories. Marvin had vowed that each of his lures carried the name of one of his former girlfriends, but only those he had seriously courted and caught. The story was always ended by a pause, by a thoughtful expression on Marvin's face, and by his claim, "I had sixty-seven of them lures, I believe it was."

Noah had chosen the name Lucky, not for the fish it had caught, but for the fact he was lucky to have lived through the war that had killed Marvin Linquist.

He left the shack, taking with him the ax he had found propped in a corner of the porch, and he went to the east side of the dam, to the place where Matthew Reynolds had entered the water.

The ax was for killing the fish.

Even-up for Matthew's death.

He placed the ax and the rod on the ground beside him. Knelt at the edge of the lake. Leaned to the water. Put the palm of his hand on it. Held the palm steady. Closed his eyes, bowed his head as in prayer. For my mother, he thought. For Matthew Reynolds. For Hoke Moore. He could feel warmth in his palm from the electricity of the water. And then the water moved slightly, slapped at his palm, and he knew it was the fish speaking to him, saying it was time.

He stood, held the palm in front of his face and licked the water from his hand, letting the taste hold on his tongue.

"I will catch you," he said aloud.

He picked up the rod and readied it. Lifted it over his head and threw his arm forward in an easy motion. A singing came from the reel and he watched the lure arching through the air like the silver dot of a falling star, watched it pop against the water, watched it dive, watched water circles curling away from where the lure had hit.

He stood, waiting.

"I will catch you," he said again.

Suddenly, the fish erupted out of the water ten feet from him, splitting the surface like an explosion, rolling its great head in the air. It turned in its fall, struck the water hard and the sound of it was the sound of a shotgun being fired. A spray of water misted against Noah.

"Used to try and catch him, but all he'd do was spit water at me," Hoke Moore had said.

Noah saw the fish moving, coming toward him, and then it dove to its right and disappeared.

He remembered another thing Hoke Moore told him: *"Never seen a bass do that. Not one that big. Not coming out of the water so high. It was like he was telling me I weren't good enough to catch him."*

A flutter crossed involuntarily over Noah's chest. He rolled the handle of his reel twice, tugged at the line, let the tip of the rod dip toward the water, then let it rest. He braced his feet on the shoreline, waited.

The surface of the water seemed to bristle with movement and he remembered his dream of fish rising up, taking flight, leaving the lake to follow the see-through bass. He glanced at the water near the shoreline. In the days he had spent at the lake he had never seen a fish, not even a hatchling, in the shore water, and he had understood why the people of the valley believed no fish were in it. Now, he saw a cloud of small fish stretching along the shore, some nibbling at the top of the water, making popping sounds.

He had learned that a large bass—a bass fifteen pounds or over—did not have the fight of a smaller one. Not like an eight-pounder. An eight-pounder had a mean temper. An eight-pounder would try to rip its head from its body to shake the hook. Yet, he knew this fish was different, big as it was. Had fight in it. Had to, coming so high out of the water as it did.

He felt a vibration in the rod, saw the line go taut, and he pulled hard, whipping the tip of the rod upward. A violent jerk ripped at the rod, bent the shank of it, almost tearing it from his hands, and he knew the hook was set in the mouth of the fish.

He released the drag on the line, let it play out, then stopped the run.

It would take time, he thought. And he remembered a long story—a funny lie, it was—from Marvin Linquist about going west to become a cowboy, and why he had given it up. Horses. He hated horses, Marvin had said. Hated the way you could lasso one and corral it and put a saddle on it, but you couldn't break it until it got ready to be broken. He didn't mind the lassoing and the riding, Marvin had said. It was all the in-between time that aggravated him.

The fish was like a horse, Noah thought. It would not be pulled to the bank until it was ready to be broken.

Behind him, the morning sun made pale spears through the trees. The mockingbird kept up its solitary song.

And he began the fight.

He could feel the fish through the line and through the rod, could feel its jittery thrashing, its large head shaking against the hook, its muscles curling for the dive it would take before turning and hurling its way to the surface of the water. The beating of Noah's heart drummed against his chest; heat coated his face.

The fish made a run toward him, turned, broke the water's surface with its head, its great mouth open, showing the lure. Then it dove. By the feel of the line, Noah believed the fish had struck the bottom of the lake, skimming it. He glanced at the shoreline. It roiled with fish. Fish so small they seemed almost invisible.

He let the fish take the line, run with it. Then he stopped the run, pulled the rod close to his chest, its tip high above his head, made three turns on the reel, then tilted the rod forward, giving the fish a new thought of freedom. And the fish began to swim in a circle—small, even, moving tamely toward Noah.

Noah smiled. He knew the trick. It was a way of making the fisherman think the catch was at hand, making him relax, and when the grip on the rod was made loose, the fish would yank it into the water. He had seen it happen fishing with Marvin Linquist in Germany. Remembered Marvin leaping into the water after his rod, flailing around like a drowning man, finally coming back to shore grinning his happy grin, saying, "That there fish was a Nazi bass. Puts up a little fight and then runs off."

The fish yanked at the line. Noah bent at his knees to keep his hold on the rod.

"You got to do better than that," he said aloud, but in a whisper.

The fish seemed to hear him. It turned again and made a strong race toward the center of the lake. Noah released the drag, letting the wet, braided line fly from the reel, singing its song of water and air.

And then it became a game of rhythm, of give-and-take, played with the muscle of fish and man. Noah could feel an aching in his shoulders and in the bridge of his abdomen. His wrists burned with pain, his fingers cramped. Beads of perspiration bubbled at his hairline and dripped from his face. Yet, he knew the fish was also tiring.

Twenty minutes later, the fish relaxed, stopped its yanking and diving and rising, and let itself be pulled gently toward the shoreline.

At water's edge, the fish lifted its head to Noah, its wide eyes staring up at him, and Noah thought of his promise to Hoke Moore. He said to the fish, "Hoke Moore's been thinking about you a long time." He paused and added, "So will I."

He held the rod firmly in one hand and reached with the other for the ax beside him.

The fish swayed in the water. A muscle rippled down its body.

For a moment, Noah did not move, and then he dropped the ax. The fish did not kill the boy, he thought. The boy died from being who he was. Nothing more. Nothing more at all.

He reached into his pocket and removed his pocket knife. Raised it to his mouth and opened the blade with his teeth. Then he eased the tip of the rod to him and cut the line and watched the fish slide back into the water.

He sat on the grass of the cleared-out spot, holding his fishing rod, gazing at the lake.

He did not know how long he sat. An hour, maybe. The sun was above the tree tips, warm on his back. His arm muscles still ached. He could still feel the weight of the fish in his hands. Guessed it at more than twenty pounds, maybe more than George Perry's fish.

The lake was calm, quiet.

He sat, letting the water drain from the lake bed into his memory, and he did not see the man approaching him, until the man's shadow fell across the grass beside him. He turned his head, looked up.

"You the one called Noah?" the man asked.

"I am," Noah answered.

"I come looking for you," the man said. He paused, added, "My name's Littleberry Davis."

Noah stood. Littleberry Davis was lanky, his face thin and pinched, the kind of face with a hawk's look. His eyes were small and dark beneath the straw hat he wore down on his forehead.

"You been fishing?" Littleberry Davis asked.

Noah glanced at the lake, then looked back at Littleberry. "No sir. Just sitting," he said, not regretting the lie.

Littleberry motioned to the rod that Noah held. "You got your rod with you." His voice carried doubt over Noah's answer.

"I been working on it," Noah told him.

"What's the ax for?"

"I was thinking of cutting down the tree where we found the boy," Noah answered after a pause. "But I guess I'll let it stay. It's not my land."

Littleberry made a sound of clearing his throat, shook his head. "I sure hated hearing about that. Howard Reynolds is as good a man as you ever want to meet, and I liked that boy. Always grinning, like he was about to bust out laughing."

"Yes sir," Noah mumbled.

"Everybody's saying you the best at fishing they ever saw," Littleberry said.

"People like talking," Noah replied.

Littleberry nodded, lifted his chin to let his eyes study Noah. "I was looking for you at the fishing yesterday."

"Decided not to do it," Noah said.

"You weren't afraid of me, was you?" The question was asked in an easy manner, almost a tease.

"No sir. Just wasn't up to it."

"Just pulling your leg," Littleberry said. "Wish you'd of been there, though. It's the first time I ever won it when I had the feeling I come in second. Shows the power of talk, don't it?"

"Yes sir, I guess it does," Noah replied.

Littleberry nodded again. He looked at the lake. "They's nothing out there to catch," he said. "They died out."

"What I heard," Noah said.

"Take a look at the shoreline there," Littleberry said, pointing toward it with a long finger. "You don't see nothing, do you? Not even a minnow. A lake that's got fish in it has always got some little fellows swimming around in that shore water, like they just hatched out and they scared of the deep water."

Noah looked at the shoreline. The fish were gone.

"You got time, I can take you over to the Chatuge. Just me and you. It's got some good size bass in it," Littleberry told him.

"I appreciate it, but I got to be leaving," Noah said.

Littleberry removed his hat, showing a bald spot on the top of his head. He ran his finger along the sweatband in the habit of farmers working out thought. After a moment, he said, "Sorry to hear that. I'd sure like to fish with you."

"Maybe next time I come through," Noah replied.

"Uh-huh," Littleberry mumbled. The look on his face carried disappointment. He turned his body toward the shack. "You been staying in Arch Wheeler's place up there?"

"Yes sir," Noah said.

"Lord, last time I was down here was years ago," Littleberry said quietly, still holding his hat. "Used to be this old fellow who was always talking about a fish the size of a barn out in that lake, and I come down here with two or three boys to see about it. We stayed the night there. Only bite we got was from mosquitoes. Made old Hoke mad, the jawing he took about that fish."

"What did you say his name was?" Noah said.

"Hoke Moore," Littleberry answered. "Took so much joking about that fish, he said he'd come back to haunt us when he died." He laughed in a soft way, an easy chuckle. "We got to calling this place the Lake of No Fish. Old Hoke would cuss up a storm when he heard that."

"What happened to him?" Noah asked.

"He died a few years ago," Littleberry answered.

"Died?" Noah said in surprise.

Littleberry let his body nod in answer. "Unless somebody dug him up, he's still up there where we put him in the church graveyard." He laughed softly, the way a man laughs over memory, then he added, "Or, unless he shoveled his own way out just to get back at me and some of the others, like he said he would."

A shiver ran through Noah, causing his hands to tremble, causing him to go weak. He remembered asking Hoke Moore if he planned to return to the valley, remembered Hoke Moore's answer: *"About all I ever think about, you want to know the truth of it, but it's a long way off for old legs. If I go back, somebody'll have to throw me over his shoulders and carry me. You take a mind to go on down there, I'll consider I'm along for the ride."*

"Hoke was a fishing fool," Littleberry said. "After he quit farming, he took to carrying his fishing stick around with him just about everywhere he went, except maybe to church, and I guess it was in his car, even then. I used to fish with him a lot before he got put off with me over the teasing I done about this lake. Lord, Jesus, he got mad. I went to see him when he was dying, trying to make some amends, but he wouldn't have no part of it. Told me to get out of his house. Said he didn't want a man like me nowhere around him when he was about to meet Jesus."

Littleberry fanned his face with his hat. "When they buried him, they buried his fishing stick with him. Somebody—I believe it was Peavo Teasley—said they ought to put a catfish in the coffin, just so he'd feel at home. I thought about that a lot over the years. Maybe we should of done it. I liked that old man, even if he was hellfire mad at me all the way to the end. He could fish. That's God's truth. He could do that. Beat me like a drum more times than I like to recall." He paused, wagged his head. "But he was a plain fool when it come to this place."

Noah turned to the lake and let his mind bring Hoke Moore back to him, and in seeing him again, he understood why Hoke Moore had appeared to him in Kentucky and had sent him to the valley. "No sir, I don't believe he was," he said quietly.

"Like I said, they ain't nothing in that lake," Littleberry said, pulling his hat back over his head.

Noah saw the water ripple thirty feet away, a ripple so small it could have been made by wind, if any wind was blowing. He moved to the shoreline of the lake and kneeled and reached to touch the water with the palm of his hand. Held his palm on it.

Littleberry walked down beside him. "What you doing?" he asked curiously.

Noah did not answer. He kept his hand on the water, his eyes holding on his hand.

"Peavo told me about you doing that," Littleberry said. "What's that all about, anyhow?" He laughed a short, nervous laugh.

The water around Noah's hand began to darken and then to churn. Fish. Small as a blade of grass. Hundreds of them.

"God in heaven," Littleberry whispered in an astonished voice. He stepped back.

The fish nibbled at Noah's palm like the giving of kisses, flitted across the water like darts of light.

"God in heaven," Littleberry said again.

From twenty feet away, the water seemed to rise in a bow and the fish came up, throwing itself into the air like a torpedo. In its mouth was Noah's silver lure flashing sunlight, the hook caught through its lip, the cut line dangling like a rope. Up, up. And then it fell, its body making a thunderclap against the water.

"God in heaven," Littleberry repeated, his voice rising. He turned and walked away hurriedly, and he did not look back.

Noah stood, letting the water drip from his hand. He watched the rippling circles on the skin of the lake, watched the small fish slide away from the shoreline and disappear in the tea-colored water. And then he picked up the ax and his fishing rod and began to walk toward the shack, across streaks and splashes of morning light cutting through the shield of trees on the rim of the mountain.

Hoke Moore was home, he thought.

In a day, he would be, too.